Quisisana
Or, Rest at Last

by

Friedrich Spielhagen

Quisisana
Or, Rest at Last
by Friedrich Spielhagen

ISBN: 978-93-64286-65-7

Published by

DOUBLE 9 BOOKS
2/13-B, Ansari Road
Daryaganj, New Delhi – 110002
info@double9books.com
www.double9books.com
Tel. 011-40042856

ABOUT THE AUTHOR

Friedrich Spielhagen (1829–1911) was a notable German novelist, literary critic, and translator, recognized for his contributions to 19th-century German literature. Born in Magdeburg, Prussia, Spielhagen pursued studies in law, philology, and philosophy at the universities of Berlin, Bonn, and Greifswald. His diverse academic background influenced his writing, which often combined detailed character studies with social and philosophical themes. Some of Spielhagen's most significant works include:**"Problematische Naturen" (1861)**: A novel that examines the complexities of human nature and societal pressures. **Durch Nacht zum Licht (Through Night to Light, 1862)**: A sequel to "Problematische Naturen," continuing the exploration of personal and social conflicts.**"Hammer und Amboss" (Hammer and Anvil, 1869)**: A novel that delves into industrialization and its effects on society and individuals. **"Quisisana, Or, Rest at Last" (1879)**: A story centered around themes of healing and rejuvenation, set in a tranquil retreat. As a literary critic and editor, Spielhagen contributed to the development of German literature and culture. His works were widely read and discussed, influencing both his contemporaries and later generations of writers. He was known for his ability to combine narrative storytelling with deep philosophical and social insights, making his novels both engaging and thought-provoking.

CONTENTS

CHAPTER I

"Why have you roused me, Konski?"

"You were lying on your left side again, sir," the servant, who held his master clasped by the shoulder, replied, as he completed the task of restoring him to a sitting posture on the sofa; "and you have been drinking champagne at dinner, more than a bottle, John says, and that surely is ..."

Konski broke off abruptly, and turned again to the travelling boxes, one of which was already unlocked; he commenced to arrange its contents in the chest of drawers, and went on, apparently talking to himself rather than to his master--

"I am merely doing what the doctor has insisted upon. Only last night, in Berlin, as I was showing him to the door, he said: 'Konski, when your master is lying on his left side and begins then to moan, rouse him, rouse him at once, be it day or night. I take the responsibility. And, Konski, no champagne; not for the next six weeks, anyhow, and best not at all. And when you have once got into Italy, then plenty of water to be mixed with the wine, Konski, and ...'"

"And now oblige me by holding your tongue."

Bertram had remained sitting on the sofa, his hand pressed to his brow; he now rose rapidly and strode impatiently about the room, casting every now and then an angry glance at his valet. Then he stepped to one of the windows. The sun must be setting now. The high wooded hills yonder still shone forth in sunny splendour, but the terrace gardens sloping towards the valley, and the valley itself, with the village within, lay already in deepest shadow. The picturesque view, the graceful charm of which he was wont to appreciate so heartily, had no charm to-day for his dulled brain. Konski was quite right; the champagne which he had to-day taken for the first time since his illness, in direct defiance of the doctors injunctions, had not agreed with him. Well, he had taken champagne because his throat had got unbearably dry from much talking, and he had talked so much because the frequent pauses in the dinner conversation were making him nervous. The whole thing had been a positive bore; the genial host, the fair hostess had surely fallen off, changed sadly for the worse during the last three years. Or ...

could he possibly have changed himself? Did he really begin to grow old? If you get seriously ill at fifty, you are apt to go downhill with startling rapidity!

This had been the second emphatic *memento mori*--after an interval of twenty years! The first--the first had been her work. Aye, and she had kissed him a thousand times, and had vowed deathless fidelity yonder on the mountain-slope, where the giant oak still lifted its mighty crown of foliage above the bronze-coloured leafy roof of the beeches. Why the deuce did they always give him these rooms? He'd better ask Hildegard this very evening for other rooms--at once, before that blockhead Konski had unpacked everything.

"Leave these things alone," he exclaimed, turning round from the window; "I do not intend to remain in these rooms. I do not intend to stay here at all, I think. We shall probably be off to-morrow."

Konski, who was already deep in the recesses of box number two, believed he had not heard aright. He lifted his head out of the box and looked in amazement at his master.

"To-morrow, sir? I thought we were to stay a week at the least."

"Do what I bid you."

Konski replaced, the shirts which he was holding in the portmanteau and rose hastily from his knees. His master was evidently in a very bad temper; "but that kind of thing never lasts long with him," Konski was saying to himself, "and then the champagne ..."

Aloud he said-- "You can be sure, sir, that there won't be much trouble about the officers who are going to be quartered here. I know all about it from Mamsell Christine. Only a colonel, a major, a couple of captains, and some six lieutenants or so, and perhaps a surgeon-major. None of our princes, and certainly none of theirs. A mere handful for a large place like this; they'll be lost, like currants in a bun. And you can remain in these rooms, where we always have been, and you'll see none of them, for I don't suppose they'll have this blessed manœuvre in the garden below."

"I do not know at, all what you want with your everlasting manœuvres," Bertram exclaimed angrily.

He had gone back, to the open window, through which there came a strong current of air. Konski went and closed the door of the adjoining room, then stepped up to within a certain respectful distance of his master, and said modestly, lowering his voice--

"I beg your pardon, sir, but what does it matter, after all, if Miss really comes ..."

"What do you mean?" Bertram said without turning round. "What has that to do with my going or staying? Why should the little one not come?"

Konski rubbed up his stiff black hair with a certain sly smile, and said--

"Not Miss Erna; the other lady--who is never allowed to come when you are here."

"Lydia? Fräulein von Aschhof? Are you mad?"

Bertram turned round with the rapidity of lightning, and now uttered these words in a rough tone, whilst his eyes, generally so gentle, shone out in great anger. Konski was frightened; but his curiosity was greater than his terror. He would gladly have at last learned the real truth about the young lady who was not allowed to come when his master came on a visit to Rinstedt, and whom he had therefore never yet seen, although in the course of years he had accompanied his master half a dozen times. But he was once more doomed to disappointment; his master had suddenly become perfectly calm again, or at least preserved the appearance of perfect calmness, and now asked in his usual voice--

"From whom have you got your information? Of course from Mamsell Christine?"

"From Mamsell Christine, of course," Konski made answer.

"And she got it from My Lady?"

"From her Ladyship direct."

"And when is the lady expected to arrive?"

"This very evening, along with Miss Erna; and there will also come a Baron Lutter or Lotter--I could not quite make the name out; they pronounce things so queerly here in Thuringia."

"Well, well!"

Bertram now remembered that Hildegard, his hostess, had at table mentioned more than once the name of the Baron von Lotter-Vippach. Of Lydia, too, although he made it a point never to be drawn into conversation about her, she had again and again commenced to speak; clearly, as he perceived now, with the intention of preparing him to some extent for the intended surprise. But My Lady had reckoned without her host. This was a downright want of consideration; nay, worse, it was a breach of good faith. There was no reason why he should put up with it, and he did not mean to put up with it.

"Where's the master? and where is My Lady?" he asked aloud.

"The master has ridden over to the coal mines; her Ladyship has gone into the village. They left word that they would be back before you were awake again; and you had not lain down on your left ..."

"That'll do. Into the village, did you say? Give me my hat."

"Please take your overcoat too, sir," said Konski; "there's a nasty mist rising from the valley, sir; and the doctor, he did say that if you caught cold now, sir ..."

Bertram had put his hat on, and waived the proffered garment back. In the doorway he turned, and said--

"Do not trouble about the boxes. We leave again in an hour. And one thing more. If you say one word to Mamsell Christine, or to anybody in the house, now or later--you understand me--and I hear of it--we part--for all that."

He had left. Konski was now standing by the open window scratching his head, and the very next minute he saw him striding swiftly down the garden.

"Upon my word!" he murmured; "who'd think that six weeks ago he lay at the point of death?--And off this evening again--an hour hence! Not if I knows it. First, I must settle my little business with Christine, and that is not to be done all at once. Christine says that at that time the Fräulein would have nothing to say to him. I can't make it out. Twenty years ago he must have been a very handsome fellow; why, he is so almost still. Nor was he a poor man even then, though, of course, he has inherited lots since. I am devilish keen about seeing the old maid. One thing is sure and certain, she will arrive this very evening."

Then he cast one dubious look at the boxes. Perhaps it was taking needless pains to unpack them.

"But, but--he'll surely think better of it--he is not the one to run away from any woman, even if she should number forty years or thereabout; and--and ..."

And so the faithful Konski, after having given a most incredulous shake of the head, set to work, and continued to unpack his master's travelling boxes.

CHAPTER II

Meanwhile Bertram, had already crossed the bridge which spanned the brook at the bottom of the garden terrace, and was hurrying along to the village along the line of meadows. His hostess, Hildegard, had said at dinner that she meant to-day, like every Thursday afternoon, to visit her newly-founded Kindergarten; so he thought there would be no difficulty in finding her. He had been a frequent visitor at Rinstedt, and knew every lane in the village; and the Kindergarten, they said, was on the main road, not far from the parsonage. Well, and what did he mean to say to Hildegard when he met her? First, of course, make sure of the facts. But there was little need for that. Konski was a smart fellow, who was not likely to have made a mistake; and then he was on such excellent terms with the omniscient Mamsell Christine! He would ask her what had induced her to break through the agreement to which she had now adhered for the last twenty years. And yet--what a needless question! Why, women are never consistent! And in such things they always like to assist each other and work into each other's hands, even if they are by no means specially fond of each other. And now it seemed as if there were special fondness between these two. His beautiful hostess had, quite contrary to her wont, sung Lydia's praises in every possible variety of way! And then, take the fact that she had sent her own daughter to Lydia's *pension*, and had left the girl there in the small *Residenz* for three years. Poor Erna! Fancy her for three years under the care of that crazy woman! Poor Erna--the beautiful creature with the great, deep, blue eyes! That should never have happened. It was a positive insult to him. He had urged every argument against it; had found out a supremely suitable place in Berlin for her; had offered to undertake careful personal supervision; had urged them to confide the child to his care, to give the child an opportunity of seeing something of life under its larger, nobler aspect. And they had said yes to everything; had thanked him so very much for his exertions, his kindness; and at the last moment they had contentedly plumped back into the beloved mire and stagnant waters of the pettiness of life in the small *Residenz*. To be sure, My Lady herself had been brought up in that social quagmire, and still cherished with plaintive delight recollections of bygone splendour, and mourned in secret over her own hard fate which had not permitted her, like Lydia, to sun herself all the days of her life in the immediate rays of princely favour, but had doomed her to marry a man who was not nobly born--a man rich enough, forsooth, but bearing the unaristocratic name of Bermer, and having friends of similarly unaristocratic names, to whom, for all that, one had to be civil. Yes, a real Baron--a Baron von Lotter-Vippach--would, of course, be infinitely preferable! And fancy her, fancy My Lady forcing the Baron's company upon him after he had expressly urged that, being only half convalescent, he needed perfect repose; and would, if they were to have company in the house, rather in the meanwhile deny himself the delight of seeing his old friends, and would come to them in spring instead on his return from Italy!

Yes, something like this he would say to his beautiful hostess, in perfect calmness and good temper, of course, only tinged with a touch of finest irony.... And this new building by his side--why, it must surely be the Kindergarten!

So it was. But the girl who was in charge of the children who were playing on the garden-plot in front of the building, said to him, in answer to his question, that My Lady had left half an hour ago; had gone to the parsonage, she thought. A couple of boys who were running about told him My Lady had gone to the village-mayor along with the parson.

The mayor's farm was situated at the opposite end of the village. Bertram started off in that direction, but before he had got half way he bethought himself that the parson would probably walk back with Hildegard, and that in that case he would of course have no opportunity of speaking plainly to her. So he turned back, determined to wait for her near the parsonage, which she was bound to pass on her way home. And yet, how could he wait? He could not tell whether he would have time left to carry out his intended flight; nay, every moment brought Lydia nearer, every moment he must expect to see the carriage whirl her past him where he stood. What? was he to stand here like this, and be compelled to bow to her? Never! To the left a narrow lane led direct to the forest, which, higher up, almost bordered on the mansion-house. This road back was somewhat longer than the one he had come by, and was steeper too; but anyhow it was much shorter than the carriage-drive, for that branched off from the high road in the main valley at the entrance to the side valley, thus intersecting the whole length of the village, and ultimately wound its long serpentine road up the high hill crowned by his friend's stately mansion. This way he would gain an advance of a good half-hour anyhow. It was to be hoped that his friend and host, Otto Bermer, had meanwhile returned from the coal mines; they lay in the opposite direction. He'd make a clean breast of it to Otto, and make Otto take his farewell compliments to My Lady. Poor Otto! "The grey mare was the better horse," no doubt; and poor Otto would not relish the task; but what was to be done? And did not he, Bertram, anyhow enjoy the doubtful reputation of being selfishness incarnate! Well, then, this done, they would swiftly get some conveyance or other ready for him. If required, Konski could stay behind with boxes and such-like impedimenta; and in two or three hours' driving, first through the forest, to avoid the danger of meeting her, then along the high road, he would reach Fichtenau. He was fond of Fichtenau. There he would rest in that evergreen dale for a few days, and recover from the fatigue of the journey and from this day's manifold annoyances. Anyhow, he would have escaped from Lydia, have broken away from the snare which those women had set for him! He owed this satisfaction to himself, and perhaps the reflection would smooth the rough forest path he had now entered upon.

For it was rough, was that path; much more so than he remembered it being formerly. Much rougher and much steeper too; in fact, most, most-- abominably steep. Never mind; by following the tiny brooklet which was murmuring in the glen by his side, and which fell into the big brook in the valley below, he must speedily reach the little bridge leading to the opposite side; and then a smooth, or at least a fairly smooth, path would lead him on to the mansion.

What on earth could she have to do, she and the parson, at the mayor's? Something, probably, about getting appropriate quarters for those who were coming to the manœuvres; to be sure, My Lady, never idle, must needs take an interest in everything! Or perchance it was some charitable purpose, something for the sick, for the poor; in the pursuit of such noble aims My Lady never spared herself now, that is never since Royalty had set the example, and made it fashionable! And anyhow, it was hardly polite, in one so uniformly polite as My Lady, to leave the house and walk right away to the far end of the village with one guest already in the house, and with other guests expected every minute. Possibly--possibly My Lady was not unwilling to avoid the one guest; and the others, to be sure, must needs drive past the mayor's house. What more natural than, in such a case, to enter the carriage that brought the new guests; whilst driving with them through the village, what more simple than to give a confidential hint or two, just the merest suggestion, as to the treatment of the bird which she had captured--oh, so cleverly! No, no, My Lady--not captured yet ... not yet!

But where was the little bridge? It ought to have appeared long ere this. What! Climb down the steep glen, get your feet wet in the brook below, and climb up again the opposite side? Perish the thought! Why, everything seemed to go against him to-day!

At last. And a broad new bridge too. And pair fully rustic, with elaborate rustic ornaments of curiously entwined and intertwisted tree branches. And, worst of all, such a confounded bit higher up the stream than where the old bridge had been.

And the path on the opposite side, too; new, new like the bridge, new and fashionable, a regular promenade path; belonging, no doubt, to the elaborate system of paths which his noble and beautiful hostess had for years woven, like a complicated network, through the woods around. Of course, like Charlotte in the "Elective Affinities," the fair châtelaine must needs have that passion for beautifying everything; like Charlotte, but not, oh dear! no, with any tender *penchant* for her husband's well-born friends. Well, well! He himself had never doubted the unapproachable virtue of My Lady: what if she now, tried her gentle hand ever so little at this, surely it was only the outcome of the excessive goodness of her chaste, and cool, and philanthropic heart.... Heart! ... And oh the wretched pain, the horrid, horrid sensation in my own heart. Who the mischief could be philanthropical if he felt like this? Perhaps this insane running and climbing has brought on a relapse. The story might then close where it began, and fair Lydia would come just in the nick of time to see that when people talk of a broken heart, they are not necessarily talking nonsense.... What rubbish, though! If my heart breaks, it will be because it has got some organic fault, and because I took champagne when I should not have done so.

He had dropped upon a bench by, the wayside, and there he crouched, almost bent double, pressing his handkerchief to his mouth, to prevent his moans from being heard in the silence of the darkening woods.

The attack passed away. Gradually the agonising pains grew less. With the physical anguish much of the fierce passion into which he had worked himself passed away too. In its stead he felt a terrible heaviness, a dull languor in all his limbs, and there was a sort of stupor about his brain.

Supposing it had given way, he mused. Fancy, sitting alone here in the wood, a dead man, for goodness knows how long, and then terrifying a poor wretch who chanced to pass this way first! This was not a pleasing thought. But this anyhow would have been the worst. Death in itself he did not dread. Why should he? Death was but the end of life. And life? His life? If he could say that his living harmed no one, except perhaps poor Konski whom he sometimes tormented by his wayward moods--yet, on the other hand, it gladdened no one, least of all himself. The few poor students or struggling artists would have their allowances paid out to them for the time fixed, whether he lived on or not, and a few public institutions were welcome to divide the residue between them. All that would be settled in the shortest and most business-like manner. Never a tear would be shed by any human being, unless perchance by old Konski. But no; it was impossible to think of the good, easy-going fellow in tears.

He was sitting at the foot of a spreading beech tree. A crow, perched on the top, uttered a shriek.

Bertram looked up with a grim smile. "Patience!" he said.

But it was not on his account that the crow had uttered that cry, but probably because somebody was approaching. He saw a lady coming down the side-path which led from the forest direct to his bench. Again, this convulsive pain at the heart! But he forced himself to look again; and no, it was not Lydia. Lydia was taller, and her blonde hair was of ashen hue; this lady's hair was dark, very dark. And the style of walking, too, was different, very different: an easy, even, step, making it appear as if she were floating down the somewhat steep path, although he could see the movement of the feet beneath the light summer dress. And now she had come quite close to him. She gave a little start, for, gazing up to the shrieking crow, she had not noticed him, and he had sprung up somewhat abruptly from the bench. But in a moment she was collected again, and the flush faded as quickly from her cheek as it had spread.

"Is, it possible?--Erna!"

"Uncle Bertram!"

There was something wondrously melodious in the voice, but not the slightest trace of the glad emotion which he himself had experienced which he himself had experienced on seeing his darling. His heart contracted; he would fain have said: "You were wont to give me a different reception;" but he blushed to face the young beauty as a beggar, and letting, go her hands, he only said--

"You did not expect to find me here?"

"How could I?" was her reply.

"To be sure!" thought Bertram. "How could she? What a silly question of mine!"

He knew not what next to say, and, in some embarrassment, he stood silent. The crow above had been silent during the last half-minute or so, and now commenced to croak, abominably. Both had involuntarily gazed up; now they were, walking silently side by side along the path.

CHAPTER III

The evening was closing in around them. Through the thick undergrowth of wood which bordered the path on both sides but little light could penetrate; overhead the leafy crowns of the beeches interlaced and formed an almost continuous roof. At a certain abrupt declivity a few rough steps had been placed.

"Will you take my arm. Uncle Bertram?" said Erna. It was the first word spoken between them since, several minutes ago, minutes which had weighed like lead upon Bertram, they had left the bench under the beech tree.

"I was just going to put the same question to you," he replied.

"Thanks," said Erna. "I know every step here; but you--and then, you have been ill."

This might, of course, have been meant in all friendliness; but there was a coldness about the tone, something like giving alms, Bertram thought.

"Have been," he made answer; "but quite well again--quite well."

"I understand you are going to Italy for the winter--for the sake of your health."

"I am going to Italy because I hope I shall be rather less bored in Rome than in Berlin--that is all."

"And suppose you are bored in Rome too?"

"You mean, bores are bored everywhere?"

"No, I do not mean that; indeed, it would have been most disagreeable on my part had I meant anything of the kind. I only wanted to know where people go to from Rome, if they desire still to travel on. To Naples, I should say?"

"To be sure. To Naples, to Capri! In Capri there stands amidst orange groves, with sublimest view of the blue infinity of the ocean, a fair white hostelry, embowered in roses, Quisisana. Years ago I was there, and I have longed ever since to be back again. *Qui si sana!* What a sound of comfort, of promise! *Qui si sana!* Here one gets well! Even those who ate fairly well, physically, have something to recover from. Why, life itself--what is it but a long disease, and death its only cure?"

Another pause. He had intended that there should be no new break in their conversation and yet the very words he had just uttered, still under the impulse of the invalid's peevish humour, were little likely to induce the beautiful and taciturn girl by his side to talk. He wanted to make heir talk. It never occurred to him that her silence was due to a lack of ideas, or even to shyness. Quite the reverse. She interested him more and more every moment, and he was strongly impressed that he was dealing with a girl of marked individuality, reposing securely in her own strength. Of her whom he had known and loved as a child, and whose image he had cherished in fondest, truest memory, never a trace!

"You know, Uncle Bertram, that you are going to see Fräulein von Aschhof--Aunt Lydia--to-night?" she resumed abruptly.

Bertram started. That name--from her, fair, chaste lips--had a doubly hateful sound.

"I know," he answered; "not from your parents, but I know."

"They will have shrunk from telling you," Erna continued. "Mamma was most reluctant to sanction Aunt Lydia's coming; but Aunt Lydia begged so very hard to be allowed to see you once more, and she thought that now, when you have been so very, very ill, and when you are going away for such a long time, you might be in gentler mood. And yet she was afraid to encounter you. She grew so nervous as we were driving along, that I believe she was uncommonly near getting out and leaving us to continue the journey without her. At last I could scarcely bear to witness her uneasiness any longer, and I felt considerable relief when I got out myself in order to walk across the hill--from Fischbach, don't you know--and as I was coming along, I was debating whether, if I reached home before them, I might not beg you to be a little friendly towards auntie. You ... but I am not sure whether to go on ..."

"I beg you will do so."

"I only wanted to add: you owe it to her."

"Do I?"

"I should think so; for her only fault has been that she has loved you and still loves you, and you ..."

"My dear child, I beg you will go on without any shyness. I am anxious, very anxious, you should do so."

"And you ... left her, after you had been engaged for a whole year!"

"And then I wrote her a letter of renunciation, did I not? And the poor forsaken one, in her despair, engaged herself within four-and-twenty hours to Count Finkenburg, who had long been vainly suing for her hand? And the old gentleman was so enchanted that scarce a week after he died from rapture and paralysis combined, without even having time to remember his fair bride in his will! Was it not so?"

"Let us change the topic, Uncle Bertram," Erna replied. "I hear from your words and from your tone that you are excited, and I now feel doubly how awkward I was in turning our talk, for auntie's sake, to a subject I ought to know nothing of, and which I certainly should never have mentioned."

"I cannot let you off like that, alas! my child," Bertram said in reply. "I must still ask you from whom your information is derived. From Fräulein von Aschhof, of course?"

"I cannot find it unnatural," Erna said, "if Aunt Lydia, in the excitement she has laboured under ever since your visit here was announced, and since she determined to see you again, has unburdened her overflowing heart to me, and has told me all which--or the greater part of which--I knew or guessed. And she has urgently entreated me not to repeat a word of this to you, and I am sure she is convinced that I would do nothing of the kind. But I gave her no promise, for I have always been very fond of you, Uncle Bertram, very, very fond; and I was so sorry that you ... that I now could no longer be fond of you. I have always in my heart taken your side, when they were saying that you were cold and selfish, and cared for nobody but yourself. I have always thought: he has never found any one worthy of him! And now I know all, I should like to say: perhaps Aunt Lydia was not worthy of him either; she has many qualities which I do not like at all--but she would surely have turned out differently if you had not betr ... had not forsaken her. How can a girl remain good, if she is forsaken by the man she loves! How can she, if her heart is easily touched, become aught but a coquette, and assume manners that people will laugh and jeer at; or, if she be proud, and ashamed of her misfortune, she must needs grow cold and heartless, and full of contempt for all men, nay, for all mankind!"

The calm, low voice had remained the same to the very last word, but in striking contrast to that calm and that self-control there was the passionate gleam of the great dark eyes, which now looked up to Bertram with wondrous firmness, such as the ancients may have imagined the gaze of the gods--"whose eyelids quiver not, like those of mortals."

The narrow path had widened to a glade; there they stood for a few moments gazing in each other's eyes; and Bertram felt the fascination of that wondrous firmness, felt, too, that no consideration could condemn him to stand before those eyes as a contemptible wretch, and that, at any cost, he must tear to pieces the dark curtain which unscrupulous lies had woven and spread between her and him.

He took her arm, as though to make sure that she would not escape from him, and, striding swiftly along, and almost dragging her with him, he said--

"And now hear me, too, and despise me, if you still can do so after you have heard me! Forsaken, did you say, forsaken and betrayed? Yea, verily! But she it was who practised the treachery--most infamous, most horrible treachery, with never the shadow of an excuse for it, if indeed anything ever can excuse treachery. I loved her--I will not say more than ever man did love--I know not how other men love--I only, know, that I loved her with the best and purest strength, of my heart. I was no longer a youth when, at your parents' wedding, I made the acquaintance of your mother's friend. I was almost thirty years of age, and was living, as you know, in Leipzig as a mere private scholar--*Privat-Gelehrter* they call it. I had planned my scheme of study on a very great scale, and, being very much, in earnest about science and art, as indeed about all things I take up, I was wont to devote years to tasks which other men, with less time or more genius, accomplish in as many months. Moreover, I had what I required for the expenses of living, perhaps even a little more--I, am not given to paying attention to that kind of thing. Now everything became changed at once. I loved her, I fancied myself loved in return. We had met here again, and, more than once, and had become engaged, though at first, and at my own special request, in all secrecy. I comprehended that a man engaged to so high-born and gifted, a girl as Lydia von Aschhof, must needs be something better than a mere obscure private scholar, and I readily 'pulled myself together,' determined to reach my goal. Some time, of course, was required before my great work could be completed. Some time; too much for her patience. Perhaps she doubted its ultimate success. Perhaps she cared naught for the success, notwithstanding the enthusiasm which she pretended to feel for my efforts, notwithstanding her being so very kind as to assure me a thousand times that my genius, my talent, had made her my captive, and would hold her my captive, yea, though a crown were laid at her feet. As it turned out, no princely crown was needed; only a plain coronet--and one surmounting a grey, decrepit head into the bargain. Oh! she wrote me a most touching, most generous letter of renunciation. 'I am but hindering you in your lofty striving; an artist, a scholar must be free, unshackled; your fame is more to me than my love,' and so on, and so on. Two or three pages more, high-sounding phrases in daintiest handwriting, concluding, of course, with the announcement of her new engagement, by which, as by a *fait accompli*, she must needs assist her wavering heart.

"The letter was written from here, from Rinstedt. I hurried to the railway; at the last station I got hold of a vehicle. When we got to Fischbach, the poor overdriven steeds could not get on any further. By the shortest, steepest path I climbed to the top of the Hirschstein, the hill you have just come by; here, on the top, I fell down like one dead. I gathered myself together again, and staggered on, on, until I reached your father's house. She must have had some foreboding that I would not submit to this in all patience; she had left your father's house an hour before, driving to Fichtenau, taking the road by which it was impossible for me to come. Afterwards I came to be grateful to her for her circumspection and her precaution, for I think I must have been simply raving mad; and it was well for both of us that my power was broken, that I could not pursue the fair fugitive, but had to remain here, a burden on your parents, sick unto death, given up by the doctors, until some six or eight weeks' after, I surprised them all by recovering, enabled to live on as best one can with a sorely wounded heart--and a heart injured, not in the physical sense alone. What good, do you think, did it do me whilst I was struggling with death here, and afterwards dragged myself on crutches through the terrace-gardens, that my work had appeared, had taken the world by storm, and made me, once for all, what they call a famous man? What good that, just at that time a childless old miser of an uncle took it into his head to die, and that, in default of other heirs, his whole huge fortune fell to me? I had had enough of the lying and cheating of humanity. Fame, love--I cared no longer for these things. I became what I am, what my acquaintances know me to be, what they have called me to you--a cold egotist. What if for all that I do not cross my hands idly in my lap but work on, and now and again utter a word of freedom which others, less independent, might lack the courage to utter; or if I start and encourage works of general utility; or if here and there I help some lame dog over a stile; these things I surely do not for the love of the Lord, nay, solely, so as not to lose that modicum of self-respect which belongs to the indispensable stock-in-trade of a discreet egotist. And talking of self-respect, dear, I begin to perceive with pain that I am lessening the aforesaid modicum considerably in telling you all this. For, in affairs of the hearts a gentleman should always spare the lady the utterance of the first word and leave her the last, and if she asserts that he is Don Giovanni and she Donna Elvira, why, he has but to bow and thank her for assigning so brilliant a part to him. And now, my dear child, now try to be fond of your garrulous old uncle once more, will you not?"

The girl made no reply. A feeling of shame had gradually stolen over Bertram as he spoke, and he had tried in vain to weaken it by concluding with a semi-humorous turn. Now this feeling grew intensified by Erna's silence. How had, it been possible for him to forget himself so far as to reveal to a young girl, one almost a child still, one without comprehension for such sad, ugly, painful experiences, the deepest secret of his heart--a secret which he had trained himself to pass by, as it were, with his own face turned away? And he had told of this, to a girl who stood to the object of his vehement denunciation in the peculiarly tender and delicate relation of pupil! How mean, how ignoble of him! He had acted like a raw, immature lad! He wished himself a thousand miles away; he cursed his want of determination, inasmuch as he might have left the place abruptly an hour ago, and thus have escaped all this horrible confusion. Now he must needs depart at once, this very evening, if possible without seeing, without speaking to, a soul; most certainly without entering upon any explanation whatever. He had just tasted the delight of such explanations, and it would be long before he lost the bitter after-taste of them!...

They were quite cleat of the wood now, and were approaching--walking across some meadow land--a tiny gate in the thick old wall, which led to the courtyard.

Suddenly Erna said, "And you have told nobody all this?"

"No," he answered; and it cost him a curious struggle to get the one brief word--out.

They passed through the tiny gate; it was almost dark in the yard now. Before the entrance to the house stood a large open travelling carriage; servants were removing the belongings of the travellers who had already alighted. Through the main gate, on the opposite side, a cart, laden with the heavier articles of luggage, was entering.

"Uncle Bertram," whispered Erna.

Just as they were about to cross the threshold of the tiny gate she had seized his hand with gentle pressure. He had involuntarily stopped. Again she was gazing up at him, but not now, as before in the wood, with a stern expression. Was it a reflection of the radiance of the young moon, just then rising above the gloom which was enfolding the buildings around--or could it be tears that glistened in the great eyes?

"You want to leave us, Uncle Bertram?"

"Who told you so?"

"It matters not. You want to leave us?"

"Yes."

"Stay! Pray, stay--for my sake!"

She dropped the hand which she had clasped until now, and hurried across the yard to the mansion-house, while he ascended the stairs to the side wing where his own rooms were situated, his whole soul full of the image of this wondrous girl, whose words, whose looks, had so potent a spell over him, that he no longer seemed to have a will of his own as against hers.

CHAPTER IV

His master's long absence had at length commenced to disquiet faithful Konski considerably. True, he knew from his ten years' experience that he need not pay much attention to any orders that master gave him when in a state of great excitement; and, of course, the later it grew, the more improbable it became that the departure, although announced, would really take place; but then, supposing some accident had happened to him? The doctor in Berlin had most strongly urged him to take every possible precaution lest, during the first few weeks anyhow, his master should over-exert himself in any way--and master had hurried down those terrace steps like one possessed! And all on account of this infernal old maid who was never allowed to visit at this house when they, master and he, were here! Oh, why had he not held his silly tongue, and not brought the great news at once to his master!

He would have liked hurrying after him into the village, but dared not leave his post. And now their host came in and inquired for master, and seemed greatly concerned when Konski, to soothe his own anxiety as it were, hinted that his master had not been over pleased when told that additional guests were expected; and Konski added, as a sort of conjecture of his own, that he had probably gone out for a walk, so as to avoid having to be present at their reception. And meanwhile My Lady had returned and had sent for him, and Konski had to repeat to her Ladyship--for whom he entertained the most confounded respect--what he had already told her Ladyship's husband; and her Ladyship had looked so hard at him with those piercing brown eyes of hers, that he was jolly glad when he was back at his post of observation at the lobby-window, whence he could survey the whole extensive court-yard. And there--an open carriage was just entering it; only two people in it--a lady and a gentleman--thank Heaven, one lady only! In the gathering twilight Konski could not distinguish, the lady's features or figure, but, if there was only one lady, why, who could it be but dear Miss Erna? And from her, master was not likely to run away; and all was well now, if only he himself were safely back.

The door below was opened. Konski heard his master's step upon the stairs and hurried to meet him, joyfully telling him all that he had observed; and did master know already that Miss Erna was the only lady who had arrived?

His master had thrown himself into an arm-chair in the sitting-room, where careful Konski had already lighted a liberal supply of candles, and was staring hard in front of him, passing at intervals his hands over brow and eyes. Suddenly he sat bold upright and said:

"What did you say?"

Poor Konski had said nothing at all during the last few minutes, but inquired now whether his master would not dress for supper; he thought it was getting quite late enough.

Bertram rose and passed into the adjoining bedroom where Konski had laid out such a costume as he deemed appropriate for the occasion. He lent him the necessary aid, and marvelled greatly that his master, who was wont to talk to him during the process of dressing more than at any other time, did not say a single word to-night. Another curious thing was this: quite contrary to his custom, the master looked hard at himself in the mirror again and again, and, strangest sight of all, he pulled and twisted his moustache about! However, seeing that master, though looking very grave, did not appear either annoyed or angry, Konski was quite satisfied. To-night then, anyhow, their departure need not be provided for.

There was a knock at the door. Their host entered as hurriedly as was consistent with his being so very stout.

"Thank Heaven that you are here!" he exclaimed, shaking both his friend's hands again and again, as though he had been 'long looked-for, come at last!' "Thank Heaven; we have been quite frightened about you. Hildegard was very angry that I had left you alone. I said to her, 'Why, he is not a child, requiring to be watched at every step;' that is to say, I did not actually say so in so many words. I ... thought so. My wife is terribly nervous to-day. I had told her at once ..."

Here he noticed the servant's presence, and in some embarrassment broke off abruptly. Bertram having now completed his toilet, the two gentlemen left the room together. As they were walking through the long passage which led to the main building, his host put one arm round his friend's slender waist and said confidentially, lowering his voice by way of precaution--

"I had told Hildegard at once that you would be annoyed; at least I did not say so in so many words, but I--hinted it, for, you know, my wife cannot beat contradiction; and I soon found out that the two women, between them, had determined that the meeting should take place. Now Erna tells me--she is a darling, is she not? a little peculiar, a little odd, but always good to me; how nice that you met on the hills--well, Erna tells me that you were not particularly angry that Lydia had accompanied her; that is to say, Erna does not know anything of the old stories, or has only heard some vague rumours that you cannot bear each other, or that you cannot bear Lydia. Never mind, it's all the same now; only tell me that you are not particularly angry."

"I was at first, but I am so no longer."

"That's all I ask for. And after all, old chap, well, misunderstandings and all that sort of thing! But the blame is sure to be yours, or almost entirely yours. Why, it's always the man who is to blame, eh? I should know that much, having been married these twenty years!"

He laughed. Bertram, to change the conversation, asked where the others were.

"The ladies are on the verandah; the Baron was still in his room when I came away."

"By the by," Bertram asked, "who is this Baron? You were talking about him once or twice at table, but I confess I hardly listened."

"Lotter?" his friend said. "Look here; you'll like him immensely. Stunning fellow, Lotter. Has read every mortal thing; plays the piano; paints--portraits, landscapes, anything you like. Has come home to do some painting; studies at our academy, don't you know?--and is a constant guest at Court, of course."

"Does he belong to these parts?"

"Oh; dear no! hails from Würtemberg. A very, very old family; Lotter-Vippach. His father was a General, I believe; his uncle a Minister of State; that sort of thing, don't you know? He has been in the army himself; was in the '70 campaign. But he is a bit of a rover. Has been up and about a good deal; in Algiers, South America; that, sort of thing. I pressed him to come and stay here during the manœvres, to help me to do the honours, as I never was in the army myself. He is awfully anxious to make your acquaintance; has read all your works and--and--but where on earth are our ladies? I'll go and look. You stop where you are; do not come out bareheaded."

The last words had already been spoken in the garden saloon, the great French windows of which, leading to the verandah, stood wide open. His host had hurried off to look for the ladies, and Bertram, left alone, strode up and down in the large, half-darkened room. Had he not, perhaps, yielded all too readily to Erna's command? If obedience was to be easy to him, nay, if it was to be at all possible for him, she ought to have stayed by his side. And now her very image was gone from his inner eye, and its place had been taken by her whom he had once so passionately loved, as if twenty years had not gone by since he last saw her, as if she had only passed a minute ago with her beautiful friend and hostess into the garden, thence to return immediately under some pretext or other, to rush to his embrace, to shower hot, passionate kisses upon him--here, in this very saloon, as she had so often, so often done--here, where the faint fragrance of violets still seemed to float, that she was so fond of, and which in those days he was ever associating with her presence!

He was standing in the semi-darkness, his back turned to the verandah; a gentle rustling sound was coming up the steps. He turned. Framed in by one of the doors against the brighter background of the evening sky, appeared the shadowy outline of a lady, lingering a moment or two on the threshold, then hastening with raised arms towards him, as he stood motionless, spellbound.

Before he could prevent it, she had sunk on her knees before him, had seized his hands which he was involuntarily stretching forth to lift her up, and now she was pressing them to her bosom, to her lips. A dense cloud of violet perfume came floating up to him.

"Mercy, Charles, mercy!"

"I entreat you, My Lady, ... for Heaven's sake ..."

He had been barely able to stammer out these words; he felt the most acute physical anguish at his heart; cold beads of perspiration stood upon his forehead; ice-cold were the hands which Lydia had held till then, and which now she dropped, terrified, rising as she did so from the ground.

"My Lady!" she murmured, "My Lady ... Ah, I knew it!"

The convulsive pain at his heart had ceased now; it beat on, but slowly, heavily; even so his anger and pain were giving way to compassion.

"Let bygones be bygones," he said.

"If it were possible!" whispered Lydia.

"It must be possible."

She knew from his gentle but firm tone that, for the moment, she dare go no farther; and though she had to confess to herself that she had been deceived in her fond hope of reconquering his affections by one grand assault at starting, something was secured anyhow, and something desirable and even necessary--a fairly satisfactory footing when they met in society.

"The dear voice!" she whispered; "the old, dear, gentle voice! But ... those hard, cruel words! Yet I have no right to complain, and I will not lament; it must, indeed, be possible!"

Much to his relief Bertram was spared the necessity of replying, for his host and hostess were just then coming in from the garden, accompanied by Erna and Baron Lotter. At the same moment a servant opened the folding-door which led to the dining-room; the two gentlemen were introduced to each other; the Baron offered his arm to the lady of the house, Lydia was clinging to the master, and thus Erna fell to Bertram's share. They were lingering a little behind the rest.

"How good you are!" whispered Erna.

"Am I?" he made answer. "I feel most contemptible."

CHAPTER V

In very truth the feeling that he had done wrong in thus opening his heart to Erna had come back in renewed strength to Bertram, since he had to admit to himself that he had emphatically broken his own dictum that bygones were to be bygones. The past was no longer a secret between those concerned; and what would henceforth happen--each word, each look which they exchanged, all, all would have a sense, a meaning for somebody else--for the beautiful girl who was so grave beyond her years, the girl with the great, still, godlike eyes.

Thus Bertram was profoundly in earnest when he declined to accept Erna's praise; but, anyhow, he hoped that the worst was over now.

How greatly he was mistaken in this, came most painfully home to him with the first stolen glimpse which he ventured to take of Lydia's face in the pitiless radiance of the bright candles which shone upon the round table in the dining-room, where he sat opposite her. Was that really ... Lydia? Or had some mischievous imp, by cruel witchcraft, put a caricature of herself in her place, and changed the picture of the bright and gifted girl, overflowing with jest and fun, with humour and wit; the girl with the somewhat irregular but most piquant features, with the big, light-blue, mischievous eyes, fresh and rosy of colour, with wild, fluttering, blonde locks, into the picture of an aging coquette, for ever pouting her thin lips, even when she laughed, so as to hide her false teeth; now lowering, now lifting her eyelids, like an actress, in vain endeavouring to give some light to her eyes--a light as treacherous as the all too bright pinkiness of the lean cheek, the all too dark carmine of the ears, adorned though they were with sparkling diamonds? An ugly old woman, who now let the gold embroidered white silk shawl glide from the scraggy shoulders, only to draw it up again immediately and attempt a more picturesque drapery--which was not a success, so that the game had to be renewed forthwith!

And he had once loved this painted, dressed-up, revoltingly coquettish person; had loved her with the best, purest strength of his heart, as, but a little while ago, he had assured Erna with passionate eagerness. It was horrible! Would Erna believe that yonder withered shrub had ever blossomed in vernal brightness and beauty? How could she believe it, when she looked at the friend of Lydia's youth, her own mother, whose majestic beauty was barely touched by Time in his flight? Her great brown eyes had lost none of their velvety softness, her raven hair still shone in undimmed splendour. And if the difference in appearance, in manner, was now so great between the two ladies, must it not always have existed? And must not the taste of a man, whose feelings could at any time have led him so far astray, have been at all times most lamentable?

And if the pitiless brightness had brought so terrible a discovery to him, how would he himself appear before Erna's searching gaze? Had not some horrible change taken place with him too? Why, these twenty years had altered Erna's father, who at college had been rightly surnamed 'The Beauty,' into an excessively stout gentleman, with a somewhat bloated countenance, and a mighty skull, which was getting painfully bald in the region of the temples! And he himself had never been distinguished for personal attraction; true, his hair was as dark as ever; and, before supper, in the glass, he had thought that he saw a pale and grave, but not a worn, face. But then the complaisant mirror of vanity might make one fancy one saw all sorts of things. No doubt Lydia had just such a mirror in her room!

Bertram felt more and more sad at heart. He no longer dared lift his eyes, but kept them fixed upon the plates, which the servants changed without his having tasted any of the dishes to which he helped himself mechanically. So he sat on, scarcely hearing a word of the conversation, which was principally carried on by Lydia and the Baron. Apparently they were talking about some Court affairs, and very amusing and piquant they would appear to be. Anyhow, there was much laughter, chiefly on the part of Lydia and the Baron, and My Lady held up her hand once or twice, and reminded the two of the respect due to the Grand Ducal family. Then the conversation touched upon the approaching manœuvres, and the Baron proclaimed his minute knowledge of every detail, and endeavoured to explain to the ladies, with the help of spoons and forks and what not, the original positions both of the attacking party and the attacked, and duly weighed the various events which might or must occur, according whether the commanding officers did or did not take certain steps. Under any circumstances, the decisive portion of the sham-fight must come off in the immediate neighbourhood of Rinstedt itself, if not in Rinstedt itself; unfortunately, the ground being singularly unsuitable for cavalry, the ultimate issue would lie between artillery and infantry. He himself, said the Baron, having formerly been a cavalry officer, was very sorry for that; but, anyhow, the ladies, could look forward to a glorious sight. What, a pity, he added, that in spite of his having so many friends in the army, he did not chance to have any personal acquaintances among the officers of this particular regiment.

"Well, I know a number of them," said the host. "The 99th were stationed at Erfurt until a twelvemonth ago. I used to meet the officers over and over again out shooting."

"Then," said the Baron, turning to Lydia, "you must know some of them too. They are sure to have attended some of our Court balls."

"Of course," the lady replied; "and they were also in the habit of coming over in shoals to the play; but who is to distinguish one red collar from another? Not I! I love plain, quiet, civilian colours. Ask Erna; she is sure to know. She spent six weeks last summer with her Aunt Adelheid in Erfurt, and there the officers, are constantly coming and going. Is it not so, Erna?"

"You are forgetting," said Erna, "that aunt was in mourning at the time. Of course there were no parties then."

"But still," the Baron observed, "people go to a house without being actually bidden to parties, inspire of the family being in mourning, if there are six marriageable daughters in it, as is the case in your aunt's house."

"Possibly; then my power of discriminating between different red collars is not more strongly developed than Aunt Lydia's; anyhow, I do not remember any one of the gentlemen."

This was uttered in such a stern tone, as of one who would decline to pursue the subject, that Bertram looked up involuntarily. Her dainty features were perfectly composed, but the blue eyes, which she was bending upon him, not upon her interlocutor the Baron, seemed to have a deeper radiance than that of suppressed annoyance. This was the first time that their looks had met across the table, and a curious thrill passed through his frame. He felt the hot blood surging to his temples; and to mask his growing embarrassment, he asked who was in command of the regiment in question.

"Colonel von Waldor," the Baron replied promptly.

"I knew an officer of that name," said Bertram, "long ago, in Berlin; at that time he had been told off to the Military Academy of that town. For some years I kept up a correspondence with him, but somehow I lost sight of him afterwards. But I rather think that was not his regiment?"

"No," replied the Baron. "You are quite right; he used to be in the 210th. He got the colonelcy of the 99th about a year ago. He made quite a name for himself in the '70 campaign."

"Even at the time I recall, my friend was considered a very smart officer," said Bertram.

"No doubt, no doubt," replied the Baron; "it must be the same man. As far as I know, there are not two Waldors in the army, at least not among regimental commanders, for I think I know all their names by heart. Your Colonel is a queer fish, anyhow."

"What is a 'queer fish'?" asked Lydia, touching the Baron's arm with her fan.

He laughed, and said: "Well, that question is more easily asked than answered."

"Then, pray, do not answer it at all," said Hildegard, the hostess, glancing at her daughter Erna.

"Why not, my Lady?" the Baron exclaimed. "It is harmless enough to let the facts speak, and it is a fact that Waldor who--I do not know him personally, but Dr. Bertram will assuredly confirm my statement--was known throughout the army not only on account of his gallantry, but also on account of his manly beauty, and who had consequently broken countless hearts, is still a bachelor."

"You say 'consequently,'" exclaimed Lydia, "and consequently you think very meanly of our sex."

"How so?"

"Well, you seem to assume that manly beauty suffices to touch--or, as you are pleased to call it, to break--female hearts. Alas, my dear Baron, how little do you know our sex!"

"I beg a thousand pardons--but I really said nothing of the kind. Venus and Mars--the alliance of valour and beauty, you know--your poets know something of this. Why, there is a poet here among us--let him speak up for me!"

With these last words the Baron had turned to Bertram; his tone and the accompanying gesture had something insultingly patronising about them; in fact, in Bertram's eye the whole demeanour of the young man, almost a giant in stature, was saturated with an arrogant sort of self-complacency, which seemed to take unanimous applause for granted. Nevertheless he replied with calm politeness:

"I neither consider myself a poet, nor am I, to the best of my knowledge, considered one by anybody who has read the few miserable trifles in verse which I published years ago."

"I protest against this most emphatically," exclaimed Lydia. "I have read those 'miserable trifles in verse,' as you call them--what a horrible expression. I know them by heart, and I consider the author to be a poet--a poet by grace divine."

"I am extremely obliged to you," replied Bertram. "However, surely what a man is born for is wont to announce itself, sooner or later, in a man's own heart. With me that voice is absolutely silent; and, therefore, I might surely claim the right of refusing to give the evidence required of me. But not being specially qualified, and being absolutely impartial, I would fain warn my friends not to repose overmuch confidence in poets on that particular point. Anxious for the applause of the many, as their trade seems to demand, they accommodate themselves but too readily to the taste of the many, who, as we all know, like very children, seize eagerly upon anything bright, glistening, motley-coloured. Therefore, why should they not picture the heroine as beautiful beyond compare, the hero as valorous beyond comparison, and heap any number of additional titles to fame upon their blessed heads! Whether one quality does not perchance exclude another, whether the measure dealt out does not, anyhow, exceed all that is reasonably possible--dear, dear, there are few who'll ask that question; and if any one does, why, then, he is a pedant, and for pedants the heroes of romance have no existence, any more than real heroes have for their valets."

"Oh! you scoffer--you wretch!" exclaimed Lydia. "Why, you will prove next that beauty, that valour, that every virtue in the world, belongs to the region of romance. What a terrible thing scepticism is! But our friend was ever thus. Did I not say a short while ago: Hildegard, I cannot believe that he has changed; he cannot change! And behold, he is exactly what he always was!"

"Well, that's coming it pretty strong, seeing it's twenty years since ..."

The corpulent host had laughingly given utterance to these words, then, feeling his wife's dark eyes bent upon him in stern disapproval, he broke off abruptly with Ahem! poured some wine into his own glass, which was but half emptied, and then wanted to know why the gentlemen present were not doing justice to the wine that night.

Bertram, wishing to relieve his friends in their evident embarrassment, came to the rescue, saying, with smiling, easy politeness: "Fräulein von Aschhof only proves by her kind assertion of my immutability, that she is indeed looking upon the world and mankind with a poetical eye. But let us remember this--the poets themselves allow only the fair sex to participate in the pleasing prerogative of the calmly careless ever youthful gods; and the poets may venture on this deception, because the listener is willing to be deceived. 'Breathes there a man with soul so dead,' who ever ventured to count up the years of an Antigone, an Iphigenia, a Helena? They are what they were--else they are not. But, even the poet's flattering arts cannot keep the man from aging; and if the poet would grant perennial youth to a man, he must needs let him die in his youth--like Achilles."

"I protest against this theory," Lydia exclaimed eagerly. "I assert that heroes age as little as heroines."

"Even that," Bertram replied with a smile, "would not help me, seeing that I am no hero, assuming even that you were right. But I may be permitted to indulge in some humble doubt. At best the hero of the Odyssey appears distinctly as a man of mature age,--to put it mildly,--and Pallas Athene must practise upon him her divine art of beautifying before she ventures to introduce him among the Phæaci."

The Baron was meanwhile playing with his spoons and forks again; he was evidently annoyed at having been so long kept out of the conversation.

Bertram went on as though he did not notice it at all; he very surely was not speaking for that fellow's sake. He only cared to clear himself in Erna's eyes from any suspicion that he, like the aged coquette opposite him, was laying claim to a juvenility which had gone by for ever; and seeing those eyes steadily bent upon him, he took heart of grace, and went on in the same tone of easy, good-humoured banter--

"Göethe, a modern, and in this case a tragic, poet too, in his Nausicaan fragments, wisely forebore to bring in that art of beautifying, which is only lawful for the epic poet in his antique naïvety, and in order to bridge over the mighty difference and distance of years, and to change the evidently improbable into something at least credible, he takes refuge in illusion, causing it to arise from the child's very heart, like a fog enveloping those pure eyes, that clear mind--

'That man must ever be a youthful man,
Who is well-pleasing to a maiden's eyes.'[1]

Thus the aged nurse, taking the unspoken words, as it were, from Nausicaa's chaste lips. A touching saying, touching, like children's belief in the omnipotence of their parents! And about that youthfulness, which exists nowhere except in the glorious dreams of a young, inexperienced, generous soul, well, Göthe has told us something with exquisite humour, not, as true humour indeed never is, without a touch of melancholy, in the novelette of the man of fifty. Poor old Major! I have always been heartily sorry for him. Remember how he begs the services of the valet (skilled in the use of cosmetics) from his friend the great actor; how that adroit official uses his balm, and his stays, and his wadding for the aged gentleman, and yet cannot save the diseased front tooth, and certainly cannot keep fair Hilarie from falling vehemently in love with young Flavio, solely because she sees him in raptures with the clever widow, solely because in Flavio's raptures she beholds for the first time a representation of genuine, ardent, youthful passion. All this is as true as it is charming, as charming as it is melancholy, at least for the reader who is in a position to test the hero's experiences and sentiments by his own sentiments and experiences."

"Of course; 'there's no fool like an old fool,' and I suppose that really is the final outcome of the whole business," said the Baron.

"How dare you talk of things you know nothing about, you prosaic individual?" exclaimed Lydia, bringing her fan down upon the giant's arm. "There is no talk of old people here. A man of fifty is not old, he is in the prime of life, and is often ten times younger than your used-up so-called young gentlemen. But I must really say something for Göthe against our 'learned friend.' Yes, yes, my friend, I know the novelette well; I read it aloud to the Court barely a week ago. Who bids you take a comedy in that tragic way?--for the novelette in question is a comedy--a 'Comedy of Errors.' Hilarie fancies she is in love with the uncle, and really loves Flavio; Flavio fancies himself in love with the young widow, whilst really he loves Hilarie; and how the Major--well, I think the final scene at the inn proves emphatically that he had only turned his feelings to--to--to--the wrong address, if I may venture upon the expression; and that he and the clever widow subsequently became a happy pair is perfectly clear to me. Or, do you think not?"

A warning glance flashed from Hildegard's dark eyes. Lydia positively blushed through her layers of paint. She had shown her hand too plainly!

Bertram struggled successfully against a strong inclination to smile; nay, curiously enough, something like pity for her indiscretion stirred within him. He went on--

"To be sure, you are right, right, above all, in calling the novelette a comedy. How little Göthe cared to have a tragic conflict is evident from the fact that he chose circumstances as favourable as possible for a happy conclusion, and that he from the very beginning secured a line of retreat for every one concerned. The Major is the uncle of Hilarie, the only daughter of his widowed mother, and he has doubtless acted the part of father to her--has, up till now, loved her as his own child. His rival, in whose favour he resigns his claims, is his own only son, to whom he is also very much attached, and with whom he is on excellent terms, whom he in fact treats like a comrade. Again, behind Hilarie, as she vanishes from him, stands as it were the young widow; and in her arms the Major will speedily forget the small humiliation. And lastly, and this seems to me to be the chief point, Göethe has wisely avoided to introduce the one element whereby he would have been enabled, nay compelled, to turn the comedy into tragedy; he has ... but I beg pardon of our fair hostess for being so garrulous. To be sure, it is high time we rose from table!"

Truly enough, the turn which the conversation had taken had, for Erna's sake, been unwelcome to her mother. So she seized the opportunity and rose from table. Erna, who had sat without turning her gaze from Bertram, took a deep breath, like some one who is being recalled from deep dreams to the consciousness of present realities, and followed the example of the others. She and Bertram were the last couple that left the dining-room on their return to the garden-saloon, which had meanwhile been lighted up, and Bertram thought she was walking very slowly--on purpose.

"What was the one element, Uncle Bertram?" she asked.

"What one element?"

He knew what she meant; but he had broken off at table, because he himself dreaded the utterance of the word. So he delayed his reply, and just then his host appeared, bringing cigars: the gentlemen might smoke on the verandah, whilst Lydia would give them some music.

"You remember, Charles, do you not," he went on, "the *sonata pathétique*--that used to be your favourite piece? And Lydia has practised it often since, I think."

Lydia was ready. Bertram, however, begged to be excused from remaining. He felt, he said, after all, tired with the day's journey, and it was but the charm of their company which had made him forget that he was still a convalescent. He barely gave Hildegard time to draw him aside, and to say to him in a whisper--

"You really are most amiable. How good of you to take it so kindly. I had not at dinner to-day courage enough to make my confession. Indeed I have to confess, to say much to you--to-morrow ..."

"To-morrow be it, fair friend," said Bertram, kissing the lady's hand, bowing to the rest, and making hastily for the door. He had not reached it before Erna was by his side.

"You used to say good-night to me less formally."

He did not venture to press a kiss on the proffered brow, but only took her hand.

The great grave eyes gazed at him as though they would fain read what was passing in his inmost soul.

"Good-night, dear child," he said hurriedly.

"Good-night," she replied slowly, letting his hot, trembling hand glide out of her own cool little one.

"It is lucky," said Bertram to himself, after he had dismissed Konski, and as he stood alone by the open window in his bedroom, "it is very lucky, indeed, that it is not very easy to read what is passing in somebody else's soul. She would have found queer reading!"

He leaned out of the window and gazed into the darkness. Not a breath of air. From the garden below the fragrance of mignonette was wafted up; the brook murmured aloud; a thin white veil was spread over the valley, with here and there a dim speck of light. The sky was cloudless, of deep blue, almost black colour; the moon looked like a mass of gold, and one solitary star near it shone forth in red splendour.

Bertram recalled just such a night, long years ago, when a friend, the assistant-astronomer, had given Erna's father and himself the opportunity of witnessing, from the Bonn Observatory, the transit of that same star-- Aldebaran--through the moon! Afterwards he had accompanied Otto back to Poppelsdorf, and Otto had in his turn walked back with him to the Pförtchen in Bonn; and so backward and forward, all through the mild summer's night, until the light of morning had come, and the birds were beginning to twitter in the leafy crowns of the chestnut trees. And they had been raving of friendship and love--of the love they both, most fraternally, cherished for one and the same black-eyed beauty, the daughter of one of their professors, and they had both been sublimely happy, all their misery notwithstanding, for the black-eyed one was known to love another--"Great Heaven, how long, how long ago? A generation, and more. And now ...?"

"Now," he went on, "you are about to fall in love with the daughter of the same man whom then you rivalled in absurdly exaggerated, donkey-like phantasies--with a girl of eighteen, whose father you could be. And this time you would not get off with raving incoherently for a night of two, and with scribbling a few mediocre sonnets! Be reasonable, old man. Let it go-- let it go! You know full well you can have no abiding place here, any more than the horseman in the Piccolomini. Behind you, too, as you ride along, crouches the lean companion and clasps you in his bony arms, and every now and again taps at your heart, to test if it is still stupid enough to throb for a beauteous maiden who is seated by the window among wallflowers and rosemary.

"And behind the curtain stands her lover, and bends across her, that he, too, may look upon the mad horseman, who is stretching out his neck to see his darling. And the clumsy fellow with the bull's neck wrinkles his silly brow, twirls his mustachio, strokes his beard, mutters *Mort de ma vie!* and shakes his coarse fist. But she pouts, and giggles and bursts out laughing, and falls on the neck of the jealous one ...

"No, no; it cannot be! You only want to hear from her lips that it cannot be. And then--away, away--ride out of the gate--to swift, honourable death. And God's blessing on thee, thou gentle, lovely, and beloved child!"

He closed the window gently, and so to bed; to bed, but not to sleep. He could not find that repose he stood so much in need of. The brook murmured so loudly, or was it the hot bloody surging to his temples?

And was he about to sink into slumber, he would start up again immediately; he seemed again, to be holding her by the hand, and she bent her forehead to be kissed by him.

"No--no! Lead me not into temptation! Do not ask me what the one thing is! I would not say it, even, if--what God forbid!--it were so. I will not let you beguile me into a tragedy, any more than from one comedy into another."

CHAPTER VI

This thought, which had at length quieted Bertram's, wildly tumultuous spirits, was also his first, when late next morning he awoke from deep and dreamless slumbers--neither tragedy nor comedy! Calm and clear observation, as best becomes a solitary individual who has done with life; who neither hopes nor fears anything from Fate for himself; maintaining a benevolent interest in the fate of others, where benevolence is merited and interest is justified; cherishing throughout the conviction that, after all, every one makes or mars his own life; that interference and advice are rarely of much use, and generally distinctly hurtful; and that, even under the most favourable circumstances, the task of mediator is ever, of all tasks, the most thankless.

In the clear light of these contemplations and of the delicious morning which was resting in sunny radiance above the lovely landscape, last night's scenes appeared to Bertram like the confused darkness of a feverish dream; nay, he derived some comfort from the thought that he probably had been ill, and was therefore only partly responsible for his extraordinary demeanour. Still, he was gravely responsible for one thing--he ought sooner to have become conscious of his condition. He might well thank his stars that in his excited state he had not behaved even more strangely; above all, that to-day, for the first time since his last long and severe illness, he felt as fresh and strong as in his best days. Assuredly with the morning all things seemed to have become better--much better than he could have expected-- than he deserved!

The master's disposition was singularly serene, and he gave it a most friendly expression in the course of his toilet, showing himself ready for a friendly gossip with Konski; but Konski, strange, to say, was out of temper, and refused to be gossiped with.

At last Bertram said: "What ails you? If you are displeased, at what I said yesterday about our speedy departure, you may calm yourself. We still remain here for the whole time we had originally arranged. I see you have unpacked already."

"We may leave to-day, for aught I care!" grumbled Konski.

"What's up now? Out with it, Konski! You know I cannot bear sour looks. Anything in connection with Mamsell Christine?"

"Of course it is!" replied Konski; "and I wonder who's to keep from sour looks under these circumstances! I had written to her that this was to be my last trip with you, and when we returned from Italy in March we might go and be spliced. I did not want to tell you at all, but don't you see, sir, one gets older every year, and it has to be some time or other, and ..."

"And now you wish to marry at once, and I am to give you your discharge?"

"Marry at once, indeed!" sniffed Konski; "she won't marry at all now--leastways, not me--and that, after we have been engaged these five years! But there is no trusting them women, and especially the old ones! She is five and forty years of age, she is,--a year older than I am myself; and now she's going to marry a young greenhorn of five and twenty!"

It was some time before Konski, generally so calm and patient, could explain in detail to his master how badly he had been treated. According to his account, Mamsell Christine had written the tenderest letters to him until a few weeks ago, and had declared herself agreeable to all his suggestions and proposals; and now it appeared from the statements of the other servants whom he had cross-questioned, and whose evidence the faithless one could not but corroborate, that she had been "carrying on" for a long while with one Peter Weissenborn, who had formerly been head-gardener at Rinstedt, and who had been settled in the neighbouring town for the last six months, and who was now, it was said, likely to be appointed one of the Court gardeners, thanks to the protection of the Herr Baron. The Herr Baron, Konski went on, had also induced My Lady to give Mamsell Christine leave to quit her service at any time without formal notice; and, indeed, the servants all said, that the way to get My Lady's consent to anything, was to get the Herr Baron on your side; that made success quite certain. And My Lady was said to be quite in favour of this marriage between Christine and the future Court gardener. In that case she would always have two of her former servants at hand when she came to town, and that was likely to be an event of frequent occurrence now; if, indeed, she did not go to live there altogether, as some of the servants asserted--Aurora, for instance--My Lady's maid, who was her second favourite, next to Christine.

Bertram endeavoured to comfort the poor fellow. He pointed out to him that he should be glad to be rid of a person who had evidently never meant honestly by him, and who would in all probability have been as faithless in marriage as she had now proved before. This conviction led him to reject any wish there might exist to get the matter rectified again, as was done sometimes, and in much higher social circles too; otherwise he would have been willing to use his influence with My Lady, which presumably would have been at least as telling as that of the Herr Baron.

Konski shook his head. "I am extremely obliged to you, sir," said he. "I am quite content if you will still keep me on, after I have proved myself to be such a thorough ass. And, as far as talking to her Ladyship goes, that would be in vain--the Herr Baron is cock of the walk there. I could tell you a good deal more about that, but I know you do not like that sort of thing!"

Bertram was startled. The man's last remark could have but one meaning, and the image of the girl among the wallflowers and with the jealous lover, emerged in singular distinctness from last night's feverish phantasies. He would fain have for once broken through his rule of never going out of his way to listen to the gossip of kitchen and servants' hall, but, as Konski did not volunteer any further remarks, he was ashamed to put any direct questions. Just at that moment, too, there came a knock, and a servant brought a message from her Ladyship. She had learned that the Herr Doctor had risen, and might she request the Herr Doctor's' company on the verandah to tea?

Bertram lost no time in following the invitation. Hildegard, who had been sitting in a shaded corner of the verandah at the deserted breakfast-table, came forward to meet him. As she moved towards him with well-balanced step, he could not but recall last night's talk about the never-changing beauty of a poet's heroine. He gazed upon the lofty figure in its youthful slimness, the clear, deep colouring of the incomparably beautiful countenance, the blue-black splendour of the ample hair, smooth at the temples, and crowning the glorious head with a dense braid.

There was a smile on her dainty lips, and if deepened a little as she saw her guest's speaking eyes bent upon her in undisguised admiration. She was making tender inquiries about the state of his health, leading him the while to the table and making him sit beside her, with the kettle bubbling in front of them.

"Otto," she said, "is, as usual, somewhere about the estate. The Baron is painting a portion of the village from the bottom terrace, and Lydia is, I believe, keeping him company with a book. Erna, you will probably find later on in her favourite place, under the big plantain tree. I have sent them all away, because I so long to have a comfortable confidential chat with you. Yesterday we did not manage to have one. And first of all, dear friend, accept my hearty thanks for having so kindly pardoned a breach of confidence of which I--not from choice--had been guilty. Nay, do not refuse the expression of my gratitude. I saw how hard you found it to appear unconscious and serene; I thank you all the more. But I knew that with your wonted cleverness you would at once find the only correct point of view--that of pity. Whatever has been done and sinned between the two of you,--she is the one to be pitied. A poor girl, growing old, even if she is in favour at Court; and although the Grand Ducal family could not be kinder, yet all this cannot satisfy the cravings of her eager mind--but I perceive that this is a painful topic for you!"

"It is not painful for me," replied Bertram; "or at least only so far as the description of a dissatisfied, unquiet soul must ever be painful for us, if it is hopelessly out of our power to bring satisfaction and peace to it."

"I understand you," said Hildegard; "and you will understand me when I beg of you not quite to rob the poor soul in question of its utterly foolish hopes to which it clings, alas! with incredible tenacity. You can do this so easily: you need but be amiable and, courteous to her, as you are to everybody--no more, but, to be sure, no less--do you consent?"

"I will try, since you wish it--on one condition!"

"And this condition?"

"I have come to the following determination--indeed, it is a matter of course for me. In the drama of human life I will not henceforth ever again leave, my well-won place in the stalls, and under no circumstances will I take a part on the stage itself--no tragic part--and still less a comic one!"

"From the latter," replied his fair hostess with a smile, "you are safe under any circumstances, through your own cleverness; from the former----"

"Through my age."

"I meant to say, also through your cleverness; or, if you prefer it, through the cool, unimpassioned frame of mind which you have grown into, and which I often envy you!"

Bertram looked up in amazement, and then quickly busied himself with his tea-cup. Hildegard, to envy him his coolness! Hildegard, who had ever appeared to him the very embodiment of conscious equanimity!

"You may be surprised to hear this from me," she continued; "but must we not all, sooner or later, learn the lesson of resignation? And my time surely has come. Indeed, it has been so all my life. What have not I had to resign in the course of my life! Or do you think that the husband's wealth can blind the wife, if she be proud, to the consciousness that she is not loved as she longs, and as, may be, she deserves to be loved?"

Bertram knew these phrases from of old; but he said to himself that to-day particularly he must make the best of everything, so he exclaimed--

"Is it possible, my friend, that you still cherish this hypochondriacal fear which you have given utterance to before, but from which I deemed you cured long ago? How can you complain of a deficiency in love, when your husband positively adores you? You can utter no wish, simply because what you could wish for is already fulfilled. Or you need but have a wish, and it is forthwith fulfilled."

"You are pleading for the friend of your youth," she made answer, raising her dark eyebrows. "Do not forget this: I am bringing no charge against him. I am resigned. Were I to die to-day, what would his loss come to? What would he miss?"

"The brightness of his life," Bertram replied gallantly.

"As if he cared for the brightness of his life!" said his wife. "Is it so? Does he share one of my fancies, my harmless *penchants*? Does he not vainly strive to appear interested in the things of beauty with which I love to surround, myself and to decorate our dwelling? Did he not consent wit evident repugnance to have the mansion-house restored in a style befitting a whilom princely residence--to let me seek out and renew the old, tangled paths through the Park? Does he support me in my humane undertakings? Have I not had to beg the few thousand thalers from him that I required for my Kindergarten and for my poorhouse? Why, he lives solely for his porcelain factory, his sugar refinery, his coal-mines, his new railway project! I say again: I have accepted all this as inevitable, and as a matter of course, as long as I alone was concerned, as long as I alone suffered. But, indeed, to bring Erna into this life of trivialities, to leave the dear child in a sphere where she sees nothing, hears nothing, that could give the slightest nourishment to head or heart, where anything and everything revolves round Mammon, is sacrificed to Mammon--that is beyond me, beyond my strength!"

"Then, if I understand you aright, you wish, to get Erna married?"

Through the soft, velvety radiance of the deep-brown eyes flashed something like a deeper light. The question was evidently not expected-- at least not yet--but the next moment already her eyes had resumed their customary expression, and she forced those beautiful lips to smile, as she said, in a tone of gentle reproach--

"Let us express it rather less egotistically. I should like Erna to find a husband worthy of her."

"A most natural wish too! One which every mother cherishes for a grown-up daughter. And as an old friend of the family I heartily join in the wish, and do not for a moment doubt that we shall readily agree as to what we shall expect her husband to be."

"I am not so sure on that point."

"Let us try anyhow. Firstly, he should be noble!"

"That is not your conviction."

"Then let it be a concession. If people wish to come to an understanding they must be prepared to make concessions."

"This concession I accept gladly. Go on, please."

"He should not be a scholar by profession; but have a good--a man of the world's--education, and a taste for the fine arts. In fact, we want a cavalier, of course, in the best sense of the word."

"Agreed."

"He need not be wealthy. In fact, it would be preferable that he had no fortune, he would in that case be all the more indebted to Erna."

"Most true!"

"He should not be a landed proprietor, or at least not a man who feels it a duty and an absolute necessity to live in the country and devote himself to agriculture. Best of all, he should have no definite calling, or, anyhow, only one which did not impose difficult and troublesome duties; say a position which should have it as a natural consequence that the man in question moved in the best society, and even came occasionally into pleasant contact with Court circles."

"Best of friends, how strangely skilled you are in reading a mother's heart!"

"Let me, then, look to the very bottom of it, where possibly the name of the individual in question is already written. If I read the characters correctly, they form the name ..."

"Now I am truly keen to know."

"Baron Kuno von Lotter-Vippach."

"Lydia has told you!"

"No. Neither Fräulein von Aschhof nor any one else has spoken to me, I give you my word of honour."

"But it is most strange ..."

"Why so strange? Am I not a very old friend, to whom you have many a time talked on most important topics, and whom you have many a time honoured with your most intimate confidence?"

"Then it is all the better, all the more deserving of my gratitude; and I thank you heartily, sincerely ..."

She had seized both his hands; her beautiful countenance, now lighted up with a flush of gladness, had never been more beautiful; yet to Bertram it appeared like some hideous mask.

"I cannot accept your thanks," he said, withdrawing his hands with slight and very hurried pressure. "I could but do so honestly, if I shared those wishes of yours which I have guessed. That is not quite the case. The impression which Baron Lotter made upon me yesterday was not specially favourable; to be quite open, the impression was unfavourable."

"That," Hildegard replied eagerly, "leaves me very calm. You men seldom like each other at a first encounter, and at a second you find one another charming. In the Baron's case no second encounter has even been necessary; he overflows with your praises; he calls you the cleverest and most amiable of men; he is charmed to have made your acquaintance; and I am convinced that you, too, my friend, will soon modify your judgment--I should almost like to say your prejudice--once you come to know the Baron better. He is somewhat spoiled, like all very handsome men; somewhat conceited, if you like; but at bottom very modest, easily led, good as gold. He will please you, believe me, and more than please you! You will come to esteem and love him!"

"Is the more important question, to me the most important, already settled? Does Erna think as favourably of the Baron? Does she love him? For that he loves her, I must, I suppose, assume."

"That is beyond all doubt," Hildegard made answer; "as for Erna, I hope so, I believe so; anyhow she does not express herself unfavourably about him, and that, with Erna, means a good deal, for she is not at all easily pleased, and is not accustomed to conceal her dislike, if dislike there be. It is of course difficult to form a correct opinion of Erna's sentiments; doubly difficult for me, because she has been so long from home, and we are not always in accord in our views and tendencies. Again, in Lydia she has never placed full confidence--which, by the by, I can scarcely wonder at. I only know one being whom she thoroughly trusts--and you dear friend, are the one!"

"I?"

"Are you surprised to hear this? Surely not? Has not the child always been so fond of Uncle Bertram, that we, her parents, might have grown jealous? Has she not ever been your favourite? If she is so no longer, for goodness sake do not let the poor girl see it. She would be inconsolable."

"Now, you are laughing at me."

"Indeed, I am not. Ask Lydia. That Lydia often speaks of you, you will find natural enough, and that now and again a word of bitterness slips in, you will find pardonable. Erna does not pardon it. In her eyes you are once and for good raised above all reproach. You are, as it were, her ideal. It is a downright case of infatuation, and it goes so far that she once assured us, with all a child's gravity--she was still almost a child--that if ever she married, Uncle Bertram must be her husband and she got quite angry when Lydia and I laughed at her."

The beautiful lady smiled, and Bertram succeeded in forcing a smile too.

"How very funny," he said; "but then very young girls are proverbially prone to conceive infatuation for some one or other of their masters, and I think, in Lydia's eyes, I have always been one of her instructors, in literature and what not. Poor girls! they give their affections to old Mentor, but they mean young Telemachus. Well, and there is apparently a young Telemachus on the stage already, if you have seen aright."

"Just to decide that point," replied Hildegard, "Mentor must not yet resign his functions. On the contrary, I must entreat him most urgently to help the mother with his clear vision and his advice, and to use his old influence with the daughter. I may rely upon this, my trusty friend, may I not?"

She held out her hand to him with these words. He raised it deferentially to his lips and said--

"You may rest convinced that Erna's well-being is dearer to me than anything else in the world."

Hildegard had wished and had expected another, a more definite, answer. It was still doubtful whether she had really acquired an ally in him. However, the main point was gained; she had taken the initiative, had represented the affair from her own point of view, had appealed to Bertram's friendship, had asked for his assistance, had given him a proof of her confidence, which he would doubtless accept as unconditional. This sort of thing is always flattering to a man, always makes him feel indebted. Of course, a woman must flatter a man if she would make him feel indebted.

Just then it was anyhow impossible to obtain a more definite assurance from Bertram, for the Baron and Lydia were ascending the main steps of the terrace; the Baron, in his temporary capacity as artist, clad in a costume of brown velvet, and a straw hat with a stupendously broad brim, and Lydia in such a grotesquely fantastic morning costume as to suggest the idea that she had been acting as model for some wonderful sketch of the artist. And indeed she did figure upon the canvas, but only as a bit of the foreground, which represented a portion of the terrace, across which you looked down into the valley and at the village, with the wooded hills rising behind. The Baron was evidently much pleased with his work, although he declared again and again not to have half finished it; it was not fair, he added, to apply to a hasty sketch the same standard of judgment as to a regular studio picture, in which everything would of course turn out quite different. This, Bertram could not but think, would be most desirable, but hardly very probable. This so-called sketch was evidently a picture which had already been touched and retouched, some portions had been painted over two, even three times, and divers desultory dilettante endeavours had failed to bring anything like harmony into the composition. Nevertheless he politely agreed with the ladies' words of praise, which flowed freely from Hildegard's lips, while Lydia, as was her wont, launched out in extravagant eulogy: wonderful, was it not, what progress the Herr Baron made day by day? At last there was once more a painter with a mission for historical landscapes on a grand scale! The resemblance of his genius to that of a Rottmann, a Preller--became more and more apparent. Nor did she alone think so. Only the other day, at Court, when they were talking of the pupils at the Academy of Arts, and some one mentioned the Baron's name, Princess Amelia said, and said with marked emphasis, "No pupil he, ladies, nay, a master, and a great master! The Baron is a distinct acquisition for our School of Arts; he represents a triumph!"

"Yes, it is true; the august lady is very graciously disposed towards me," asserted the Baron, stroking his natty beard. "I wonder what she will say to my new sketches."

Fortunately for Bertram, who was planning his escape under some pretext or other from this painful scene, his host now came up to greet his friend, and to ask if he felt strong enough and was inclined to go for a little drive with him; only to the porcelain factory, they would be back in an hour. Bertram declared his readiness.

"The Baron would surely like to go with you," said Hildegard, exchanging glances with her husband; "but I fear there is barely comfortable room even for two in your little trap."

The Baron hastened to assure her that he could not go, anyhow, as he had promised Miss Erna to try the accompaniment to some new songs with her.

Hildegard asked Bertram if he would not, before starting, say good morning to Erna, who would be hurt if he left without having done so.

They called for Erna in vain. It seemed to Bertram that Hildegard only wished to find time enough to beckon him aside, and to whisper to him that he need not conceal from her husband what they had been discussing in reference to Erna. On the contrary, she was anxious to learn Otto's opinion of the whole matter; he would probably speak with less reserve to his friend than, alas! to her, and that Bertram would take her side she felt sure now.

"But Erna is not coming, I see," she exclaimed aloud; "I will not keep you gentlemen any longer. *Au revoir*--an hour hence."

CHAPTER VII

The little trap was so light, and the road was in such good condition, that the friends were able to drive at a very fair pace, in spite of the not inconsiderable gradient. Soon they passed into the wood. The easy, comfortable motion, the perfect beauty of the morning, the fact that the friends were for the first time in undisturbed companionship--all seemed to favour a confidential exchange of thoughts. Yet both men were silent, and barely exchanged a word or two on indifferent topics. At last Otto said, after he had taken a stolen side-glance or two of his friend--

"What do you think, Charles--shall we walk a bit? The road now will be virtually level for some distance."

Bertram nodded assent. The carriage stopped. Otto bade the man drive slowly on in front of them, in the direction of the factory.

"You never can be sure," he began, as they were striding along the well-kept footpath by the side of the road, "that these beggars do not hear more than they should; and I particularly want to ask you something. Tell me--but quite honestly, mind--how do you like the Baron?"

"Let us come to the point at once," replied Bertram; "I have had a talk with your wife."

"Oh! indeed!" exclaimed Otto, hiding his embarrassment as best he could by bursting out laughing, and abruptly leaving off again. "That is to say, I rather thought you would. I should like to have done the same--I mean had a talk with you--yesterday, in fact; but my wife told me not to ... and, don't you know, the ladies always claim precedence."

"Very well; then let me commence at the point where my conversation with your wife came to an end--with the question which she either could not or would not answer when I pressed her, and which seems to me of paramount importance--Does Erna love the Baron? Have you, between you, or have you yourself, any proof of--any support of this? Have you made any observation from which you could conclude such a thing?"

"Look here, old man," said Otto, "you are asking a lot at once. I can't follow you. Proof--support--observation! Good Heaven! Who can look into a girl's head and heart? She has said nothing to me, and rather than ask her--ask her--it's such a queer question to ask, and possibly one might only do harm by it, and learn nothing in the long run, or at least not the truth. Of course she is fond enough of me, and has confidence in me. Heaven knows how fond I am of her! but father and daughter, you know--or rather you do not know, for you never had a daughter--that's a curious business!"

He had taken off his hat and was scratching his head in his perplexity. Bertram understood that he was not likely to get anything out of him that way. After a pause Bertram said--

"Well, let us assume--although, to say the truth, I find it very hard to do so--let us assume that Erna does love this man. Would you then be able to say Yea and Amen with a good conscience? In other words, are you convinced that the man would make Erna happy? That he has, anyhow, the qualities which according to human reasoning and experience, render her happiness at least possible? That he is a man of honour, of fit and upright disposition;--in a word, that he is a gentleman?"

"A gentleman!" exclaimed Otto in amazement "Why, good Heaven!--a man belonging to such a family--bearing such a name--a constant guest at Court--invited to every ball, every evening party there; besides joining their private circle, once or twice every week--why, he must be a gentleman!"

"The deuce he must!" exclaimed Bertram angrily. "If you have no better guarantee than Court balls and such like humbug!"

"But what more would you have?" said Otto. "What more would any one have? If that is no guarantee I wonder what you would call one. I have it as a matter of certainty from Lydia, that his nomination as Chamberlain is made out, is lying ready for signature in the Grand Duke's cabinet; and Lydia ought to know, for, between you and me, she, with the help of our Court Marshal, an old friend of Lotter's father, has been urging the matter strongly at Court. Lotter is very grateful to her, and says quite frankly, that but for her he might have had to wait much longer; and I think that is, a trait in his favour--although I am convinced--but you must please not give any indication that you know--although I am convinced that Lydia has not tried her hardest for Lotter's own sake, but to conciliate my wife, who is bent upon seeing her future son-in-law hold some Court appointment. And the reason why Lydia had to keep in my wife's good graces is not far to seek; and, old fellow, she has had her way at last, and is allowed to sojourn once more under the same roof with you. You see: *manus manum lavat.*"

"So I see, indeed," laughed Bertram. "And now Hildegard must again keep me in good-humour, that I, in my turn, may keep you in good-humour. It were strange indeed, if, under these circumstances, we were not, all of us, in the very best humour!"

"This hardly seems to be your case as yet," said Otto, "your laughter notwithstanding."

"Nor, I hope, yours either," exclaimed Bertram.

"Why do you hope so?"

Bertram made no answer. His Heart was full of sorrow and wrath. He saw that the whole affair was arranged--among the two women anyhow--and the easy-going henpecked husband by his side would be sure to say yes to everything, had probably done so already, and this was but the second scene this morning in a nicely-arranged comedy, with all the parts carefully distributed beforehand. Evidently the drive had but one object--to give Otto an opportunity of saying his part. And he, himself?--Why, barely an hour ago he had solemnly protested to the fair stage-manager that never more would he act again! And she had listened to his solemn protest without laughing in his face! Well, well; there might yet be a chance of interpreting some passage in a way that the clever lady had not thought of!

Otto broke the silence, after they had been walking side by side for some little time, by saying somewhat humbly--

"You are angry with me!"

"What right could I have to be so?" replied Bertram. "I am no relation of yours. I am nothing but a friend; and, as such, I have no right whatever. It is only my duty to give an honest answer if you consult me on a matter of importance. And there is properly no consultation in this case. You are not in need of any advice; you, her parents, are resolved. Nothing is wanting, but the merest trifle--Erna's consent. And, as that is sure to be given in good time, the whole thing is clearly settled, and we may as well talk of something else."

"No, no!" exclaimed Otto, "nothing is settled; and the matter is by no means clear--clear--not in my mind, anyhow; and Hildegard has not the faintest conception how things really stand. She thinks it is only my want of resolution that ... And because she knows how much I value your judgment--if I could only tell you everything ..."

"But you cannot, and you would be, sorry for it afterwards. Therefore, you had better not try."

"But I must at length tell some one, and there is no one else in the world whom I could say it to. Listen: I ... I ..."

A kind of spasm passed over the full, round, good-humoured face; the blue eyes, which he kept rigidly fixed upon his friend, seemed to struggle against rising tears.

"I--I am ruined!"

He had just managed to pronounce these words hoarsely; then he broke, down and sunk upon a log of wood which was lying by the roadside.

Bertram had, at first to struggle against the terrible notion that his friend had suddenly gone mad. But his look, though one of utter despair, was not that of a madman.

"What is this you say, Otto? Impossible, impossible!" he said, sitting down upon the log by the side of his friend, who seemed bereft of all strength. "Go on, anyhow, that I may judge what it comes to. I am quite convinced--beforehand that it comes to nothing at all. But speak, for goodness sake, speak!"

Otto nodded assent, and murmured--

"Yes, yes, I will speak. Come to nothing, forsooth! I have seen it coming--for a long time past--for the last four years at least--ever since I started, in addition to all the other things, that confounded sugar refinery. We made it a Company; but I hold all the shares myself now--I could not bear to ruin the poor beggars who, trusting in me, had taken up the rest. This has cost me untold money; and the whole thing was a failure, and the building is ready to be pulled down again--would already have been pulled down if that, again, did not require money. Besides, a thousand acres of my best soil planted with beetroot--food for the pigs now. And yonder is that porcelain factory, year by year a balance on the wrong side; and then the mines--yes, yes, formerly, but not now ..."

There had been one long series of enterprises, each of which had turned out more unsatisfactory, and, in the long run, more ruinous than the other; and with increasing swiftness they had swallowed up ever bigger sums, and had now at length given at least a most severe shock to a very considerable fortune. This much Bertram gathered clearly from the statements of his friend, although he only understood a small part of the technical and mercantile details.

"But how on earth," he exclaimed, "could a quiet, sensible man like yourself ever dream of venturing on this 'inclined plane'? How could you graft one reckless, foolhardy speculation upon another; neglect, ruin those splendid estates, the legacy of your fathers; stake your peace of mind, your happiness? And if it had been a question of yourself only! But your child-- your wife ..."

He paused abruptly.

"Poor chap!" he murmured. "I think I understand after all--poor, good chap!"

He was pressing Otto's hand warmly. Their eyes met. His unhappy friend was smiling, and a most melancholy smile it was.

"To be sure, to be sure," he said; "I did not want it cried from the house-tops; I knew you would find the reason. I myself--dear, dear--I would not have cared to increase my gains. I should have been more than satisfied with the estates and the mines, or with the estates alone, if the mines ceased to yield a profit. You know how as a young man I used to be quite ashamed of having so much money, never a farthing of which I had earned, when I saw how my betters had to toil and moil. And I knew too that I was not good enough for her--that it was great condescension on her part to marry me at all--that I must needs ever be in her debt. From the very commencement I let her have her own way--she should never be able to say that I, the *bourgeois* proprietor's son, was ignorant of what befitted and became a beautiful young lady of high degree. I even--don't laugh at me, man--even tried to procure a patent of nobility, she wished it so very much; and I have made many a sacrifice with that object. This whole, ill-starred porcelain factory, for instance--I had been told that at Court they would like me to establish one, and indeed they buy here what they require, though, to be sure, only for kitchen and servants' hall--and there was many another thing besides. And then she wanted the terraces and the park and the mansion-house restored--in the true style, I think they call it--and she takes delight in all this, trumpery rubbish of dim old mirrors, and shaky old chairs, and worm-eaten old cabinets, and coffee-coloured, pictures, and abominable old pots and pans; and I, great God! would willingly buy the whole world for her--lay it at her feet--if only she would love me a little in return. But--you see, Charles, it has all been in vain--quite in vain!"

The big man had buried his face in his hands, and was sobbing like a child. Bertram's soul was filled with pity. The wretched weakness of his friend in reference to his beautiful and beloved, but cold, unloving wife, and its mournful consequences--he now understood it all too well not to be ready to pardon--to a certain extent. But that, husband and wife must settle, must bear, among them--only Erna should not be dragged to ruin, should not also be sacrificed to her mother's unbounded selfishness. And perhaps this was the one bright spot in the dark picture which his friend had drawn of his position.

"You have not endeavoured to give the Baron a clear view of your situation?" he asked.

"For goodness sake--no; certainly not," exclaimed Otto, rising in terror from his stooping position. "Anything but that!"

"And yet you will have to do so as soon as he formally asks Erna's hand from you."

"How can I tell him the truth? He would withdraw immediately."

"Otto, are you not ashamed of yourself? And you would really give Erna to such a cur?"

"What am I to do?"

"What you are simply obliged to do as a man of honour, not to say as a father!"

"And he'll talk about it--here, in the town, at Court--and everything, everything depends upon my credit remaining unquestioned, at least a little longer. If the projected railway is made to pass through here in lieu of through the valley below, it would be done mainly on account of my establishments, my factories, and what not. And in that case I am saved-- nay, I must needs grow wealthier than ever I have been. But the ultimate granting of the concession--our local Parliament notwithstanding--rests with the Government; and Lotter, with his divers relations, his well-known influence ..."

He paused, then resumed in a somewhat less confident tone--

"If, therefore, I do not reveal everything to him at present--and, by the by, there is no need for it yet--I am not acting dishonestly, but in everybody's interest. You will grant me this much."

"To be sure," replied Bertram. "I only fear you will not be able to continue this profitable silence for any length of time. For any day it may happen that the young people come to an understanding, and--to-morrow, perhaps, or this very day--they may come and ask for your blessing."

"It would kill me!"

"It would, anyhow, be extremely awkward! Therefore, I beg to make the following proposal to you. I am already authorised by your wife to sound Erna; I now ask you to give me the same commission; and you will tell your wife that you have spoken to me about it. Thus you will both have placed the matter into my hands as it were. Now I shall find Erna either distinctly favourable to your plan, or else distinctly unfavourable, or undecided. In the latter case, I will try to confirm her in that state of mind; and would prove to your wife that to advance with inconsiderate rashness must needs be risking, and, probably, spoiling everything. But even if Erna, really loves the Baron, or, on the other hand, if she is satisfied in her own mind that he is not the man who corresponds to her ideal--all girls create such an ideal for themselves--well, I think I have influence enough with her--or, in case of need, I possess diplomatic talent enough, to get the ultimate decision put off one way or the other. For how long--we shall judge by and by, once you and I are so far agreed."

"My dear boy, I put myself entirely in your hands. I'll not take a step without you. Gracious me--what a lucky thing that you have come! I do not know what would have become of me, and of the whole business."

He shook and pressed both his friend's hands in the excess of his gratitude, looked upon his situation already in a much more hopeful light, turned the conversation again to the new railway and to the stupendous chances which would come to him in case the decision was favourable, and that it would be so, he suddenly assumed to be probable, nay, certain. He never noticed that Bertram had made the little carriage turn which was waiting for them at the end of the wood, and that now they were driving back the way they had come. The suggested inspection of the factory had only been a pretext for having an undisturbed hour with Bertram.

His friend was now sitting in silence by his side. Otto kept on talking to him, lowering his voice on account of the driver's presence. Bertram hardly heard what he said. He hardly saw, either--or if he saw, it was like in a dream--the golden lights flash down through the top of the giant firs, and play around the brown stems and along the mossy ground; he saw but as in a dream the lovely vistas which opened here and there, giving glimpses of loveliest landscape beauty in the valley far below. His busy mind was working and modelling away at the part in the family drama which had, after all, been forced upon him, and which he had not dared to decline--for Erna's sake.

CHAPTER VIII

For Erna's sake! How often he repeated that phrase to himself in the course of the day! He wanted nothing for himself. What, indeed, could he have wanted for himself? Nothing more than a man who should see a child lost, in danger, among a crowd of carriages, and who should bound to the spot and carry the child away to some place of safety; nothing more than a wanderer, who sees a fellow-traveller start upon a road of which he knows of old the insecure state, and who warns the heedless man to take some other road instead. One does so because it is one's duty as a human being; one does so because one's heart urges one to do it, because one cannot help doing it.

Yes, a man acts and speaks in such situations as he would hardly act or speak for his own sake. He is more courageous or more anxious than he would be, if his own weal or woe were at stake. One grows beyond one's self, or else sinks beneath one's own everyday moral level.

"And the latter is meanwhile my case," said Bertram to himself, as he played his part with due zeal, and, as he thought, with great success. It was a natural consequence, of that part that he lectured Hildegard (after the event), because she had not yesterday taken him at once into her confidence; that he exchanged with his friend Otto looks of the completest accord and understanding; that he used with Lydia--to her evident delight--a tone of mingled melancholy and fun, which appeared half to express and half to hide a deeper emotion; and that with the Baron he completely dropped his calm manner of the day preceding. How else could he form an opinion of the man? And how could he be a faithful counsellor to Erna without having formed an opinion?

So he examined the Baron's portfolio with patient attention, whilst that nobleman turned over the leaves and gave explanations. The collection would have been a priceless treasure if the quality had corresponded with the quantity. There were sketches from almost every country in Europe; the northern coast of Africa, too--Algiers, Tunis--was largely represented. And then the painter's talent embraced all styles and kinds of painting:--landscape, architecture, still-life, portraiture--nothing had escaped the unwearied brush, nothing had appeared too difficult. On the contrary, there were the most unlikely effects of light and shade, the oddest scenes, the most *risqué* situations, involving the wildest inroads on the laws of perspective and the most reckless foreshortening--and the daring sketcher seemed positively to have revelled in these. And yet Bertram had to confess to himself that a not inconsiderable talent, which, with patient and careful schooling, might have borne beautiful fruit, had been recklessly wasted-- and, indeed, generally recklessness did seem to him to be the Baron's leading characteristic. Anyhow, the painter's fluent comments on his own sketches quite corresponded to the reckless style of painting. Everywhere his ideas, good ones and bad ones, and some really original ones, were clothed in the same hurried, flurried, sometimes absurd form, showing a ready, but never a profound insight into human relations, into manners and customs of nations; much, but most desultory reading; extensive, and yet scattered knowledge. The man spoke as he painted, and painted as he played music. Reckless, superficial, inconstant, like his work and his talk, will and must his love be too, thought Bertram.

Could love like that lastingly suffice for Erna? It seemed impossible. But is there such a word as impossible in connection with the magic world of the human heart? Are not the natures of truly noble women at times visited by irresistible and undying passion for wavering, unstable, yes, even for morally worthless men? Does it not well-nigh seem to have all the stability of a law of nature, that totally opposed characters, all inward resistance notwithstanding, feel drawn to and fascinated by each other?

Was this fatal fascination visible in Erna?

Bertram kept his attention unconsciously fixed on that one decisive point, but without being able to come to any definite result. True, he had to confess to himself that even a still keener observer would have vainly tried his hand at the task. Erna joined to-day even less directly than on the previous day in the general conversation; nay more, he thought he noticed what had not been the case yesterday, or what had at least escaped him then, that her gaze, usually so firm, seemed at times fixed on vacancy, then again appeared directed inward, anyhow was not dwelling on her surroundings- -a symptom which by no means pleased the observer, because from it one might surely conclude that there existed a deeper sentiment, one which absorbed her inner life. And this sentiment was not likely to be one of aversion to the Baron, to whom she talked more, in her own calm way, than to anybody else; with whom she played music two or three times during the day; and with whom she played chess after supper in her own grave, attentive manner. Hildegard came and explained all these details to Bertram ...

"Believe me," she said, "I know Erna. Mind, my words of this morning. She may be long in confessing her preference for any man, but if she were to dislike any one, he would find it out pretty soon."

"I fear that I am experiencing something of the sort," Bertram replied.

"How so?"

"Have you not noticed that she has not said three words to me all the evening?"

"Insatiable man! Are you not satisfied with Lydia who is ransacking her repertory for your sake? Would you have all womankind at your feet? I shall warn Lotter against you as against his worst rival."

"Do not destroy our budding friendship. But, joking apart, can there be a rival?"

"What are you thinking of? And if there were, I should be sure to know it through Lydia, who, like all elderly girls, is apt to err on the side of seeing too much rather than too little. Moreover, we two, Lydia and I, have never lost sight of the child, and in Erfurth, where, it is true, she went alone once or twice during the last few years, she was always in the company of my sister and her six girls, and I never heard a word, nor the slightest hint. One of the girls, Agatha, the third, Erna's bosom friend, is coming here, by the way, in a day or two; and a good, modest, sensible girl she is, though not as pretty as the rest. But you surely remember Agatha? Well, I'll question her a little when she comes, but I know beforehand that she will not have anything to tell. Oh, you'd better concentrate your jealousy upon Lotter!"

Hildegard surely felt very certain of her ground, else she would not have jested--a rare occurrence with her. Bertram took up a similar tone, and during the game of whist to which he and Otto soon afterwards sat down with the two older ladies, he was remarkably merry and talkative.

But two hours later Konski found him all the more gloomy and taciturn, and so silent that he did not even reply to the "good-night, sir," of that faithful servitor.

"It's the old one," soliloquised Konski, as he meditatively brushed his master's boots in his own little room, "who is bothering him. 'Dear Mr. Konski,' here, 'My good Mr. Konski,' there--I know what she is after. And then, to give me a whole dollar! And she has not any to spare, I can see that much, in spite of her grand airs and her trimmings. And she to rule the roast for master and me! Not if we knows it! And now we'll both marry; and marry smart young ones too! And may the devil fly away with all old women!"

CHAPTER IX

For this morning, after breakfast, a general expedition had been planned--a drive to a certain eminence, from which the Baron was desirous of expounding to them all the arrangements for the forthcoming manœ vres. Bertram had at the last moment made an excuse: much to his regret, he sent Konski to say, that he had forgotten to write some really important letters, and must needs stay at home to do so now. Would the others, please, on no account give up their drive for his sake.

"At first they would not go without you, sir," Konski reported; "but I got them to do it, and they are getting the horses ready now; the ladies are to drive, the gentlemen will go on horseback. So you may stay quietly in bed and try to get another hour's sleep. I am afraid, sir, you have had another awful night!"

And indeed it had been a worse night for Bertram than the preceding one, and this time the morning had not improved him. That he had to admit to himself when, after having first vainly endeavoured to follow the faithful servant's advice, he had at length risen in very low spirits and dressed, trying whether a stroll along the terrace garden-walk would cool his fevered brow and refresh his weary heart.

He had no right to be wearied. He was bound, when they came back, to meet them merrily and serenely; that belonged to his part. How could they give their confidence to one who appeared to have none in himself, in his own strength, his own courage?

And he would need all his courage to look, if it could be done, deeper than hitherto into Erna's eyes, into Erna's heart: and he would need all his strength if that look were to confirm what, yesterday, he had deemed impossible, but what, during the awful night, had come to appear to him as thoroughly possible, nay, as probable. If it were so, then the whole elaborate plan which he had yesterday confided to his friend, had therewith fallen to the ground. Otto's embarrassments were scarcely as great as he had represented them; and even if he had not, according to his wont, exaggerated things, what would be the use of delaying the decision? On the contrary, the more swiftly it came, the better for all. If the Baron was a man of honour; he would not withdraw on learning that the maiden of his choice was not wealthy; if he had influence at Court, if this influence really amounted to something considerable, he would now try all the more to use it for his future father-in-law. They might then make their own arrangements, as best they could; and they would make arrangements; sacrifice some things on both sides, give up some hopes. What would one not sacrifice, what would one not give up, if one loved from one's very heart? But to have to look on at such hearty love, love delighting in sacrifice--never! To run away would be cowardly, no doubt. But then valour, like honesty, is appropriate only when it is needed, and when it will be of some use. He would have to think beforehand of some suitable pretext which should render a sudden departure possible.

Thus lost in mournful thought, Bertram was pacing backward and forward along the terrace-walk, now past sunny espaliers, along which ruddy grapes were already commencing to shine through the dense clusters of vine-leaves, anon between rows of beeches, which were entwined overhead and formed dusky arbour-like groves.

Having reached the end of one of these groves, he paused as one terrified. In front of him, on the platform where the terrace widened, Erna was seated beneath the great plantain tree which overshadowed the whole place with its broad branches. An open volume lay upon the round table before her; she was writing busily, bending over a blotting-book. The graceful form, the finely-chiselled features, stood out in clearest profile against the green terrace above her. In this subdued light the dainty cheek seemed even paler than usual; and as she now paused, pen in hand, lifting a long eyelash and glancing meditatively up at the leafy roof above, the great eyes shone like those of an inspired Muse.

"One draught before I pass onward--on the shadeless remainder of my dreary road," Bertram muttered to himself.

He might have stepped back without being noticed, but he did not do so; his motionless eyes clung to the beautiful picture before him, as one perishing of thirst might gaze upon a brimming cup, when, lo! she turned.

"Uncle Bertram!"

She had said it quite calmly, and now, slowly, she laid down her pen and closed her blotting-book, rising at the same time and holding out her hand to him as he came up.

"I felt that somebody, was looking at me."

"And you wished, to remain unseen, or at least undisturbed. But could I have guessed that I should find you here? Why are you not away with the others?"

A smile flitted over her face.

"I had important letters to write, too."

"Well, you have written, anyhow."

"And have you not? For shame. If you make any excuses you should yourself take them in earnest; then you will come to fancy afterwards that the excuses were really valid."

"I'll remember this in future. But what makes you tell me to my face that my important letters were but an excuse?"

"I thought that you did not care to go; and I think I know the reason why."

"Indeed! I am curious to hear it from you."

"I will tell you. I wanted to say so last night already, for then I noticed quite well how gladly you would have made an excuse, only you could not at the moment think of a suitable one; but I could not have said what I wished to say in a few words, and so I determined to try and have an undisturbed talk with you. Shall we not sit down?"

They sat dawn, Erna with her blotting-book before her, Bertram on the seat opposite. Her large eyes were lifted up to him. But a minute before he had greatly longed to be able to see deep, deep into these eyes, right to the innermost recess of her soul; and now, when it could be, when it was to be, he shrank from it, he wished the time deferred. He would in any case learn the secret all too soon.

"Uncle Bertram, I wanted to tell you that ..."

The dark eyelids had closed after all; well, she anyhow did not see the breathless excitement with which he hung upon her lips. In his mind he heard already the words--"that--I engaged myself last night to be married to the Baron." The pause she made--of a second or two--seemed to him an eternity.

"My dear child," he said in a voice well-nigh inaudible ...

"That ... you shall not for my sake lay upon yourself a burden which you can no longer bear."

The large eyes were gazing firmly at him again, while he bent his own in deadly confusion.

He murmured--

"I--I do not understand you."

"You are too good to wish to understand me; but the excess of your goodness weighs me down and frightens me. I know that you are fond of me, that you do it only because you love me. But I love you too, Uncle Bertram, love you very much, more than formerly, when I did not really know you, did not at all understand you. I am no longer a child, and therefore you should not treat me like a spoiled child and do what I ask, especially when I see that I ask for something to which I had no right. I had no right to ask--I should not have entreated you to be kind to Aunt Lydia. And now I beg of you not to be so any longer, or to the same extent. I cannot bear it. She has harmed you as terribly, as terribly as only an evil heart can harm a good one. And she to be allowed to take your hand, look into your eyes, jest with you, as if nothing had occurred! If this had happened to me, I would not tolerate it--never, never!"

Her voice quivered, her lips trembled; the pale cheek was flushed now, the great eyes were flashing. She said she had not known him, had not understood him--and he? What had he known of her? of the strength of feeling of that heart of hers which had seemed to him to beat in such steady measure? His gaze was fastened on her now in raptured amazement, like the gaze of a mortal to whom something divine is being revealed.

But next moment the wondrous girl had conquered that passionate impulse, her features regained their usual expression, and she went on, calmly enough--

"And you, Uncle Bertram, should not tolerate it either--you, least of all. You cannot lie, cannot play the hypocrite. Let others do so; it befits you ill, it is unworthy of you. I cannot, will not see anything unworthy in you. I will have one human being whom I can believe and trust unconditionally. This one you are, you must be; is it not so, Uncle Bertram?"

She held out her hand to him across the table. He could not refuse it, and yet, as he touched those slender fingers, something thrilled through him as though he had been guilty of some act of desecration.

"You think me too good, too great," he said. "I can only reply, I will try to deserve your confidence."

"And I will give you an opportunity at once. I am not contented with myself either. I too--for the sake of others, to please papa and mamma who seemed greatly to wish it--have been kinder to somebody than at heart I felt justified in being, and I must henceforth change my conduct towards him."

"He has proposed to you?"

"Proposed? To me?"

A scornful smile played round her exquisite lips.

"I beg your pardon, dear Erna. He was so remarkably assiduous in his attentions to you yesterday. You admit yourself that you have been kinder to him than now you care to have been, and he strikes me as being one of those men who grasp the whole hand the moment you hold out your little finger to them. And moreover, I know that your parents encourage him much, and he is surely aware of that too. Thus my question was not wholly groundless; still, I beg your pardon."

"And indeed you need it in this case, Uncle Bertram. Or, have I perhaps behaved so childishly that even a clever man like you could deem such a thing possible?"

"No, no; pray, try to forget what I said without thinking, or take it for a proof that I was right, that I am neither so good nor so clever as you thought."

The words sounded diffident, almost submissive, but his heart was swelling with proud delight, and the songsters perched above in the shady recesses of the big plantain tree seemed to have been silent till now, and to be then commencing all at once to twitter and sing and make sweetest melody; and from the terraces beneath there was wafted up to them in fragrant cloudlets the perfume of carnation and mignonette. What a beautiful, divinely beautiful morning it was!

"Henceforth," said Erna, "we will be open to each other, and then such misunderstandings will not occur again. This one, truly, should make me blush. The Baron is the very last man in whom I could take the very slightest interest. I find nearly everything he says stupid and silly, and if a fairly good idea turns up, as it does every now and then, it is impossible to enjoy it, for the question is sure to obtrude itself: 'What nonsense will he talk next?' I am only now making his acquaintance; he, it is true, has been often here before, but in my absence; and in town, when he came, as he sometimes did, to see Aunt Lydia, I always avoided having to meet him."

"You have met few young men yet?"

"And those few have not made me anxious to meet any more."

"This sounds very hard; but, to say the truth, you are not the first girl whom I have heard talk like this."

"My only wonder is that all do not talk, or, at least, think like this. My own idea is, that men are naturally selfish, frivolous, and vain, and only become with advancing years good, and noble, and amiable, and this applies only to the few exceptions; for I suppose the bulk remain as they were."

"Are you serious?"

"Perfectly. And that is why, the night before last, I could not agree with you at all when you asserted that a young girl could not love a much older man, or was at least committing an act of folly if she did so, which, to her sorrow, she was bound to realise sooner or later, and therefore the sooner the better. Nor is it at all this consideration which makes Hilarie change, and which throws her into the arms of that youth who is behaving so childishly and insanely, that Flavio;--there is quite a different reason for it."

"Then you know the novelette?"

"No; I only read it now; and I had to hunt a long time for it, until I found it in the *Wanderjahre*. The book is lying there. And now I also understand the 'one element,' which you said the night before last that Göthe had excluded, or had not made use of--which is the right expression in this case?--because otherwise the comedy would have been turned into a tragedy."

"And this 'one element,' what is it?"

"The fact that her uncle is not in love with her at all. Was not that it?"

"To be sure. I only wonder at your having found it out."

"And my only wonder is that Hilarie did not discover it sooner. She must have been very blind not to have seen that her uncle returns--or rather does not return--her love from sheer kindliness of disposition; that at best his *penchant* is but the faintest reflex of her passionate love. Look at this passage: 'You are making me the happiest man beneath the sun! Exclaiming this, he fell at her feet.' How feeble, how strained! And it contents her, makes her happy. I should have been ashamed of the whole business."

"You must make some allowance for the spirit of the time, for the manner and expression of the period; in that case, these things do not look or sound quite as bad. But now for the other side of the medal: You hold that Hilarie did truly love her uncle, and would have remained faithful to her love, in spite of any number of Flavios, if her passion had been returned?"

"Most certainly!"

"Well, be it so. He loves, loves passionately. Enter Flavio, loving, loving passionately, too. The father perceives it. He sees that his own love would seal the doom of the son whom he loves. Moreover, he is sure--if he is not a conceited fool, but a man of heart and head, he must be sure--that Hilarie would undoubtedly, return his son's passion, if he, the father, the uncle, did not unfortunately stand between them; that the girl's love for the young man, and *vice versa*, is the only natural--that means, the only right thing; that therefore Hilarie cannot truly love him; that her love rather, if it be not absolutely unnatural, is anyhow an error, an aberration, from which she shall and must turn. Given these things, am I wrong in asserting that then, indeed, the comedy changes to tragedy--a tragedy the secret and silent stage of which, I admit, will be solely ... the elderly man's heart? Do you not agree with me?"

"I must, I think; if I have first granted your suppositions and assumptions, particularly this: that a girl's love for a man much older than herself must needs in every case be an error, an aberration. But then, again, I do not see why the elderly man's love for the girl does not also tend to self-deception, to a fact which he, being more far-sighted, clever, experienced; is bound to realise all the sooner. And then, where is your tragedy?"

Once more the great eyes flashed, the dainty lips quivered, an angry cloud lay on her brow. There was a wild voice in his heart crying: "Where?--here, here--for I love, I love thee! and it is impossible that into thy maiden heart, there should ever fall one spark of the wild conflagration raging here." But he succeeded this time, too, in subduing the tumult in his heart, and he said smilingly--

"I hoped, nay, I knew that you would make this objection, which is absolutely correct, and which helps the Master to regain that absolute sovereignty and undeviating correctness in matters of the heart in which I, wantonly, tried to argue Göthe was deficient. Of course, so the matter stands, turn and twist it as you will--Hilarie's love is an illusion; or, more correctly, it is a foreshadowing of that true and genuine passion which she will feel one day. The Major's love is a reminiscence of what his heart once, in the bygone days of his far-away youth, was glowing with, and what it never again will glow with now. Anything of a warmer feeling that haply still survives, may be sufficient for a sensible, reasonable marriage, with the clever widow, in whose sentiments towards him again reminiscence acts the part of a kindly mediator, and ... but surely ... why, they are back already! Shall we go and meet them?"

From the verandah Lotter's loud voice was heard. Lydia, too, was calling out; she was calling Erna. Bertram had risen, glad of the interruption; he felt his strength very nearly exhausted. He was resting his hand on the back of her chair, lest Erna, if they shook hands, should feel how his hand trembled. But Erna was gazing straight before her with a very gloomy expression of countenance.

"I should like to finish my letter first," she said.

"Then I will disturb you no longer."

He had gone; had gone without offering her his hand. Erna sat for a while without looking up; then she re-opened her blotting-book, and read the last page she had written:--

"I see him always, absent or present; I see his noble, pale countenance, the deep, thoughtful eyes, that mouth which can jest so delicately, and which yet (for me) quivers so often in sorrow for a wasted life, a lost happiness. For me! The others never see it; how should they? To them he is the cold-hearted egotist, the bitter jester, who believes in nothing, least of all in love. To be sure--once betrayed as he has been--alas! Agatha, that is the very thing which draws me irresistibly to him. I can now gaze deep, deep into his noble heart, can feel all the pangs that have torn it, and must be tearing it again now in the presence of the viper who--oh, I do hate her! ... And he manages to be quite friendly in his demeanour to her, because I asked him to, before I knew all the circumstances. But he shall do so no longer. I cannot bear it, when he turns his good, truthful eyes to me, as though he would ask: 'Is it right thus?' No, it is wrong, a thousand times wrong! But is it not wrong, too, that I should be allowed to read in his heart, and he not in mine? Shall I tell him ... all? It is ever on my lips, but then ... no. I should not be ashamed in his presence, he is so kind, and he would understand me! Resting on his protecting arm he would let me shed the last of those hot, angry tears, which will yet persist in sometimes rising to my eyes, and which I brush away indignantly; and I would gratefully accept his mercy, but on one condition only, that I may go on resting on that arm, that he would permit me to love, to serve him, to-day and for ever, as his friend, his daughter, his slave! ... Shall I tell him?"

Erna gave a bitter smile, and took the sheet of paper in both her hands in order to tear it in pieces. Then she laid it down again, and seized her pen once more.

"She who has written this is a conceited little fool, and deserves exemplary punishment for her conceit, and the said punishment is to consist in her sending these lines to her granny, in order to receive by return of post the requisite scolding, even if granny, and this is an urgently repeated request, is coming here the day after to-morrow. For between granny and me there shall not be said one word on this subject, and even less about the other thing and the other one; and now, dearest granny ..."

"Ah, there is Miss Erna!" exclaimed the Baron, issuing with Lydia from the terrace walk.

"We have been looking everywhere for you," said Lydia. "Heavens! how the child has flushed and heated herself over her writing! To Agatha, of course!"

"Ah, if one could read the letter!" exclaimed the Baron.

"There is nothing about you in it, I can give you that assurance, if it will set your mind at ease," said Erna, closing her blotting-book with the unfinished letter in it, and rising.

CHAPTER X

"Have you availed, yourself of the opportunity to talk to Erna?" Hildegard asked Bertram as soon as they were alone.

Bertram had expected this question, and had sought and found time to prepare his answer to it. His first impulse has been to taste the full delights of triumph, and to assure Hildegard, in strict accordance with the actual truth, that the Baron need never expect to gain Erna's affection. But then he considered that so brusque a revelation, would, without the slightest doubt, cause the proud lady to burst forth into a tempest of indignation, would bring Erna into a disagreeable position, and possibly involve her in extremely awkward scenes. Her feeble father would be no support to her whatever--on the contrary, he wished the decision to be put off as long as possible. And, lastly, he saw now quite clearly that Hildegard's pressing invitation to make a lengthened stay had had the very definite aim to secure in him, as in a very influential friend, an ally in the execution of her plans. Now he had failed in his diplomatic mission, and though they would not openly deprive him of his confidential position, they would very surely not consult him again. Future events would then occur behind his back, and the sooner he went away the better for them. And was he to go now? He felt as though he could as readily bid farewell to life and light.

And so his answer came to be nothing but an adroit evasion. He had, he said, done his best, and Erna had met him in the heartiest and most confiding manner. But on this very ground he considered himself justified in stating that there was at present no trace of any definite *penchant* for the Baron on Erna's part, and that he could only advise them all to possess their souls in patience, to bide their time, and to hope for the best from the gradual, but all the more sure, influence of daily intercourse.

The apparent genuineness of conviction with which all this was expressed deceived Hildegard completely. Her assumption that Erna took a special interest in the Baron was chiefly founded on Lydia's assertions, and Lydia, poor soul, was for ever weaving matrimonial projects, was much addicted to exaggeration, and to the making of molehills into mountains, and would, in this particular case, to get into Hildegard's good graces and maintain herself there, amply confirm anything she might be desirous of hearing. Now, when Hildegard was for the moment looking at things through friend Bertram's clearer and, as she thought, perfectly unprejudiced eyes, she was bound to admit the justice of his observations; indeed, in Erna's manner to the Baron there was very little indication of anything like a warmer sentiment, so little in fact, that the varying ways in which she treated him might almost seem matters of congratulation. Bertram asked himself why Hildegard did not give up a project which looked so very unlike fulfilment, since Erna, in all the charm of her young beauty, would assuredly have no lack of suitors, while her mother, not having the slightest suspicion of her husband's awkward financial situation, must needs, as indeed she did in her matrimonial plans in reference to Erna, reckon wealth among the attractions. There seemed to be something self-contradictory here, anyhow it was passing strange; and yet, as he went on meditating, he thought he had found the key to the enigma. Fair Hildegard herself was most pleasantly impressed by the Baron's striking appearance and confident manner, and was much flattered by the homage he paid to her beauty, her cleverness, her kindness, a homage to which, he gave even in company a very perceptible, and in their not infrequent *tête-à-têtes* probably even a more emphatic expression. And then the circumstance which, by the by, the Baron by no means concealed, that, to use his own words, he was as poor as a church mouse, she looked upon as a distinct point in his favour.

"Herein," she said to Bertram, "I see the finger of a just and compensating Fate. I know, my friend, that you are too wise and enlightened not to pardon an aristocratic fancy of mine, namely, that it is best if the aristocracy marry among themselves, and the *bourgeoisie*, for whom I have the greatest respect, also among themselves. Well, I, being a very poor lady with a long pedigree--for, indeed, the traditions of our family are reckoned by centuries--have had to break with these traditions, and was in this way the first to contract a *bourgeois* alliance. I do not complain of my lot; it was my lot, and there's an end of it; but I have never ceased to pray to God that my only daughter might be granted a different fate. And if a family, which is still older than mine, is enabled to resume its rightful position in the world, I really do not know what better I could wish, assuming always that Erna, as would doubtless be the case, gets a husband who loves her, and who--not to reckon his little cavalier's foibles, in reference to which a wise woman will be judiciously blind, knowing that this kind of thing is sure to stop of its own accord--is in every way worthy of her love."

"And whom," added Bertram mentally, "I hope to bring as completely under my control as my husband."

He was convinced that this thought was the leading one in the calculations of the selfish lady, in spite of the great care with which she endeavoured to avoid even the faintest appearance of any egotistic motive. Even as she was fond of representing her life as one long chain of sacrifices made by her on behalf of others, so she would now appear prepared to give up her own comfort for Erna's sake. Of course, she explained, it would not be possible to leave the poor child alone in town, among indifferent strangers; and she and Otto must in consequence make up their minds to spend the winter there in future. This, to be sure, would necessitate the purchase of a house of their own in town; but the question of expense was not to be taken into consideration where the happiness of their child was concerned; and, by a lucky accident, there happened to be for sale, and at quite a reasonable price, a newly-erected villa close to the Park, surrounded by a pretty garden, and roomy enough to enable them all, parents and children, to live comfortably together. And it would be quite feasible and not very expensive either, to build a studio for the Baron, she added. Perhaps Bertram would not mind driving to town with Otto, to look at the house? When? Why not to-day? Otto, as usual, could not make up his mind, although it would be an excellent investment, even supposing--supposing--but no, that case was not likely to occur, the momentary, somewhat unfavourable, aspect of things notwithstanding.

"For in this, too, my friend," she said, in concluding her explanations, "you will agree with me: the more carefully we prepare all things needful, and thus show the child, as it were, an image of the safe and sure and peaceful happiness awaiting her, the more swiftly and fondly her fancy will busy itself with that image, and from the fair image to the fairer reality--*il n'y a qu'un pas*. But first we must settle about the villa. There will be no difficulty if you speak seriously to Otto."

"I promise," replied Bertram.

The incident was most opportune, he thought. Here Otto, already harassed on all sides, was threatened, with huge additional expenditure, before which even his fatal readiness to yield must needs pause at length, as before an absolutely insuperable obstacle. The consequences were clear. He could not simply meet his wife's request by a refusal. There must be a full explanation between husband and wife; there would be a fearful storm, but it had to come, it was absolutely required to clear the sultry atmosphere, to disentangle the wretchedly involved situation. Hildegard's frivolous scheme would burst like a soap-bubble, and at one stroke Erna would be freed from an importunate suitor, and her father from an unworthy and intolerable position. Yesterday already he had been determined to stand by his friend through all the anxieties, embarrassments, and perils which were bound to ensue. To-day his heart beat anxiously, eager as he was to face those perils, for every peril cleared out of her path and victoriously conquered, was a trophy laid at her feet, hers, for whom he would have willingly shed his heart's blood drop by drop.

Fancy his terror and his indignation when, driving to town with Otto later in the day, he found his friend more removed than ever from any manly resolve.

"The purchase of this villa, dear me--why, if Hildegard cares for it so much--would, after all, be a comparative trifle--really. And then, what I told you yesterday regarding my situation, why, dear me, you know me well enough, old man, to ... to know how I am influenced by passing moods. That makes me look at all things accordingly; things are either black or white to me. And yesterday, why, I had a black, a very black mood. To be sure, my factories are not a success, and, indeed, may now and again involve a loss. But, then, look at those fields, and think of the crop we'll have; and with such a prospect I can afford to leave myself a very fair margin, the more so as the harvest in Russia and in Hungary promises to be very bad--so the reports say--and in that case we shall make no end of money. And then--look here--just you read his paragraph in the paper about the railway question. Eh--and the paragraph, I feel sure, is from the pen of the President of our own local Parliament, who is, by the by, a great friend of mine, and has for years been my lawyer. Well, what do you say now?"

"I say," replied Bertram gravely, "that things are exactly in the position which you described yesterday. Your friend here clearly represents only his own, or, if you like, your views and wishes; and will, moreover, naturally put some pressure upon Government, by representing it as impossible for them to decide differently from your wishes and hopes."

"But the Government--which means the Court--is already more than half won over. Lotter assures me...."

"For Heaven's sake! leave him out of the business."

"Oh, of course, of course; if you are so prejudiced against him that you refuse him even the common credibility which you allow otherwise to everybody!"

"There is no question here of credibility or incredibility," exclaimed Bertram indignantly; "but the thing is this: you are mistaking your illusions and hopes for realities and facts; you are voluntarily blinding yourself lest you see the abyss into which you are about to plunge. And mind this: by your miserable hesitation you are really accelerating the coming of the dreaded moment; nay, you render it only the more dreadful. There is still time; this very day you can go and say to your wife: I have met with losses, terrible losses, and we must needs retrench, and therefore.... Why, man, you will let it come to this, that you must confess to her: We have nothing further to lose; all is gone! Think of this, friend, I entreat you. Your boat is overloaded; away with the ballast which all but sinks it now; overboard with it all! Were it a question of yourself alone, you would be manly enough not to hesitate; and with wife and child on board, whose ruin is certain unless you act at once, you ... cannot, will not act!"

Otto would say neither yea nor nay. Bertram was silent in his despair. What would come of it all?

And so they arrived in town, having hardly exchanged a word more. They looked over the villa, and again hardly a word was exchanged; just an indifferent remark here and there, nothing more. Otto was apparently annoyed at something, but Bertram saw well enough that this appearance of annoyance was but assumed to hide his irresolution.

"I know, I know," Otto said at last grumpily, "we are not likely to agree as it is. Had we not better call together upon my lawyer and hear his opinion about the whole business? He is, moreover, on your side, in politics, and will be delighted to make your acquaintance."

Bertram seized eagerly upon so sensible a proposal, and to the lawyer's they drove accordingly; but when they had got to the door, Otto remembered that he had to do some commission for Hildegard: he even explained--

"About those officers who are going to be quartered upon us, don't you know?--extra provisions and that kind of thing. She can never, she thinks, have too much on hand, in case.... Well, well, it's her nature to ..."

And so the broad-shouldered figure of his friend passed down the lonely sunlit street; and Bertram added, speaking to himself, this comment, "And your nature is ... to do things by halves only, unless you mean, in this case, to throw the whole responsibility upon my shoulders."

And in this view his friend's lawyer completely confirmed him.

"Look here," said the latter to Bertram, when, after a hearty, mutual welcome, the two had swiftly grown to be confidential with each other, "you may take my word for this, he is most anxious we should have a perfectly unrestrained talk about his affairs, and has backed out of being present simply to avoid having to hear all the disagreeable things we could not spare him; moreover, he might oppose to you and to me, separately, a certain resistance which he would not have the courage to do if he, found us confronting him together. Under these circumstances I do not consider it indiscreet, but I think I am acting according to the wishes, and I know I am acting in the interest of our common friend, if I now add a few words of explanation to what you know already; then, indeed, you will be thoroughly acquainted with the state of his.affairs."

The lawyer then proceeded to describe Otto's position in detail; and to his amazement Bertram found his own conception confirmed throughout. Why, even his own image of the ballast which required to be heaved overboard to set the ship once more afloat, figured in the exposition. To be sure, Bertram now learned for the first time how weighty that ballast really was. Thus, to give but one example, Otto had never mentioned, had not even hinted at the fact that Hildegard's elder sister, the widow of the late Secret Counsellor von Palm, and her whole family, lived entirely upon Otto's bounty. "And that," said the lawyer, "is an awful item! For the lady in question is, in every respect, a true sister of your friend's wife. She thinks that death and the end of all things must needs be at hand, if she and hers cannot live on a very grand scale indeed. And then her house in Erfurth is a sort of gathering-place for all who, by rank or position, may aspire to the honour of appearing in such sublime surroundings; half-pay general officers and colonels galore--and the little town was ever full of them--and, of course, the whole number of officers actually on duty in the garrison, and so on, and so on. The girls--and there is half-a-dozen of them--are as bad as their mother, always excepting one dear, sensible creature--not one of the pretty ones, though--whom, I understand, you are about to meet in Rinstedt. Well, if the daughters are extravagant, the two sons--both, as you know, in the army, go on as though their uncle's cashbox had no bottom to it. Three times, four times, already he has paid the debts of those young men, whom, by the by, he cannot bear at all, and this, and all this, simply *in majorem gloriam Hildegardis*, his well-beloved wife, a lady of such an old family that the scions thereof cannot, of course, be measured by the same standard as common mortals."

"And do you not perceive any way of escape from this vicious circle our friend is wandering in?" Bertram asked.

"Only the one you have already pointed to," the lawyer made answer. "But how the deuce can you advise a man who will not be advised, or rather, who accepts all the advice you give him and never acts upon it for all that ...? And there is one thing yet in which you have, too, judged aright. It is by no means too late yet! If he give up those factories of his which will never pay, even if--and on that his whole hope is now centred--the new line of rails passes straight through his estates, and if he meets My Lady with a *sic voleo*, *sic jubeo,* and if, with one determined cut, he severs the boundlessly costly train from My Lady's garment, leaving it, for all that, a very respectable garment, he would be enabled to discharge his other liabilities gradually, or at once if somebody would, at fair interest, lend him a biggish capital. This, of course, times being bad, will not be very easy to manage, more particularly if people begin to talk about his being embarrassed."

"And how large, think you, should that capital be?"

"I think that I could settle everything if I had a hundred thousand thalers at my disposal, without there being any formal arrangement with his creditors, or even a voluntary surrender."

"In that case I beg to put the sum mentioned at your disposal."

The lawyer looked up in amazement.

"I had no idea that you were so wealthy," he said simply.

"It does not represent half my fortune. Anyhow, I am not running any risk."

"No, to be sure," replied the lawyer; "I should be able to secure you against any loss; the rate of interest, as I observed before, would be low. But I may tell you beforehand that your generous offer will be refused. I know our friend. He would rather borrow from the most unscrupulous cut-throat of a usurer than from you, for whom he has, as I know, the profoundest respect. For, though you may be the best of friends, you are not his brother, not his cousin, not a kinsman at all. If you could say to him, you owe it to our family to do so--such an appeal to the family honour, which he holds in the highest esteem, he would comprehend much better. But as it is, his very pride, or his vanity rather--for vanity is distinctly his ruling passion--will be hurt; he will appear to be immensely grateful to you, will say that you are his good angel, and--will not accept a farthing from you, as long as he sees, or fancies he sees, any other way out. He may possibly come to his senses when his last hope, the railway, proves illusory. I fear--I am a keen promoter of the project myself, but on different grounds--I fear that will occur presently. Meanwhile, try your luck, or his rather, by all means. But I repeat, you will not succeed with the mere appeal to your friendship."

Bertram, as previously arranged, then called for his friend, and as they drove home together he made his attempt The lawyer's prophecy was literally fulfilled. Otto overflowed in expressions of the greatest gratitude for an offer so thoroughly characteristic of his generous friend, and which, for the sake of their long friendship, he would unconditionally accept--if there were any occasion for it. But that, thank goodness, was not the case.

And then came the wretched old story which Bertram knew by heart already, and to which, for all that, he now listened; not, as before, with disgust, but with an odd feeling of anxiety and doubt. To be sure, mere friendship was not sufficient. He would have required another title, one giving the right to demand what now he begged for in vain. Should he venture upon the word that was trembling on his lips, and that yet was ever beating a cowardly retreat to the tremulous heart? Cowardly? No! It would have been cowardice, miserable cowardice, if he had spoken it; cowardice, trying to take by miserable money-bribes a fortress invincible to valour and high courage; cowardice and treason, treason to the sanctity of a love which had hitherto been unselfish and as pure as the heart of the great waters. If things came to the worst, if it was a question of guarding the beloved child against common want, she would be noble enough not to refuse the helping hand of a protecting friend. But woe to him if that hand were not unsullied; if even the shadow of a suspicion of selfishness fell upon it!

And as they thus drove homewards, with the evening darkening around them, he fixed his eye on high, where now the heavenly lights were appearing in ever-increasing numbers, with ever-growing splendour; and he reverently repeated to himself the poet's great saying of the stars above, in whose majestic beauty man should rejoice without coveting their possession.

CHAPTER XI

But no poet's word could henceforth stay the wild conflagration which raged in his heart; and every thought by which his mind strove to obtain rest and clearness proved a faint-hearted hireling soldier that takes the first opportunity of deserting to the ranks of the more potent foe. In vain did he recall the arguments by which, in a certain memorable conversation, he had tried to refute Erna's assertions--it had been a lie, a lie--or, at best, mere theoretical twaddle. His love a reminiscence merely? And of what, pray? Perhaps of that mournful aberration when his heart, his thirty years notwithstanding, was still full of faith and devoid of experience? Or of the coquettish phantom-fights and ugly caricatures of passion with which a heart that has ceased to believe, in love, endeavours to deceive itself regarding its own needs? Thee, he exclaimed, thee I have always loved. My whole life has been one unbroken longing for thee; and when now at length I have reached the land of promise, am I solely to see it, bless God, and die? I am no longer weary of life. Nay, life has never yet appeared so fair to me, and never yet have I so felt the desire and the power to enjoy it. Die we must; die, however empty life may have been; but oh, how better far to die in the full bliss of love! No, no! If I love her, my only reminiscence is one of weary deserts traversed until I reached her: if she could love me, her love should be no mere mirage of an oasis in the future; palms should rustle above her fair head, silvery brooks should run at her feet. Love surely has this potent spell: it can create a paradise on earth!

And from these fairy dreams of future bliss he was startled by the thought that Erna's heart must have already once received some mighty impression. For it was surely passing strange that she knew so well how to interpret some of the mysterious symbols in the book of passion; that she evidently liked to read in that book. But since all his cautious questioning led to no result, since she spoke of the few young men whom she seemed to know at all either with indifference, or even, as in the case of her two cousins, with a perceptible touch of irony, he could not but conclude that his suspicion was unfounded, and he became more and more familiar with a fond hope, from which he at first recoiled as from a temptation to sheer madness.

But he still had the full use of his senses, and they, had never been so acute as now. How was he to explain that her voice, whenever she turned to him, and particularly when they were alone, was quite different from its usual tone--softer, deeper, more intense? How was he to explain that she--surely without being aware of it--kept sometimes, at table, if he happened to speak eagerly, her gaze fixed upon him for several minutes--that strange, fixed gaze which he had never before met from any human eye, and which reminded him again and again of the gaze of the gods,--

"Whose eyelids quiver not like those of mortals;"

and then when he ceased to, speak she was like one awakening from a dream, drawing a long breath, which caused her maiden bosom to rise and sink!

Nor were other promising tokens wanting. He had, for good reasons of his own, disregarded Erna's request to be henceforth less kind to Lydia; nay, he had doubled his attentions and courtesies, not only towards the coquettish lady, but towards the Baron too. It seemed so easy now to pardon, to show indulgence, to look at all things from the best and most amiable point of view; and politeness is a veil behind which one may hide so much. At first he had been prepared for opposition or serious displeasure on the part of the proud, self-willed girl; but nothing of the kind occurred; she either seemed not to notice his disobedience, or actually to approve of it; and once or twice, when he somewhat overdid his part, a meaning smile played about her mouth. Nay, more, she followed, though with evident hesitation, his example; she no longer met Lydia's fantastic exaggerations with short and sharp replies, or with that frigid non-recognition which is more cutting than direct blame: she continued, as on the first evening or two, to sing and play with the Baron; she even suffered herself to be put into the famous terrace picture, and was patient enough to sit to him for a couple of hours, in which the Baron, with his brush, was constantly taking one step forward and two backward, as it were; while he vowed again and again that this was the most grateful, but also the most difficult, task which he had ever undertaken in his life.

And there was yet one thing more which had struck him as peculiarly strange and important. Erna was accustomed to repeat her interlocutors' names frequently in the course of conversation, and to add them, even to quite trivial phrases or questions. From the first days of his visit he still recalled with delight her sweet "How are you, Uncle Bertram?"--"Yes, Uncle Bertram"--"No, Uncle Bertram." But sweeter, sweeter far it seemed to him that he now no longer heard it--no, not once--that her conversation now was plain yea and nay, as enjoined in Holy Writ, and quite in accordance with the wild wish of his heart. Hilarie, too, had surely ceased to call her lover--Uncle. Poor Major! But it served him right, after all, for it was not youth so much that he lacked, as the courage and force of genuine passion.

> "That man must ever be a youthful man
> Who is well-pleasing to a maiden's eyes!"

And he does please her well, because she feels with the unerring instinct of true love that he can and will give love for love.

And as though he would force Fate to grant him all, because he was staking his all upon it, he looked on with a happy smile, whilst the fire of his great love burned up with increasing vehemence with every day, with every hour, spreading around and engulfing his entire being. He was proud that he could no longer feel anything else, think of anything else, but always her, and her alone. If she was away, how empty, how barren did the whole world seem! With what painful impatience did he await the moment when he should behold her again; and when he beheld her again, it seemed as though he had never beheld her before--as though the Creator had but just uttered the command: "Let there be light!" and as though the world lay before him in all the dewy freshness and brightness of the morn of creation.

Then, when the torment of delight became overpowering, he fled from her, to dream, often for hours, in the solitude of the forest, in lone, rocky caves, or on sunny summits--to listen in the deep silence around for the echoing of her sweet voice within his heart, to whisper her loved name to the discreet herbs and trees; to hear that name in the murmur of the brooks, in the rustling of the breezes, in every note of the birds' songs; to see her fair image smiling down upon him from among the dainty white cloudlets that flecked the deep-blue sky, or gazing at him with musing gravity from the dusky shadows of the towering trees, gazing with those great, still, potent, godlike orbs.

That those orbs were now smiling more rarely, that they were fuller of gravest thought, often gazing with a certain sweet fixity of intensest concentration, he had not failed to observe, and he had not interpreted it as a symptom unfavourable to himself; how should, how could it be otherwise, if there fell into her young soul even the faintest reflex of the bright radiancy that was filling his own to its deepest depths?

But he had not failed to observe either, and this he knew not how to explain, that this musing gravity from which his own love in its hopefulness drew sweetest sustenance--like a bee from the chalice of a budding blossom-

-was turning to a gloomy indignation, which not only was for ever veiling the beloved eyes, but was not unfrequently enfolding the fair face with its fine, energetic features in darkest night, luridly illumined by wrathful flashes.

This startling change had occurred quite suddenly, coincident, strangely enough, with the day, almost with the hour, of Agatha's arrival.

CHAPTER XII

On the occasion of former visits at Rinstedt Bertram had repeatedly seen Agatha, and had always been on the best of terms with the ever equally pleasant, amiable child. Now, of course she had, like Erna, developed during the last few years into a maiden, though one could not say that she had gained by the process of metamorphosis. The blonde hair now was almost red, freckles abounded unpleasantly on brow and cheek, and an awkward tendency to one side had become an undoubted lurch; so that, taking all these things together, one might indeed be tempted to take the nickname "Granny," which Erna had bestowed upon her cousin and bosom friend, not in its moral meaning alone. But the bright blue eyes had faithfully preserved the old, dear expression; nay, even more openly than of old, there spoke out of them a heart full of kindliest goodwill to all men, desirous of riving in peace and friendship with all men, and seeming not so much to loathe as simply not to comprehend the evil emotions and passions of the human heart.

So gentle a creature, made but for sympathy in joy or in sorrow, could scarcely have found the requisite courage to destroy even the commonplace illusions of a commonplace heart, and would most likely have recoiled from the mere attempt to lay violent hands upon a heart like Erna's, deviating as it did so greatly from the humdrum, everyday pattern. And, again, Bertram had to drop the suspicion which at first had come to him in his perplexity; to wit, that Agatha had, whether in carelessness or intentionally, blabbed about something confided to her by Erna. Such a thing would have been in downright contradiction to the character of the girl, who was as clever as she was good; and, lastly, that he himself should have betrayed his feelings to the rest--that was absolutely impossible. He was only too painfully conscious of having from the very first moment put a most careful guard on his conduct, of having weighed his every word, controlled his every smile and look: of course he had! Why, he recoiled in horror from the very thought that Erna might discover his great secret; it was certain that she had not discovered it, and how could others have done so?

But why should they, again, not have seen, and seen in envy, uncharitableness, and terror, what it was the utmost delight to him to see? Though he, in the full consciousness of his love, in the anxious doubt as to whether that love was not a folly, a crime even, had put the utmost restraint upon himself, yet Erna had assuredly not been equally careful in expressing her feelings, whose real significance she might guess at, though most assuredly she could not measure it. Why, the most harmless and innocent things in the attentions she was spoiling him with, the many kindly little offices which she did for him without any fuss, *en passant*, as it were--all these things might have been malevolently criticised and viciously explained, suspicion being once aroused one way or the other!

And that such must be the case he could scarcely doubt any longer, when he submitted the demeanour of the others towards him during the last few days to a subsequent examination. Thus, in the light of newly-won knowledge, sundry things stood out in a very marked way, which, under other circumstances, he would either not have heeded, or anyhow have interpreted differently. His beautiful hostess, who used to avail herself of every tête-à-tête with him to turn their talk to Erna and the Baron, had not resumed her favourite topic of conversation; and, on the other hand, Lydia now manifested infinite interest in Erna, and never wearied of starting contemplative talks in reference to the qualities of her former pupil, wondering how one should represent to oneself the future of such a singular being as likely to develop itself. The Baron had still, on each Occasion when Bertram and he had met, overflowed with civility, but had yet tormented him less often with challenges to billiard-matches and to contests in pistol-shooting, but had on the other hand undertaken more frequent solitary shooting expeditions--neither Bertram nor Otto, their host, cared for shooting, as it happened--and had extended them farther too. Otto himself had certainly and most clearly avoided him. At first he had thought that Otto did it to avoid new and painful discussions in reference to his financial position, but Bertram now assumed that it was done lest Otto should distinctly show that he was angry with his friend for Erna's sake, or, what--with his natural weak readiness to yield--came virtually to the same thing, that he had been bidden by the ruling spirit to be angry with Bertram.

These were curiously mixed feelings which were roused within him by his recognition of the new position he so suddenly found himself in. He said to himself that the things which caused anxiety and terror to his adversaries were for himself objects of joy and triumph, and constituted the clearest proof that he had not only dreamed a dream of rapturous delight. And to be sure, his love could not for ever remain in the far-off regions of starry splendour; it was bound some time to approach this earth, to become visible to the dull, mole-like eyes of these men. But then again, putting himself in the place of these others, and examining himself and his love, as these others were undoubtedly doing, he would hear anew, and this time from the lips of unjust accusers, the old evil questions which he thought had long ago been done with, to wit--Is your longing and your desire really and truly free from every vestige of selfishness, from every frivolous admixture? Has the satisfaction of your own vanity, inasmuch as you may prove that you, a man of fifty, are able to win the love of such a youthful, and, in every respect, such a highly-favoured and gifted girl, against the wishes of her own parents, before her who had once spurned your love, in the presence and to the shame and discomfiture of so much more likely a rival--have these considerations nothing, nothing whatever to do with your love?

And supposing he were to allow himself to be urged by pressure on the part of his foes to make a declaration before the right time; or supposing there never had been and never would be such a time at all--supposing he and all of them had blundered;--supposing Erna's heart knew nought of love, and rejected his love, amazed, terrified, insulted--what then? Ye Heavens above! what then? Where was then that line of retreat which Göthe had so wisely secured for his hero?

He realised it to be one of those horribly hideous contradictions of human life that, while before his inner eye the possibilities of his future fate concentrated themselves as in a focus, he was busied before the mirror in exchanging the cravat which Konski had put out for him for the early dinner, for another (the first dressing-bell having just rung), in reference to which Erna had once said that it suited him particularly well.

He stepped, annoyed, from the mirror to the open window. There came floating through the balmy, sunny air a gossamer thread and fixed itself on his shoulder. He sighed wearily, he felt unutterably sad.

There was always one line of retreat open, and that was--Death. Perhaps his life was really hanging on as slight a thread as this bit of gossamer. But then, was not his love for that very reason both madness and sacrilege? Was that love which at bottom thought, after all, of itself only, and thought not first and last of this? Could one, according to human judgment, really undertake the guarantee for the well-being of those whom one ... made believe one loved? Whether, for her, weal would not swiftly change to woe, whence, even though time and that youthful vigour which refuses to be crushed were to heal the grievous wounds, there could never again blossom forth a full, whole happiness? And thus, and for this reason, to have henceforth, like humdrum everyday folks, to dread death, when he had already again and again looked into his hollow eyes!

There was some noise behind him, and he started in terror. It was only Konski who had come back bearing a letter. The post which was due in the morning had arrived now, and there had been lots of letters for the other ladies and gentlemen too, and some of them would seem to be mighty important, for My Lady had given orders to put dinner back half an hour, so the Herr Doctor could anyhow read his letter in peace.

Konski had gone away again, and Bertram held the letter still unopened in his hand. How odd that his physician and friend should write to him just now--that the busiest of men should so swiftly reply to his own letter, in which, on the second day of his visit, he had, as requested, given news of his state of health, a letter which really called for no reply at all. Was his friend now going to tell him that he ... was doomed to speedy death? Well, the letter could not have come at a more opportune moment.

With trembling hand he broke the seal and read this--

"Dearest Friend,--Laugh if you like. On reading your letter a second time--your letters are not, like most others, consigned to the waste-paper basket--I have even more strongly the same impression which the first perusal had given me; namely, that, possibly unknown to yourself, there is to be read between the lines of your letter a question, which can be answered only by omniscient Fate and by 'Yours Truly;' and which, seeing Fate is not altogether to be relied upon in this respect, Yours Truly has the honour and likewise the great pleasure of answering herewith. Reduced to its simplest formula, then, the question comes to this: May I marry? Seeing that you do not laugh, but, on the contrary, look extremely grave, I will not keep you needlessly on the tenter-hooks of expectation, but will reduce my reply, too, to the simplest form, viz.:--Yes, best of friends, you may marry, in spite of your late serious attack; nay, oddly enough, all the more because of it. For although even before your illness I had no doubt that your curiously powerful nature would for years continue to hold its own against the severe damage done (to deny or reason away the existence of which was unfortunately impossible), I now have hardly any misgiving in that respect. For your last illness was simply and solely a remarkably energetic attempt at self-help on the part of nature, and the attempt has all but succeeded. What remains to be done to complete the cure is but little, and that this little be done as swiftly and thoroughly as possible, you can yourself greatly help. How so? Well, by marrying! You, having always been over-conscientious and abnormally scrupulous, having ever lived but for ideal aims and for the benefit of other folk, should now at length begin to live for yourself, should now at length find that quiet happiness which you so richly deserve, and be happy in that happiness; though, to be sure, for the last condition more good sense is required than what the majority of mankind have been ready to employ. You, my good friend, have that amount of sense. *Ergo*--marry for goodness' sake, marry for your own good, marry for the good of those whom you love, and, lastly, marry with my full consent, without which I know you would not do it at all.

"But now, seeing that you are too accustomed to suffering of some sort to be able to dispense with it altogether, I owe you a fresh supply to make up for what I am depriving you of, and I am going to saddle you with one of the most awful kinds of suffering a free man can be tormented with in these hard and distressing times--you must stand for Parliament. There is no help for it; we must have you in the *Reichstag*. Good old S. can bear the burthen no longer; he is going to retire. I should have insisted upon it on medical grounds if he had not at length come to see himself that there was no help for it. He is done for, and doomed to speedy death. And you, who are vigorously advancing to complete restoration of health, shall and must take his place--by order of the Electoral Committee, who met at a late hour last night and ultimately came to a unanimous conclusion on the subject, all, finally, voting for you! There is no reason why I should keep back the fact that, to begin with, O. and B. were opposed to it, and so were a few others, asserting that you could be of greater use to the common cause as an outsider. They went on arguing that your absolutely independent position within the party had hitherto enabled you, and would continue to enable you, to ventilate certain grievances which really require to be ventilated, and which it is impossible for ourselves, sitting as members of the *Reichstag*, to bring forward, because, sitting there, we must pay a certain regard to ... what not. This great and invaluable activity of yours, they wisely contended, would be rendered absolutely barren by your entering the serried ranks of a definite political phalanx within the House itself. Right they are, I know well enough, none better; for I have, as you know, always maintained the same view. But, for all that, you must stand. The need is imperative. We have, alas! none but you; and therefore our arguments prevailed: and the requisition I am now forwarding to you in the name of our common party is, as aforesaid, unanimous. Knowing you as well as I do, and knowing therefore with what a struggle you make up your mind, ever determined to adhere unswervingly to a resolution you have once arrived at, I'll give you three days to think it over. Perhaps you'll talk it over with our friend G. in W., whose acquaintance you have probably made ere this; not to get him to appeal to your conscience--small need for that in your case--but because an old veteran like him may be able, from the fulness of his experience, to give you some hint or other which may be of use to you in your candidature. It is very probable that you may have to appear speedily in the arena. The Government would appear to feel very confident of success, and will not delay the election. Four weeks hence everything may be settled. That would leave you another month before the meeting of Parliament to recover from the fatigue of the electioneering campaign. The Italian trip will have to be given up, it is true. But no one can serve two masters; and as for the mistress, if my conjecture be correct, I do not dread her jealousy. If it were permitted to harbour any doubt whether you have chosen wisely, or if there were any need to apply a special test, there could be no surer touchstone than this. The true gold of a genuine woman's love never shines more brightly than when a sacrifice has to be made for the sake of letting a man's worth stand out clearly. Commend me cordially to the fair unknown, and accept my own affectionate greetings."

The second dinner-bell had rung, and Bertram still sat staring at the letter. Could this be true? It looked like witchcraft. By what wonderful ingenuity had his friend rightly interpreted the state of his heart, judging from hints which were not intended to be hints at all? Well, if it was a miracle, it was a very auspicious one--one that could only have had its origin in the great strength of truest friendship. Impossible for the tempter to have assumed the guise of the best and noblest of men!

He pressed the letter to his lips, and gazed upward to the blue sky. And, lo! as he moved, the gossamer thread floated away from his shoulder, away into the sunny afar.

With glowing eye he followed its flight.

"Right, right! Fly and float with it, ye cowardly thoughts of retreat! Who fears not death has already half won the battle!"

CHAPTER XIII

Below, in the garden saloon, Bertram found only Otto and the Baron, who abruptly stopped an eager conversation as Bertram entered. Otto looked greatly embarrassed; the Baron gave him one angry look, then turned away to the young ladies, who were walking on the verandah.

"I seem to have disturbed you," said Bertram.

"Don't be annoyed," replied Otto. "The Baron had, last night already, disagreeable news from home, which is confirmed to-day, and will compel him to travel back; and just now, in this time of tension, he wishes of course--it is extremely awkward ..."

"In one word, he has officially asked you for your daughter's hand?"

"Not exactly officially; we really do not know about Erna. You had undertaken to put us *au courant*, to advise and help us, and now you are not helping us at all, and--and my wife is rather annoyed with you on this ground."

"So I have observed; and therefore, to make up for previous omissions, I'll give you my advice now: get rid of him as quickly as possible, and spare Erna the humiliation of having to refuse the fellow."

"Humiliation? The fellow? How oddly you talk!"

"I talk how I feel. He is unworthy of Erna, absolutely."

"So you say; but why?"

Bertram made no answer. What good could it do now to have a dispute with Otto about the worthiness or unworthiness of the Baron?

"You see," said Otto triumphantly, "you have no real reason to give!" Then, seeing his friend look extremely grave, he went on--"I know of course that you mean well by Erna, by me, by all of us. Perhaps you are right, too, at least in this--that Erna may say: No. If she does, well, then there is an end of it, and Hildegard and he may see how they can best put up with it. If only it had not happened just now. I have my head quite full enough as it is--all these officers coming to be quartered here to-morrow, then the final debate on the railway question, and then I just remember that I have also to redeem to-morrow a certain mortgage, not much, only five thousand thalers, but it happens most inopportunely, I wanted to talk to you about it before, but I did not like to disturb you in your rooms; perhaps after dinner, or to-night sometime--there is my wife coming, for God's sake no fuss, I entreat you!"

Hildegard entered, Lydia followed soon after, the young ladies and the Baron came in from the verandah, and they all went to dinner. Conversation somehow flagged; every one was busy with his own thoughts, and, if one were to judge by looks, these thoughts did not seem to be pleasant ones, except in Hildegard's case. She kept smiling mysteriously to herself, and at last, when there had been a pause of some little duration, she held up a couple of letters which she had laid by the side of her plate, and said--

"It is really too bad; here, I am sitting with quite a treasury of most interesting surprises, and none of you take the trouble to show the slightest symptom of curiosity. It would really serve you right if I were not to say a word to you; but I will be gracious, as usual, and let you participate in my joy. First, then, your mother, Agatha, has after all yielded to my entreaties. It is most kind of her. She has a big party to-morrow, too; some twenty officers, she says, and can ill spare any of the girls. Still, she understands that I have even greater need of them in our solitude, if the crowd of uniforms is not to become intolerably monotonous--*enfin*, she'll send Louise and Augusta. They will arrive to-day; so we shall really be able to have a dance to morrow evening, if we invite the girls from the parsonage and a few others. Well, what do you say?"

Erna made no reply; she seemed hardly to have listened. Agatha said--

"You are very kind, aunt," but it did not sound hearty.

"Is that all?" exclaimed Hildegard. "Of course I am kind, far too kind to you ungrateful *blasée* girls, who cannot rise to enthusism even with the prospect of a dance! But you, Baron?"

"I envy the gentlemen," replied he, "who will benefit by your kindness; I myself, as you are aware, will scarcely be able to participate in it."

Hildegard raised her eyebrows.

"I thought," she said, "that the matter was settled. Your relations may see how they can best do without you. I wish to hear nothing more upon the subject. This is my ultimatum, and I beg you will respect it."

The Baron bowed, and muttered something about *force majeure*. Hildegard paid no heed to it; she had already taken up the second letter.

"I must beforehand apologise for my bad French accent. The letter is from the Residenz, and I ought to mention ..."

"From Princess Amelia?" the Baron asked eagerly.

"Not from our gracious Princess," replied Hildegard with a courteous smile, "but from a princess, for all that."

"Perhaps you would translate it?" suggested Otto timidly.

"Very well," replied his wife. "I was thinking of doing so anyhow, for I know you pretend that you do not understand French. Well, then--

"Madam,--Will you pardon a perfect stranger who ventures to request a favour which it is usual to grant only to one's friends, or to duly accredited persons--the favour of being your guest for a short time? You are amazed, madam; but why do you own a mansion whose classic style of architecture and whose internal fittings are the marvel of the land? Why does every one who can judge, laud you as unsurpassed in the horticultural art? I travel through Germany chiefly with the object of studying all that is best and most beautiful in these things, in order to try and imitate it upon my estates in Livadia. I shall not, as I said, trouble you long; only a day or two. To-morrow and the day after, if I may, for I can unfortunately not dispose differently of my time. And as regards the inconvenience I must needs cause you, I will try to reduce it to a minimum. A gardener or forester to pilot me about outside, a steward to show me some of the things inside, a little corner by your fireside, a little place at your table, a little chamber to sleep in; that is all! True, already too much, if I reflect; but one should not reflect, if one is the thorough egotist who has the honour of remaining, Madam, your obedient servant,--Princess Alexandra Paulovna ..."

Hildegard looked up from her letter, and said with a smile--

"I cannot make out the surname."

She passed the letter to Bertram, who was sitting on her right.

"Well," said the Baron, on her left, "she would seem to be a Russian, anyhow."

"No doubt of that. Well, my friend?"

"No," replied Bertram, "I cannot make it out."

"Will you allow me?" said the Baron.

Bertram handed the letter back to Hildegard, who passed it on to the Baron.

"Why," he exclaimed, "it is quite plain, Bo--Bo!" He paused.

"Bo, Bo, Bo!" laughed Lydia. "Let me try." But Lydia failed too; the note was passed round the table; Otto and Agatha tried and failed; Erna passed it on to Bertram without casting one glance at it.

"Will you not try?" asked Bertram.

"No."

She uttered this so sharply that Bertram looked up terrified.

"How very unkind," said her mother.

Bertram had the same impression at first, but he knew Erna too well; there was assuredly something else going on in her mind, something which had tried to find expression in the abrupt No. She was very pale, and had pressed her teeth against her under lip, whilst her eyes looked gloomily and fixedly straight in front of her. One might have expected her to burst into a flood of tears the next moment. To turn the attention of the rest from her, and also to overcome his own feelings of uneasiness, he began once more diligently to spell away at the signature, and suddenly exclaimed--

"I have got it, I think--Volinzov--Alexandra Paulovna Volinzov!"

"Let me see, please?" exclaimed Hildegard. "Really, Volinzov; and quite plain too. How blind we have been! Dear me, Herr Baron, what is the matter with you?"

"I beg a thousand pardons," said the Baron from behind his handkerchief, which he held pressed to his face, rising from the table as he spoke, and swiftly withdrawing from the room.

Hildegard looked sadly after his retreating figure.

"Poor fellow!" she said, "I am so sorry. He is in a terrible state of excitement. And now, in addition, this home news--if I only knew what it is all about, but he is discretion personified."

Bertram, still pondering over Erna's strange demeanour, had almost mechanically cast his eye over the whole letter, and only became conscious of this on coming to a passage which he did not remember having heard in Hildegard's translation.

"Here," he said, "is one line, my fair friend, which has escaped you, and which yet strikes me as important. Listen: 'thorough egotist who has the courage to follow her letter at once, and has the honour,' &c."

"Impossible!" exclaimed Hildegard.

"There it stands; see for yourself. You passed from the last line but two on to the last."

"Oh dear! oh dear!" exclaimed the hostess. "She will be wanting to dine of course; and that is not the worst, but all the rooms will be occupied by to-morrow afternoon."

"The officers must do with a little less accommodation," said Otto. "It will be all right."

"No, it will not be all right," said his wife, "if each of them is to have a room of his own; and we cannot put less than two each at the disposal of the two Majors and the Colonel."

"Let me help you in your embarrassment," said Bertram. "You know, I originally intended leaving early to-morrow, let us adhere to the old plan; the more so, because I have just received a letter which necessitates my very speedy return to Berlin."

"That is an excuse," exclaimed his friend.

"No excuse, my dear fellow; you may see the letter yourself. But I may as well say what it is about. I have been selected by my political friends for a forthcoming vacancy in the *Reichstag*."

"But you will surely not stand?"

"Indeed, I mean to do so."

"And your Italian trip?"

"Postponed to some future day."

"But your illness?"

"Thanks to your excellent nursing, I never felt better in my life."

"But it's quite out of the question!" cried Otto. "I cannot let you. It would be downright ..."

In thus urging his friend to stay, Otto was simply following the dictates of his own good-natured heart, without any reference to his own special interests; now it suddenly occurred to him that his wife had that very morning called Bertram's presence a positive misfortune, and had accused him of standing--the one obstacle--between herself and the execution of her favourite plan.

So he broke off abruptly, casting a sheepish, embarrassed look at his wife.

Hildegard blushed to the very temples. Now she was obliged to urge him to stay, if everything she had been settling during the last few days in secret with Lydia and the Baron, and at last with her husband too, was not to lie like an open book before Bertram, and unless there was to be a real rupture, which, of course, it was desirable to avoid as long as possible. In order to conceal the true reason of her blush, she seized, as though obeying some uncontrollable impulse, both his hands, and said--

"I am almost speechless with amazement, my friend! Otto is quite right; the thing is impossible, it would be downright--abominable--that is what you were going to say, is it not, dear Otto? You cannot, must not leave us now. In a few days, if it really must be, well and good; but not now. I have--quite apart from our own feelings--revelled in the thought of the pleasant surprise it will be for Herr von Waldor to meet here, upon the threshold of a strange house, an old friend of his own. And if old friendship cannot exercise a spell over you, are you not allured by the prospect of meeting the mysterious Russian, whose name you alone were able to decipher, and who will not care to converse with any one except yourself, once she has heard how beautifully you speak French? But come--Otto, Lydia, Agatha--help me to entreat our friend to stay."

In the general excitement, every one had risen from table, dinner being finished anyhow, and now they were talking on the verandah. The Baron had reappeared too, but was keeping at some little distance; he evidently had not quite recovered from his attack. Those to whom Hildegard had appealed by name hastened to comply with her request, and were all urging Bertram to remain. He never heard them at all; he did not even see them; he had eyes for Erna only.

Erna, as though she had no interest whatever in the matter under discussion, had stepped down from the verandah to one of the flower-plots on the lawn. Suddenly she turned, retraced her steps slowly, ascended the verandah again, and approached him. Her cheeks--so pale but a short time ago--were flushed now; there was a light in those large eyes, and a defiant smile played round her dainty lips. She fastened a beautiful red rose, just about to unfold, in his buttonhole.

"I prayed you the night you came--I pray you again: Stay! stay--for my sake! Come, Agatha!"

She had seized her cousin by the hand, and drawn her away into the garden; Bertram had stepped into the billiard-room, and was knocking the balls about; the others looked at each other, amazed, embarrassed, frightened, scornful. But, greatly though their various feelings desired expression and exchange, and opportune though the occasion might appear, there was no chance in the meantime. For the very next moment the sound of a post-horn was heard coming from the great courtyard, and announced, to Hildegard's terror, that Princess Volinzov had interpreted her own letter literally, and had really followed it without delay.

CHAPTER XIV

The sunny brightness of the day was suddenly interrupted by a thunderstorm, and the evening closed in dark and stormy. Up from the valley and down from the wooded hills thick grey mists came rolling along, and violent showers of rain ensued. It was chilly and disagreeable; and the "corner by the fireside," referred to in the letter of the Princess, seemed no longer to be a mere phrase, but to embody a very natural wish, and one which Hildegard took care to fulfil, by having fires kindled in all the drawing-rooms. There was quite a party at the mansion this evening. An hour after the arrival of the Princess, the sisters of Agatha had come; then the forest-ranger, the Herr *Oberförster*, had turned up, without having brought his ladies, on account of the disagreeable weather, but there had come with him a young gentleman from the Forests and Woods' Department, Herr von Busche, who had been absent for a week, and who, as he laughingly assured them, must try very hard to make up for the many pleasant hours he had lost. He seemed determined to carry this into practice, for he was most indefatigable in suggesting new games and new jests, and kept the four young ladies in constant laughter.

"*Qu'y a-t-il de plus beau,*" said the Princess, talking, as before, now French, now German with equal readiness, "thus to hear, from an adjoining room, the happy laughter of girls, while one is sitting snugly by the fire talking to a friend. The past and the present mingle and separate again, like the red and blue flames among those coals; and sometimes there flashes between them a green one, which we may take for a light giving a glimpse of the future-- and indeed it vanishes again very swiftly. How comfortable, how beautiful everything's in your house, *ma chère*. And how can I thank you enough for admitting me to the full enjoyment of your charming home?"

She had seized both Hildegard's hands as she spoke, and seized them so eagerly that the bracelets on her round white arms jingled.

"I have to thank you, Princess ..."

"For goodness' sake, do not call me that any longer. Say Alexandra, will you not?"

"Will you say Hildegard?"

"*Cela va sans dire*--Hildegard--a beautiful name--beautiful like her whose it is! What were we talking about? The future, yes, to be sure. Well, there is a glorious future in store for you in your lovely daughter."

"Do you like Erna?"

"Like her? *Mon Dieu!* only a mother's modesty can ask this. She is simply divine. Not that I never saw more beautiful girls--you see I am quite frank--but there is something in her whole bearing, the way in which she walks or stands, every movement, every gesture, her expression, her smile, her gravity even, there is a grace and a charm about it all which completely bewitch me, woman though I am. How may men feel? Poor men! Poor broken hearts, I pity you!"

"She has scarcely had the chance yet of breaking hearts," replied Hildegard with a smile; "she has only just left school."

"But even very young ladies, I am told, manage sometimes to do it," said the Princess. "I am afraid I broke one or two myself whilst I was at a boarding-school, and it was a strict one, too! But to be serious, have you already chosen for your fair child?"

"Our girls in Germany are wont to claim the right of choice for themselves," replied Hildegard, casting a stolen glance at Bertram, who, walking up and down the saloon with Otto, happened just at that moment to be inconveniently near.

"A bad German peculiarity," said the Princess. "If a girl who does not know the world, does not know men--except her father, of whom she is afraid, and her brothers, whom she thinks ridiculous--is allowed to choose a husband according to the confused illusions of her silly little head--you may bet a hundred to one that the result will be either a *bêtise* or a *malheur*--which, according to the saying of the witty Frenchman, are, however, identical terms."

"That is quite my idea, dear--Alexandra," said Hildegard, bending her head with a courteous smile to her new-found friend; "quite my idea!"

"Clever women understand each other *à demi mot*," replied Alexandra. "But there are exceptions, and your Erna is such an exception. She would never dream of losing her heart to a man simply because he stands six feet, and knows how to brush himself up and to cut a figure, however confused things may look beneath the smoothly-parted hair, however rotten a heart may beat behind the dainty cambric shirt-front."

Hildegard did not dare to stir; she had noticed that during the last few words of the Princess the Baron had been standing within a couple of steps from them, evidently with the intention of joining them. But as neither lady seemed to see him, or wish to see him, he examined a vase which stood upon a marble table near, and turned on his heel again. Hildegard breathed more freely.

"You may be quite assured," said Alexandra, "I spoke in French on purpose when I saw him coming. I had made sure that he speaks it very badly, and understands it even worse, which, by the by, is rather curious in a cavalier who is anxious to obtain a Court appointment."

Hildegard felt very uneasy, although it was of course out of the question that the Princess should have meant the Baron when she spoke of a "man standing six feet."

"You know," she said with some little hesitation, "that the Baron is very intimate at Court?"

"I was at Court last night," replied Alexandra, "to tea. We Russians are in very good odour at your Court, you know; and, moreover, I had made the acquaintance of their Highnesses during their last visit to St. Petersburg. Princess Amelia is specially gracious to me, and she is the one who interests herself in the Baron."

"To be sure," Hildegard assented eagerly. "Pray, tell me more, it has much interest for me."

"I have not much to tell. I mentioned in the course of general conversation that I intended to pay you a visit to-day. This led to Fräulein von Aschhof and the Baron being mentioned as your guests. For that curious lady every one seemed to have a smile, nothing more, which, by the by, I can quite understand. About the Baron--well, *chère amie*, since you are interested in the young man, I must be indiscreet enough to tell you of a very confidential conversation I had afterwards in a window recess about him with that dear old man, Count Dirnitz, the Court-Marshal. He told me that the opinions regarding the Baron were at least much divided at Court. The Grand Duke himself, he said, in particular, could not overcome a certain antipathy to him, and that was the reason why his appointment as one of the chamberlains, although duly made out, still awaited the Grand Duke's signature. The Count said that he himself, although he had been an intimate friend of the Baron's father, did not know what to advise. Just then the Grand Duke came up to us; he had heard the last words of Count Dirnitz, and said laughingly: 'That, my good Count, happens pretty often to you; but may I ask what it is about?' And when Dirnitz, who, I suppose, had no option, had told him, he said: 'Well, in this case, I must admit I am perplexed myself; I should so much like to oblige Princess Amelia, and yet ...' Then the Grand Duke suddenly turned to me and said: '*A propos*, Princess Volinzov, as you are going to Rinstedt to-morrow, you might have a good look at our man. I will gladly confide the matter to your unprejudiced decision. If you think him suitable for us, *eh bien*, I'll risk it.' ... What a truly charming ceiling this is! Quite a work of art."

Princess Alexandra was leaning back in her arm-chair examining through her double eye-glass the painted ceiling.

"I see," she said, "a fine imitation of that Guercino in the Villa Ludovisi. It is superb, truly superb!"

Hildegard was in a state of painful excitement. The young Princess had, anyhow, impressed her greatly; now this unexpected, but of course perfectly natural, intimacy at Court, and specially such a mission, possibly the one solitary motive of the whole visit, and upon which the Baron's fate depended. She felt almost dizzy, and it cost her a considerable struggle to be able to say with some calmness--

"I beg your pardon, my dear Alexandra, but you have forgotten the main thing."

"The main thing! What main thing?

"What your unprejudiced opinion of the Baron now is."

"To be sure!"

She looked again at Hildegard. There was an odd smile on her lips now.

"If my opinion were only unprejudiced. But how can that be when the friends of our friends are our own, or ought to be?"

"You shall not escape thus," said Hildegard, whose sinking courage the fair visitor's smile had revived a little.

"I do not mean to escape," replied the Princess; "only I do not quite like to confess a silly trick to you which my memory, which is generally very fair as far as physiognomies are concerned, is playing me in this case. But it is simply impossible to free one's self altogether from the influence which a marked personal likeness exercises; and when I first saw the Baron, there came to me the most disagreeable reminiscence of an episode of the last journey I made with my lamented mother to Italy. However, as I ought at once to state, there is no harm in the matter, for the Baron, whom I asked, says he was not in Monaco that year."

"In Monaco?" cried Hildegard.

"Alas, my good mamma, the Countess Lassounska, you must know, was a great votary of the green cloth. Well, she could afford to indulge a passion which, among the ladies of the Russian aristocracy, not seldom survives or reappears, when they have had to bury all other passions. And in all others poor mamma had been so very unfortunate; but in this she was singularly lucky. Thus, one night--it was in autumn '72--she died next spring, four weeks after my marriage with the Prince, who had at that time followed us to Monaco, and to whom I had just, being then sixteen years of age, become engaged--good Lord, and he has been dead these two years! How time passes! But what was I going to say? Oh yes; mamma had won an immense sum one night, so much that at last she was barely paying any attention to what she was staking, and when she noticed a friend, she turned round to talk to him, without leaving her chair, until the gentleman himself called her attention to the accumulating gains, and asked if she would not withdraw them. But she said there was no hurry, and went on chattering, to the amazement of her neighbours and the terror of the bank, for they kept and kept losing on the red. At last mamma did turn round again to the table, her own curiosity roused by the divers exclamations of the bystanders; but just at that moment a gentleman, who had been sitting by her side all night, was pocketing the whole huge heap of banknotes and rouleaux of gold. Mamma claimed her property, of course; the gentleman assured her she was mistaken. Mamma knew that this was not the case, but a scene in a gambling-room, don't you know, dear, *c'est une horreur* for a lady with aristocratic nerves like poor mamma, the friend she had been conversing with wanted to interfere, so did a number of the bystanders, and play had to be suspended. Mamma said that if the gentleman asserted that the money was his, she would waive her claim; rose, took her friend's arm, and left the room. Here the matter ended, and nothing further followed, for the 'gentleman' elected to leave that very night for Nice. There, they say, he speedily got rid of his illgotten gains. At least, when we arrived there four weeks later, they pointed out a gentleman in the play saloon to us who had recently lost fabulous sums. On that occasion I saw him for the first time--I was not generally allowed to enter the gambling-rooms--and for the last time, for he had no sooner caught sight of our party, than he rose from the table and vanished from the room, and I think from Nice; anyhow, he never, appeared again during the rest of our sojourn. Mamma had given strict orders not to take any notice; whatever of the adventurer."

"And this--adventurer, had a distant likeness to the Baron?"

"A distant likeness? No, dear, a most distinct one. That's the misfortune!"

Alexandra was leaning back again in the arm-chair and toying with her rings. Hildegard was staring gloomily in front of her. The execution of her long-cherished, plan, the fulfilment of her eager desire, was now threatened by an obstacle which seemed much worse than any previous one; and she was already almost reduced to despair by the others that she had to struggle against.

"A misfortune, indeed!" she said; "a great misfortune for our friend, who, will now have to suffer so bitterly for an accident he is guiltless of."

"How suffer, dear?"

"Were you not saying yourself a short while ago that this wretched likeness was making it impossible for you to arrive at an unprejudiced opinion about the Baron? Well, it matters everything to him, of course, that your opinion should not only not be prejudiced but favourable. And--to confess the truth--to me, to us, it matters much, very much."

Alexandra drew herself up, the old odd smile was hovering about her lips again.

"Does it really matter so much to you?" she said. "Do I understand you correctly?"

"Let us assume that you do," replied Hildegard, trying as she spoke to imitate Alexandra's smile.

"Then I can only answer: *Je n'en vois pas la nécessité.*"

"Of what?"

"That this particular man should marry Erna. Where is the necessity? If she were in love with him, the matter would have to be discussed at least. Now it is not worth while. A girl like your Erna--proud, self-willed, large-hearted--will never be in love with this Baron, never! It is impossible, it is contrary to nature--I mean contrary to the nature of a gifted heart, for there are gifted hearts, just as there are gifted heads. One can, nay, one must, have absolute confidence in both, even supposing that, from very excess of feelings or thoughts, they seem not to have confidence in themselves. One must let them have their way, they cannot err long."

"But they can err for all that," replied Hildegard bitterly. "Would you not call it an error, would you think it to be in accord with the nature of that gifted heart you speak of, if the girl in question were to take a special interest in--out with it, were to love--a man who, according to years, might be her father, a man of fifty?"

The question seemed to come upon Princess Alexandra as a great surprise. She had almost risen from her chair, and was staring fixedly at Hildegard with a burning blush on her cheek. But the very next moment mien and colour had resumed their former state, and nestling even more snugly in the recesses of the deep arm-chair, she said slowly--

"This question it is impossible to answer with an unconditional Yes or No. So much would depend upon the individual. Let us speak of the girl first. You are of coarse referring to ..."

"To Erna."

The eyes of the Princess were all but closed now; something seemed to flash from beneath the long eyelids.

"Of course," she replied very slowly. "And ... he?"

Hildegard bent her eyes in the direction of the opposite side of the drawing-room, where Bertram was conversing with the forest-ranger.

"Ah!" was all the Princess said, putting up her double eyeglass and surveying Bertram curiously. Then, after a long pause--

"Are you sure?"

"Quite."

"It is so easy to make a mistake in these things."

"There is no chance of a mistake here."

"How so?"

Hildegard hesitated before she replied. But her heart was too full. The pain--repressed with difficulty--caused her by the merciless condemnation of the Baron, her displeasure in reference to Bertram, her anger against Erna--all these emotions were clamouring for expression, although her pride bade her desist. She bent over the Princess and whispered hurriedly--

"You will not condemn a mother even if, in her despair, she has recourse to desperate remedies, or, at least, allows things to be done on which she could never voluntarily determine. I was positively free from the faintest suspicion, but Lydia--Fräulein von Aschhof--who had reasons of her own for exercising minute control over the gentleman's demeanour, felt sure she had found it out. Indeed, she communicated to me observations she had made--words she had heard, looks she had intercepted--I thought the charge monstrous, incredible, abominable; but my confidence was shaken--I saw with new eyes, heard with new ears--saw and heard what caused me to shudder. And yet I would certainly have shrunk much longer from accepting a conviction which every day and every hour was urging upon me anew; but two days ago Fräulein von Aschhof brought me a letter which my daughter had written to her cousin Agatha, written but not sent--why, I know not. Nor do I know how Lydia--Fräulein Von Aschhof--got hold of the letter. I believe ..."

"Go on, go on!" said Alexandra, as Hildegard, embarrassed, was pausing. "That does not matter at all. The chief thing is that you have seen the letter. And what did the letter say? That she loved this man?"

"Not in these words, but in words which it were impossible to interpret differently."

"Have you the letter still?"

"No, I am sorry to say. Lydia has ..."

"Has replaced it where she found it; of course. It's a pity, though. It might be possible to imagine another interpretation. However, let us assume that it is so. What have you resolved?"

"To die rather than give my consent--a thousand times rather!"

Their eyes met, and they looked; steadily at each other for a few moments. Then the Princess nodded, and said--

"I see you are in earnest. I can quite understand it; nay, more, I will help you. You will not have to die. I promise my help. Will you reject it?"

She had seized Hildegard's hand.

"I shall be eternally grateful to you," said Hildegard; "but ..."

"No 'but!' I am one of these people who always do what they undertake. You shall be content with me."

"I fear, I fear it is too late."

"We shall see about that. Now, in the first instance, bring me the man, and leave me alone with him. One more condition: you are never to ask me what means I have employed. Will you promise?"

"Anything you wish, my kind, good friend!"

She would have pressed the little ringed hands, (which she still held clasped) to her lips, but the Princess prevented it by a swift movement, saying as she did so--

"For goodness sake, do not be demonstrative! People are not to see what intimate friends we have become!"

Hildegard had risen to fetch Bertram. Alexandra was again examining, with the help of her double eyeglass, the painted ceiling above; but her thoughts were not with Apollo and the nymphs.

"So now we are going to see Mr. Right! To be sure, the other one was scarcely worth the trouble. But this one it will not be so easy to subdue.

Poor Kurt--I could take such sweet revenge here! But no, no! I have vowed to myself, by the love wherewith I loved you, wherewith I love you still--as a brother--that I would bring you back your loved one though I should have to fetch her out of Inferno. I will keep my vow. I will be able to look with a clear conscience into your beautiful eyes to-morrow.... Ah, Mr. Bertram! Now I call this very nice of you. I was already beginning to feel offended. I am not accustomed to be neglected by clever people. You must try to atone for it now. Pray, sit down!"

CHAPTER XV

Bertram had no difficulty in replying merrily to the merry questions of the fair stranger. His head was full of merry thoughts, there was nothing but rapture in his heart. All the world seemed to him to be filled with the fragrance of that rose Erna had given him to-day, that rose which he had since worn near his heart, and from which the hostile looks of Hildegard and the others fell off harmless, as from a potent talisman. Human envy notwithstanding, things awarded him by the grace of the gods were coming to him, nay, had come. If he had still required any confirmation, what confirmation more delightful could he have had than the exuberant mirth to which the beloved child's melancholy gravity had suddenly turned? Like fairy music her rippling laugh seemed to him, coming from the adjoining room, where, surrounded by her cousins, she was as indefatigable in admiring Herr von Busche's feats, as that gentleman himself was in performing them. And he was willing to bear in patience that she was taken up by her friends all the evening, even as he was himself by the rest of the company, and that thus he had not found one single moment when he might have approached her, might have told her what she knew already, what no longer required to be said, what could be said only by a kiss on those pure, sweet lips.

In such rapturous dreams his soul was rejoicing whilst he was conversing gaily with the Russian beauty. And rapture, too, it was to compare this foreign beauty, from whom, in spite of her youth, the strong and not always pure breath of the great world had long ago brushed away the dainty down, with the chaste grace of the beloved maid. She needed no sparkling diamonds, no jingling of golden bracelets; she could dispense with all these over-refined arts of the toilet, this coquetterie which calculated every pose of the plump little frame, every movement of the round arms and the white hands, every rise and fall of the long lids, every glance, every smile from the black eyes! His Erna was the fairer and nobler of the two, a born Princess!

In their conversation, which was carried on, as far as Bertram was concerned, all the more eagerly the less his heart was touched by it, and to which Alexandra, passing as lightly as a bird from one subject to another, was constantly adding fresh topics of interest, they were interrupted by the loud laughter of the girls. Indeed, two of the sisters came rushing into the drawing-room to invite those who were there to come and admire a positively incredible trick which Herr von Busche had just performed, and which he was prepared to repeat--but by universal desire only. They drew the others away with them, uncle and aunt, the Herr *Oberförster* and the Baron.

"You would like to go," said Alexandra. "Do not stay on my account. I have already withdrawn you too long from the society of the others."

"You dismiss me?"

"One should never detain any one who wants to escape!"

"But what has brought such evil suspicion upon me?"

"Your eyes, which are constantly, though ever so discreetly, wandering to that door, in whose frame, it is true, the group of young ladies appears as full of charms as one of Winterhalter's tableaux. Four girls, one of whom, for the sake of contrast, I suppose, has had the superb inspiration to be ugly, while the other three vie with each other in beauty. Which of the girls do you think the most beautiful?"

"I thought the question could not be asked."

"Do you think so? But since I have asked it, I suppose you will have to be polite enough to answer it. You mean the young lady with the lovely neck and the glorious Titian-like hair? I could wager that you do."

"Don't; you would lose your wager."

"Then I declare that you are not an impartial judge, perhaps absolutely bribed; bribed by the rose, say, that you wear in your button-hole."

Alexandra had dropped the eye-glass which she had raised to look upon the group of girls in the doorway, and now, turning swiftly round to Bertram, she looked laughingly into his eyes, and said--

"That was indiscreet, was it not?"

"Not at all," Bertram replied. "This rose, it is true, is the gift of one of the young ladies, and indeed, of the one who seems to me to be by far the most beautiful--the daughter of our host, if you wish to know. But it was no secret gift. I have had it awarded to me before the whole party assembled, as a reward, by the way, for staying a few days longer than I had promised. You see in this case, as in so many others, the small merit is out of all proportion to the great reward."

"Then I was not altogether wrong," said Alexandra, "there was a certain amount of bribery connected with it, although there was no call for it. Openly speaking, I can but confirm your decision. Fräulein Erna is by far the most beautiful, most graceful, most interesting, not only of the few young ladies yonder, but of all those I have recently, perhaps whom I have ever seen. And my evidence is assuredly unprejudiced and unbribed, nay, more, it is generous, for, between you and me, Fräulein Erna is not treating me in a friendly way."

"That," Bertram asserted eagerly, "is assuredly a mistake; it may seem so, but her cousins are claiming so much of her attention, and, perhaps too, having been so little in society as yet, she may be a little shy before a lady of the *grand monde*."

"Perhaps," said Alexandra, "although the latter alternative would not be very flattering for me, seeing that I fancy, besides being somewhat of a grand lady, I have remained a good deal of the *bonne enfant*. Nor have I at all given up the hope of proving to the dear child that I am indeed her friend. I believe I have found out that she needs one. Do you not think so?"

Bertram was puzzled. But she had spoken kindly, naturally, just like some one rather given to blurt out whatever thought came uppermost.

"Who does not need friends?" he answered with a smile.

"Very true," replied the Princess, "and very diplomatic. I quite understand your diplomacy. You are the friend of this fair creature; it is therefore your bounden duty, if other people clamour for admission to the ranks of her friends, to be very critical, particularly so if it strikes you as incomprehensible whence those others derive the sudden sympathy to which they lay claim. But, *que voulez-vous?* A young woman, whose heart is wholly unoccupied, and who is driven about in the world by this aforesaid unoccupied heart, like a balloon that has lost its ballast--what other and what better thing can she do, than be interested in anything interesting that chance puts in her way? This is my occupation. Any occupation seriously pursued makes you an expert, sooner or later, in that occupation. I have always pursued mine seriously, and have pursued it long enough to claim to be something like an expert in it. Now here everything is so simple and clear that the meanest understanding can make for itself a fairly correct picture in half a dozen hours. Given: a man who would be the very pattern of a loving father for his daughter, if he were not a rare specimen of the truly obedient husband; a wife who would swear by all she held sacred that she thinks of nothing but how to make her daughter happy, and who makes her as unhappy as only a narrow-hearted narrow-minded mother can make a singularly gifted, large-hearted daughter; an aged scandal-loving, intriguing *confidante*, who likes to make mischief, the better to pursue her own mean objects in troubled waters; a young suitor, endowed by nature for the very part of *jeune premier* at a second-rate theatre; an older friend of the family whose clear, clever eyes see all this, of course, and whose whole sympathy, equally a matter of course, is enlisted for the girl whose gradual growth and glorious development he has watched. Why, I should think the matter was as plain as the 'secret' in the most casual novel. And, should you care for a more complicated ... fable,--let the friend of the family conceive a serious, passionate attachment to the 'dear child,' and then you have abundant material for volume number two."

Bertram started. This could no longer--it was impossible--be the mere inspiration of the moment, and only a harmless *causerie*. There was treachery at work here, evidently inspired by Hildegard, with whom the Russian lady had, a short time ago, conversed so long and so eagerly. And if the Princess, as was quite possible, considering the great vivacity of her disposition, had already chosen a side: which side? Erna's? or that of her mother? Probably the latter, for she spoke so very bitterly of her. One does that kind of thing to draw one's opponent out. But in that case the great lady must use greater cunning yet.

"I admire your wonderful imagination," he said, "and if I were a poet, I would envy it. How charming to see poetical elements everywhere, and also to be at once clear as to the arranging and dove-tailing which torments the poet so much. You should really make a book of it. Even if the subject is not quite new--where, indeed, could, quite new ones be found nowadays?--a clever author will see something new even in the most hackneyed subject. For myself, of course, the second volume would be specially interesting, when the old friend of the family comes on the stage; for him, of course, the business cannot possibly end well."

"I beg," said the Princess, "that you, will not spoil my text. I have by no means said that my hero is old. On the contrary, he is in the prime of life; of that age when we women only begin to find you men amiable, and rightly so, for you only begin then to become amiable; somewhere about fifty, we'll say."

Bertram bowed.

"Accept my sincere thanks," he said, "in my own name, seeing I am of the amiable age, and in the name of my many contemporaries. You are taking a load off my heart, for now, equally of course, the issue need by no means be so bad. The chances for and against are anyhow equal."

"There, again, you go too far," replied the Princess. "The bad issue, to be sure, is no longer necessary; it must, however, always remain probable."

"Always?"

"I think so, even under the most favourable circumstances."

"What would you call favourable circumstances?"

"We will talk of that later on. Let us first take a specially unfavourable case, which, perhaps, is so all the more the less it would appear to be so. It seems, for example, that our fair young friend would feel less keenly the difference in years, and all the unpleasant and awkward things connected with it, and resulting from it. She is--at least so I judge her to be, and that is sufficient for our purpose--one of those deeply serious natures who are greatly given to confounding the wild phantasies of the head with the true enthusiasm of the heart, and who will conscientiously, and to its utmost consequences, adhere to what once they have seized upon and vowed. But I presume that she is as passionate as she is conscientious; and if her passion and her conscience once come in conflict, the struggle will be terrific. She may come forth victorious from the battle, but what avails a victory that ends in resignation? There we should have an issue, which may be convenient enough for the oldish husband, but then--his convenience and her happiness are surely very different things."

"If I under stand you correctly," Bertram made answer, "you plead for the same theory which I hold, too, and which, as it happens, I have had to defend repeatedly during the last few days in our little circle: namely, that a man who is no longer young, cannot become the object of a passionate attachment on the part of a young girl; or it is anyhow in some way an aberration, and therefore cannot last."

"That is exactly what I mean," the Princess assented eagerly. "We come, then, to a law of nature, which we must accept like other laws, although they are by no means flattering, nay, downright humiliating to our pride. Perhaps, however, on the other hand, the danger of an error and of the consequent conflict is not quite so great in the case in point, since the curiously-veiled radiance of the glorious eyes of that fair child seems to imply that she has already more than a mere vague foreboding of that passion--that she has already loved, perhaps loved unhappily, and would, consequently, not have to make these bitter experiences, which teach us to be wise, and quiet, and resigned, one after the other, in actual wedlock. But who is to give us the guarantee that the last supposition is correct? I could tell you a curious story, if you care to hear it."

"You simply owe me the story, my gracious Princess, as a proof of our joint theory."

"Well, it is fortunately not a long story, and the rest of the company have given us up, anyhow. Listen, then."

Alexandra's eyes had been examining the large chamber; they were quite alone in it now, for all the others were crowding with merry laughter round the magician's table. She leaned forward in her chair; Bertram courteously, approached his own, and she began with a lowered voice, keeping her black eyes under the half closed lids steadily fixed upon him:--

"The scene is Paris; the time some two years ago; the heroine is a friend of mine, a lady belonging to the highest society in France, whose fate had been similar to my own in one respect only: she too had married at sixteen, and been shortly after left a childless widow. Claudine--I give you her Christian name alone, for the other is unimportant to us--was not only, of course, much more beautiful than I, in fact, extraordinarily beautiful and much more gifted; she was also for good--and, as I may add without boasting, for evil--a much greater, more energetic creature. Not that I have anything very bad to say of dear Claudine, or, at least, nothing worse than has been said of many a woman who could not, perhaps, claim such weighty 'extenuating circumstances.' Her mother had, for reasons of her own, persuaded her into this marriage, which had turned out singularly unhappy. Her husband, although allowing for the difference of sex, he was scarcely older than she herself at the time of the marriage--he was then two-and-twenty--had, though so young, already managed to be acknowledged as one of the completest *roués* of all Paris, in spite of the keen rivalry of his high-born compeers. He had seen in the innocent young girl only an additional mistress whom, after a brief period, one could neglect with the greater impunity, since one could feel sure of her, and since she, moreover, in spite of, or perhaps, rather because of, her pride, did not seem to belong to those troublesome women who make 'scenes.' And indeed, after she had realised what, from another side, was made clear to her, they had but one 'scene,' but a terrible one, a recurrence of which was both impossible and unnecessary. He thoroughly understood her then--and she had proved a hundred times the stronger of the two. He was allowed to continue his own way of living, on the one condition that he did not concern himself in the least about hers. And hers? Well, I told you hers was a passionate nature, and she was an unhappy wife; that combination can yield nothing but unhappiness. Fortunately for her, she was speedily set free from the worst impulse, the one which had poisoned and warped her passionate nature; for her husband died. She was free once more, and vowed to remain free. Not that she did not mean to marry again; in the circles where she lived, she could only by a second marriage escape from the bondage of those relationships into which one is forced as into a new fashion, abominable though you may think either. Her second marriage was but to guarantee her a clear position in the world; the other guarantees for peace and for freedom she thought she bore within herself. And so she made her choice.

"At this period of the story I became intimate with Claudine, whose acquaintance I had previously but hurriedly made when travelling. It was in Trouville. You know how swiftly people become intimate in a watering-place. She introduced to me the victor in the endless row of suitors for her hand. After careful examination I could not altogether agree with her choice. In most points, it is true, he answered the requirements of the programme. He was no longer young--fifty-one, or -two; held a high command in the army, and brought her as dower a not inglorious past. He had led a wild and wandering life, and been the hero of a thousand adventures, but there was not the slightest stain upon his name--at least not in the eyes of society. Moreover, though not an intellectual man,--which she would have disliked in the long run,--he was one of those who are able to captivate even the most fastidious company, by their quick perception, their lively temperament, and their varied and abundant experience, upon which they can, aided by an excellent memory and natural eloquence, draw at all times. All this was, as I said, excellent as far as it went; but one thing I thought very hazardous--it seemed by no means impossible to me that he should still be capable of a serious, passionate attachment, and--this comes, almost to the same thing--still capable of inspiring it. Now, either lay assuredly beyond the programme which my friend had sketched out for herself.

"I told Claudine of my fears. She endeavoured to argue me out of them thus: 'What you think to be real and direct light,' she would say, 'is nothing but the reflection of the sun that set long ago upon glacial Alpine summits. It looks beautiful, and people cry, Ah! and Oh! when they see it; and for their sake I would not willingly miss it. But one cannot be warmed by it, or set on fire by it! My dear child, with all that blaze you could not make your kettle boil, far less rekindle the bitter and bare embers of a heart like mine!'

"As far as the gentleman was concerned, Claudine might be right. At least the somewhat boastful and exaggerated gallantry with which he laid his homage at her feet corresponded, as far as I could judge, exactly with her prediction. But how greatly she had been mistaken about herself the immediate future was to show.

"There were delays before the marriage could be concluded. Both Claudine and her friend had to free themselves from certain tender bonds. That required tact, management, caution. Moreover, she had become entangled in a law-suit with the family of her first husband, which, for some reason or other, might end badly for her, if it became known that she was contemplating a second marriage. Enough, absolute secrecy regarding their relations and intentions was requisite for some considerable time, and they had both taken their measures accordingly. Claudine had retired from society, and lived in deepest seclusion near Paris, on the estate of a widowed sister of her friend's--she, of course, being in the secret. Her friend went to see her when he could--which was not often the case. The requirements of the service were just then peculiarly exacting, and it was not possible for him to indulge in frequent absences, which anyhow, in the case of a man whom society did not care to miss, and whose doings society carefully controlled, would have caused remarks. The situation became even more critical when, in spite of all precaution, Claudine's place of sojourn had after a little been discovered, and when she saw herself watched by her foes at every turn. At last they scarcely dared to write to each other, dreading lest by treason on the part of bribed domestics a letter should be intercepted or purloined. It became absolutely indispensible to employ a thoroughly trustworthy go-between, on whom, at the same time, it should be impossible that suspicion could fall, and her friend found one--found him in the person of a young officer in his regiment, the son of an old companion in arms who had fallen in the last campaign--a young officer whom he loved like his own son, and who was likewise devoted to his chief in most loyal love. The youth had soon an opportunity of indeed proving that love and loyalty."

Alexandra drew a long breath, as though she were fatigued by the rapid low-voiced utterance. In her deep black eyes which now, after a quick survey of the still untenanted chamber, she turned upon Bertram again, there was an uneasy light, and the soft voice quivered as she went on, now speaking even quicker and lower than before, so that Bertram could scarcely follow her--

"I must be more brief if I am ever to finish my story. And why, indeed, picture in detail to a man like you what you understand without comment, and what, understanding, you pardon! Poor Claudine! She thought she needed no forgiveness. She thought she was in the right when she abandoned herself without resistance to a passion, which indeed would seem to have brooked no resistance. I had never observed anything like this with any other woman--least of all, God be thanked, with myself. I should simply not have deemed it possible. It was like a hurricane--a cyclone; it was simply awful! I trembled for the reason, for the very life of the unhappy woman: for she could not conceal from herself that her passion was not returned, although she, being anyhow little accustomed to control herself, and being now solely engaged by her own overpowering feelings, neither would nor could hide her great love from the handsome young officer. Fortunately for her, the catastrophe was not long in coming. Nay, rather, she brought it about herself, resolute and energetic as she always was; and now feeling that so, and only so, she might yet save herself from herself, she forced from him the avowal that his heart was no longer free, that it was entirely filled by his love for a charming young girl whose acquaintance he had made in a distant garrison-town where a portion of his regiment had until recently been quartered, and to whom he had become engaged in secret. The youth was bitterly poor, the girl's parents were rich and proud; he wanted to have his captain's commission before he ventured to apply for her hand, and-- dear, dear--they were both of them so young and so romantic, and so fond of each other, and in their love they were so sure of the future. Why then be niggardly with the moment? And secrecy is like a phantastic mask through the hollow apertures of which the light in the eyes of those we love shines with doubly seductive brilliancy.

"Claudine was at first utterly crushed by a blow which, in spite of everything, had found her unprepared--for where is the loving heart that would willingly let the last faint gleam of hope die out? Then there came a fierce burst of jealous resentment, raging like a fever; then she endeavoured to wrap herself in her pride and to see in the idol of her heart the last and least of men; and ultimately she grovelled at his feet and entreated him to look upon her as his slave, and the slave of her whom he loved, and to ask from her what he would, to bid her do what he chose, and do it she would by all that she held sacred!

"Nor was it long before he took her at her word.

"One day he came to her presence, haggard of look, in a state of desperation, scarcely worse than the one over which she herself had but so recently triumphed. The girl had sent him back the half-dozen letters which he had written to her in the twelvemonth since they were separated, and the tiny collection of ribbons and flowers and other tokens with which innocent love tries to prove to itself its own fabulous fairylike existence. I know not, nor does it matter, how she had heard the story of his connection with Claudine; not of course, the true story, but a caricature, such as the clumsy hands of one's own good friends and the subtle hands of one's foes are equally able to sketch and fill in with revolting effectiveness. Anyhow, the young lady had made up her mind, and as she belonged to those energetic characters that cling tenaciously to their errors, things really looked desperate for Claudine's youthful friend. Every attempt on his part to bring an understanding about was abruptly refused; the poor fellow at last was in downright despair; he told his sorrows to Claudine, who told him that she would bring him back the loved one whom, for her sake, he had lost; he looked at her with an incredulous smile. How was she--she particularly--to manage that?

"But she had never yet let herself be baulked by difficulties if she really cared to have her own way, even though, it might have been but a whim.

And now the noblest impulse that can fill a woman's heart urged her to energetic action. Above all, she had to prove to herself, and to those to whom she had so greatly boasted, that, though she had become unfaithful to her programme, and had not guarded herself against a passionate attachment-- which she called the only real one of all her life--she yet possessed the force to subdue this passion, and to re-conquer her own peace of heart. Only personal interference on her part could now bring them to the wished-for goal; but that alone would not suffice; the friend, too, for whose sake the youth had sacrificed himself, must needs come forward. That, of course, would completely put an end to the secrecy of their connection, and this just at the moment when the lawsuit was at last about to be settled, and when so much depended upon having the veil drawn as closely as possible. For herself no such consideration existed; but she was by no means sure that her friend, who, of course, did not know her real motives, and could never be allowed to know them, and who equally, of course, took things much more coolly, thought the same; nor did she know at all whether the young man would accept the sacrifice. So it became necessary to create a situation, which should not leave either of them a choice, whether they cared to join or not; and whilst she was cudgelling her brain how to bring such a situation about, an unprecedentedly lucky accident had already arranged everything according to her wishes, nay, far beyond her most daring wishes, in the very best manner possible. To explain the full details would take me too long, and is not really called for; enough, circumstances over which they could not possibly have control, would bring both gentlemen on a given day to the house of the parents of the young lady in question. Claudine, still keeping her own counsel, managed to get a day's start of them, introduced herself--by what means I cannot remember--into the family who, I may add, was absolutely unknown to her, and she was, having presumably got hold of some excellent letters of recommendation or something of that sort, most kindly received by every one, excepting, of course, the young lady herself, who, with feelings that can be readily imagined, saw the foe suddenly in the secure camp of her parental abode, and avoided her in every way. That, Claudine had expected; she looked forward with glee to the following day which was to remove all obstacles, solve all enigmas. But who can describe her terror when she, who has eyes and ears for everything, and who, in a few hours, was completely at home on the new and strange ground, discovered among the visitors, besides a suitor *sans conséquence*, a man whom an abundance of exquisite gifts and qualities and a whole sequence of special relations, every one of which spoke for him, might turn, nay, if everything did not belie assurances, had already turned into a terrible rival for her young friend. For ..."

Alexandra paused, glancing at the same time at the other room; then she said with a laugh which sounded quite natural--

"But I really do not think it right to keep you any longer from the rest of the company, and to go on with my experiment as to whether is greater, your patience or my garrulousness. Moreover, the rest does not properly belong to the story, at least not to the story I meant to tell you. Come away!"

She had risen swiftly; Bertram followed her example so hesitatingly that she could hardly leave at once. And then, having risen, he remained standing, leaning one arm on the mantelpiece, and said--

"What a pity! What a great pity! I should have so much liked hearing the rest. The more so, as I believe it contains a new illustration to the moral of the fable. Or am I mistaken in assuming that the unexpected rival is ... no longer a young man?"

His lips were smiling; still Alexandra thought that his large expressive eyes we're resting upon her with a very meaning, very searching look; yet she managed to put on an air of surprise, deeming it absolutely requisite now.

"Indeed!" she exclaimed. "How very curious! But then there is no hiding anything from you clever men!"

"Oh yes, yes. For example, which of the two suitors succeeded--the older and younger, or the newer and older?"

"Charming! Charming! An exquisite play on the words. What a suitable language yours is for that kind of thing, in the hands of a real master, I mean. Ah! which succeeds? Why, the former, of course!"

"I should scarcely have considered it such a matter of course. I should not be surprised if, for all that, the young lady's feelings for him had never again recovered the former degree of warmth. Your beautiful and clever friend, I admire her extremely, but--do not be angry with me for what I am going to say--but I had, during your description of her, always to think of Circe. There was only one man who left the palace of the sorceress with absolute impunity, and he only by the aid of a certain herb a god had given him. Now, young and ardent officers are not said to meet the god very frequently."

"But I really cannot make the story anything different from what it truly was like," cried the Princess, half pouting, half laughing.

"Certainly not; but what became of the man who was no longer young? How bore he the loss of hopes to which he had clung all the more tenaciously because he had not many more to lose?"

"That, as a punishment for your scepticism, you are to say yourself."

"How can I? Had he been a poet he might have written a novel, after the manner of the 'Elective Affinities,' and thus cleared his soul from the purgatory of jealousy and humiliation. But being no poet ..."

"How do you know that?"

"I assume it. I am driven to assume things, am I not?"

"Well then?"

"Therefore his ultimate fate is quite problematical to me. There are so many and such various possibilities. Perhaps he killed himself, or perhaps he married your fair friend."

"My friend--Claudine? Oh, this is exquisite!" The Princess laughed aloud, and Bertram laughed too.

"It is not," he said, "after all so very laughable, or at least so very improbable. Upon the basis of mutual imperturbability, I should think one could erect and overthrow and rebuild relationships, like houses of cards."

"Mow malicious!" cried Alexandra, "and yet how true! Claudine must hear of this; I must write this to Claudine!"

"For goodness sake not, most gracious lady; or, anyhow, do not mention me by name! I travel a good deal, the lady probably too; we might meet some day by some unlucky chance, even as the luckiest of chances has brought me into your presence. How hideously embarrassed I should be!"

"Very well, your name shall not be mentioned, then. Here is my hand in pledge of this."

And she held out to him her small hand with its many rings.

"But now I really must disturb your tête-à-tête," said Hildegard, entering from the adjoining drawing-room.

"It is just finished!" the Princess called out to her; then turning again to Bertram, she said, "And thank you very much for a most charming *causerie!*"

"It is for me to say thank you, my Lady. Your story was most interesting, and you told it capitally."

He touched those slim fingers with his lips as Alexandra left him. She hurried up to Hildegard, who had remained standing, gazing with great wondering eyes at the group by the fireside, and putting her arm through that of her hostess and drawing her away with her, the Russian lady whispered--

"You are absolutely mistaken, or else the man is the greatest actor I ever saw."

Bertram had bent over the fire; with his left hand he was half unconsciously stirring up the dying embers in the grate, his right hand was laid on the rose he wore, which he wore above a heart now quivering in spasmodic agony, and he painfully whispered to himself--

"Ashes to ashes!"

His hand, nerveless, glided down.

"No," he murmured, "no, not yet; I will hear it from herself."

CHAPTER XVI

The company was breaking up now. The gentlemen from the *Oberförsterei* were anxious to avail themselves of the momentary cessation of the rain for their homeward drive; the Princess, pleading fatigue, had retired, and Hildegard speedily gave the signal for retreat to the others.

"We shall have a trying day to-morrow," she said, "we all need rest beforehand. And this remark is specially meant for you young ladies; I really must request you not to lark and laugh, as is usual with you, till a late hour!"

The unexpected visit of Princess Alexandra had considerably diminished the available spare rooms, seeing so many were reserved for the officers, who were expected on the following day; for her protest against having to accept a splendid saloon, a dressing-room, and a couple of bedrooms for herself and her maid, had met with no response. Hildegard had assured her that there was abundant room, and that she blushed as it was at having to offer such humble quarters to so valued and cherished a guest. But the two bedrooms had really been originally intended for the three sisters von Palm, who had now to be content with a tiny chamber in the turret, whilst a bed for Agatha was rigged up in Erna's bedroom. Fortunately for the young ladies, the corridor by the side of which Erna's rooms were situated, brought one after a very few steps to the door of the turret-chamber; and thus, in spite of Hildegard's special injunction to the contrary, there was for an hour or so plenty of rushing to and fro, and no end of laughing and giggling and eager secret whispering and chattering, until at last 'Granny' Agatha blew out the light in her sisters' room, and drawing with her Erna, who this evening was in the highest spirits imaginable, groped her way to the door.

"I could not bear your mirth any longer," she said, when they had arrived in Erna's room; "I thought every moment ... Good Heaven! I knew how it would be."

She had begun to undo her hair before the mirror, and now started on hearing a pitiful moan. Erna was sitting in a low chair by her own bedside, both hands pressed to her face. The slender frame seemed shaken as though by a fit of ague, the gentle bosom rose and fell feverishly, and her breath came and went with difficulty, as if she were moaning. Her friend was now kneeling by her side, and held her clasped with both arms; her head fell on Agatha's shoulder, and at last the long-repressed tears welled forth in a violent flood. She was weeping as though her very heart must break.

"My poor, poor Erna! My own sweet love! Weep, weep away! Better this, better far than that awful unnatural mirth of yours all day. You will come round now. You will be again my own sensible Erna. Poor, unhappy, darling child! All things will come right now. It is impossible for any one not to love you, and, believe me, he, too, loves you still."

"I would not have his love. I am no longer thinking of him. I hate, I loathe him!"

"Then why should you weep like this?"

Erna started to her feet, flinging off Agatha's protecting arm.

"Do you think I weep for him?"

She was pacing up and down the bed-chamber. Her long hair, which she had previously undone, fell in dark masses over her neck and bosom; her face was aglow, her eyes were flashing wildly.

"For him? Never say that again! For him, forsooth! I have wept for very shame, because that woman dares to come before me, and I must bear it! because I cannot step up to her and hurl defiance at her painted face: Away from this house--honest people live here! Even audacity should have its bounds, and hers is boundless!"

Agatha had now risen from her knees, and was sitting in her chair casting looks of pain at Erna and waiting in patience, until at least the first tempest of wrath should have passed.

"I am sure," she said at last, "that he does not even know that she is here, and--you are sure, too."

"And were it so," cried Erna, "what does it alter? The sting lies in her daring to do it at all. She would not do so, did she not know from the beginning how he will take it. Perhaps he will be terrified just at first--I dare say he will--and then he will thank her for having had the base courage to help him to achieve this vile triumph. In fact, they are a worthy couple!"

"It would be quite too terrible," said Agatha, shaking her head. "People cannot be as bad as that; it is impossible."

"Oh, of course!" cried Erna scornfully; "quite impossible; as impossible as that he will himself be here to-morrow."

"But, Erna, an officer is surely bound to go to any place to which he is ordered. In such a case he has no will of his own."

"Then he should have a pistol of his own, and rather put a bullet into his head than let a shameless woman make him figure in such a spectacle, if indeed she, the wretch, has arranged a spectacle for my humiliation. But she is very much mistaken. I shall not let her have her triumph. I, even I, shall triumph. Let her boast of her conquest, I shall outshine it and her by far. Oh! how I look forward to to-morrow's joy! What are a thousand like him to the best of men, the only one?"

"Erna! Erna!!" cried Agatha aghast, lifting both her folded hands in agonised entreaty, "I conjure you, do not go too far. Do not make yourself for ever unhappy. Do not make Kurt unhappy...."

"Do not mention his name!" Erna exclaimed. "I wish to hear no more."

"I must mention his name, for I must speak of him, and you must hear me, lest you do something of which you will for ever and ever repent."

"Why repent? I love Bertram!"

"You do not."

"Can you read in my heart?"

"Yes, dear, better than you can yourself, being now blinded by passion. And however angrily you may look at me with those beautiful eyes of yours, that I myself am in love with, and though you send me away for good and all, and though I cry myself to death for love of you--I should not be loving you, and I should not be your poor, unhappy 'Granny' if ..."

Poor child! She could get no further. Like Erna half an hour ago, she was now sitting, her hands pressed to her face, weeping convulsively, and now Erna was kneeling by her side, and tried to draw those hands away from her countenance, and begged her to calm herself, and to be fond of her again, and to be once more her own good 'Granny.'

Then--neither could have said how the change of scene had been brought about--Erna was lying in her bed, and Agatha, in her nightgown, was sitting on the edge of the bedstead, and all they had discussed during these last days in many a fragmentary talk was once more, and now connectedly, discussed between them. But if clever Agatha had flattered herself that she would thus induce the fair penitent to see that her little soul was not, after all, as black as she thought in her excitement, that hope was not destined to be fulfilled; the very contrary happened. With every word she uttered Erna seemed to talk herself more and more into a passion, in the existence of which Agatha would not, and yet all but had to, believe, when her friend now recapitulated all her relations to Bertram, beginning with that first meeting in the woods, and continuing her account, to this very evening, and when Erna tried to prove from a hundred minute details, which she strung together with marvellous logic, that there was on her part no whim, no caprice, no aberration of an extravagant fancy, no satisfaction of injured pride, no despair, no, nought but true and genuine love that knew no bounds, and knew only the one doubt whether she herself was worthy of the man she loved. But not unworthy because she had once before thought herself in love. That was a necessary error for the sake of getting her to understand herself; to convince her that love was not an intoxication, but a deep and clear sentiment attracting and absorbing all other feeling and thought, even as a mighty stream absorbs the springs and brooks around; and now in her love, like banks in the waves of a stream, were mirrored her whole existence, her past and her present, mirrored and beautified, made far more glorious than reality.

Erna's words flowed on, not unlike the object of the image in which she saw her life and love; and her voice, although pitched so low, had such a curiously intense ring, and her great eyes, which were opened wide, shone so strangely in the flickering light of the tall candles upon the dressing-table, that poor Agatha was almost beside herself with terror. Was Erna still aware of what she was saying? Was she raving? And, horrible to think of, could she be going mad?

"Erna! Erna!" she cried aloud, seizing and pressing both her hands. "Awake, awake! I have just been counting it up--when you are eight-and-thirty, like your mother now, he will be seventy--only he will never reach that age."

Erna gave a contemptuous smile.

"I thought so!" she said. "As if time had anything to do with love! As if one year during which I can serve him, love him, did not outweigh a century! O Agatha, how meanly you think of love! And if he dies to-morrow, I'll die with him! There, that is the way I count, and I think it is simple and plain enough."

Despair lent Agatha courage enough to revert to the one point on which, as she had observed more than once during the last day or two, Erna was most sensitive.

"I will grant it all," she said. "I will believe all you assert about yourself, for I cannot read your heart. But Herr Bertram's heart is not your heart, and what is going on in his heart, Heaven only knows; you do not know it, at least he has never betrayed it to you by word or look. And I hold that he would have done so long ago if he loved you. What reasons should he have for hiding his love?"

"A thousand!" exclaimed Erna. "Or is it not a reason that he should have tortured himself for days with the idea that I might be fond of the Baron?"

"That idea he has assuredly given up ere this."

"Then, that mamma will be furious."

"For all that, he might tell you what he feels for you."

"And what if he doubts whether I love him?"

"Good Heavens, dearest! how can he doubt that?"

"He can indeed. During the first few days I was not clear about it myself. And when I was feeling that I loved him, I often was odd and capricious and defiant; and above all, when I discovered that the letter was missing from my blotting-book, and I hunted for it everywhere, and when suddenly it turned up again, having in the meantime passed through I do not know how many hands, and having very surely been read by mamma too--I was so indignant, I could see that he sometimes did not know what to think of me."

"You did not make him feel your indignation; on the contrary, you gave him one token of your favour after the other."

"And in that I did right, for I was determined to let mamma see that I was not afraid of her wrath."

"And that rose to-day! and your prayer that he should stay--for your sake! Was that right too?"

"Was I to let him go to-morrow?"

"If he wanted to go, was it for you to keep him? Erna, there is but one thing wanting now. Why not say to him: 'Will you marry me?'"

"And I should not think it shame to say so, if I were sure that he wished me to do so. Yes, yes; he does wish it; I see it clearly now; he wishes to avoid even the semblance of suspicion of having beguiled and over-persuaded me; he wishes it on account of my father and mother. Well, God be thanked, now I know what I have to do to-morrow."

"Nay, the pity of it, Erna, the pity of it, that you can talk in such a way; for it is impossible that you should really think so, really do it. My proud Erna cannot forget herself so far. I entreat you, by our great friendship, Erna, follow my advice in this one thing; if it must be, let him at least say the first word--the word that then will be decisive of your fate; and then let come what God will!"

She had folded her hands as if in prayer; big tears were coursing down her cheeks. The simple expression of her great grief touched Erna. She embraced "Granny" and kissed her, and promised at last that she would do what Agatha kept asking of her again and again.

"And now get to your bed, you poor child! You are so wearied, and I too."

Agatha had already lain quietly in bed for an hour or so, mournfully thinking it all over again, and assuming that Erna, who did not stir either, had fallen asleep, when suddenly she thought that she heard subdued sobs.

"Erna!"

No answer.

"Erna! If it comes out that Kurt is really innocent, what will you do?"

Again no answer.

Had she been mistaken? Had Erna wept in her sleep? Had she really asked that question of Erna? Or had she only thought of it?

CHAPTER XVII

It was a day of tremendous excitement for all the in habitants of Rinstedt. True, the arrival of the soldiers was not to occur before four o'clock in the afternoon, but it was known that the corps to which the 99th belonged had been on the march from the north since four o'clock in the morning, in order to take possession of certain positions whence they were to operate against the fortress. And that might turn out an awkward job, for not only was the fortress strongly manned, but there was also approaching from the west, in forced marches, a large hostile corps, and against them the 99th would have to be on their guard, if they did not mean to get wedged in between them and the garrison, who were simply awaiting the moment for making a sally. Thus the attacking party being themselves attacked, might get into desperate straits.

The village-mayor had expounded this situation to the farmers, and he ought to know. He had been only three days ago to see his brother-in-law, who was employed in the War-Office branch at Erfurt. He had himself served in the French war as sergeant, and in that capacity he had, during the fighting about Orleans, been in command of a company, every officer of which was dead or *hors de combat*. And as almost half his auditory consisted of men who had served in the army, and who only required to draw upon the ample treasury of their experiences and reminiscences, in order to confirm or contradict the assertions of their chief, there had been no lack of eager discussion in the village inn. But from the very beginning the opposition had not been strong, and ultimately it was almost completely silenced. The whole village now stood like one man on the side of the attacking party, and the 99th was only spoken of as "Our Regiment." Their arrival was looked forward to with the utmost impatience, as though they were bringing relief and release from some yoke long borne.

My Lady's urgent appeal to give "Our Regiment" a brilliant reception, and to let nothing be wanting, had met with the readier a response, since she had not only, with customary liberality, taken upon herself the cost of any "extraordinaria," to use the expression of the village-mayor, but in the case of the poorer inhabitants in whose houses accommodation and larder were not of the best, had specially promised to pay for anything and everything, and had actually freely distributed money beforehand. The mansion-house was moreover setting the village a capital example. The long winding road up to the house was transformed into a *via triumphalis* with towering poles, from which fluttered the German and Thuringian flags, with garlands of fir-branches stretching from pole to pole all the way up the hill, up to the richly-decorated portals which opened upon the equally decked-out great courtyard. And at night a ball in the mansion-house, and fireworks on the village-common in front of the lowest flight of the terrace-steps, with blue-lights and what not!--No wonder that the young barbarians of the village, down to the tiniest lads and lasses, were only kept from breaking out into frantic disorder by being employed, for days beforehand, in lending a hand in the preparation of all these glories.

And yet, much to Hildegard's dismay, it seemed doubtful whether everything would be ready in time. Her own attention was fully absorbed indoors by the preparations for banquet and ball; and now, at the last moment, the Baron had to go to town on business that brooked no delay, and she had to entrust the supreme command of the department of the exterior to new hands: fortunately Herr von Busche, the young gentleman from the Forests and Woods' Office, was willing to take the Baron's place.

But yesterday Hildegard would, under no circumstances, have allowed the Baron to go, for then his star was still in the ascendant, whilst now it was sinking rapidly. For the Princess he no longer existed, after she had given her judgment upon him last night; she had not observed his entry into the breakfast room, had not returned his bow, just as though the not inconsiderable space filled by his presence had been vacant. And the Grand Duke had a certain antipathy to this man; and even his father's old friend, the influential Court-marshal, did not dare to stand up for him energetically. No one seemed to favour him at Court, except Princess Amelia, whose caprices, it was notorious, were frequently as changing as the phases of the moon. And then that ugly Monaco story! It was, of course, not possible that Lotter could be the man--gracious goodness, no! Nor had Alexandra said so! But--one ought not to have an awkward likeness to people who figure so unpleasantly in the memory of distinguished visitors; and then--and this made the matter peculiarly unpleasant for Hildegard--she was aware that the Baron, even if he was no gambler, was very fond of high play. Up to last night this had been one of his gentlemanly foibles, now it was a wicked passion which he who was wooing Erna had no right to indulge in!

It was nearly eleven o'clock when the Baron went to find Otto, to ask for a carriage to take him to town, and to tell him at the same time the drift of the disagreeable news which he had received from home. A younger brother, in the army of course, had contracted debts, and was on the point of being cashiered if those debts--in the contracting of which there would seem to have been some discreditable element or other--were not forthwith paid. His relatives, poor people every one of them, were incapable of helping the young man; as a last refuge they had applied to him, the elder brother, who, though not likely to be himself possessed of the necessary means, might yet probably be able to obtain the money on loan from the wealthy friends with whom he was on such good terms. Could Otto help him in an embarrassment that was weighing more heavily upon him than any one of his own making had ever done? It was not a big sum which he required--a mere miserable three thousand thalers!

Otto was quite distressed. His stock of cash was exhausted by the incessant demands that Hildegard had made upon him during the last few days, and to-morrow he would have to redeem that mortgage of five thousand thalers which he had mentioned to Bertram, without as yet knowing where to lay his hands on the money. The moment, of which Bertram had said that it would very surely come, was at hand, had, in fact, virtually come already; the terrible moment when he must discover his situation to his wife. And yet his wife could parry the first thrust for him. He had in the course of years given her, on different occasions, considerable sums of money as special donations, and all this was invested in excellent securities, though she was for ever spending the interest beforehand. He loathed the idea of claiming back a portion of the money from her, and he had vowed that he would not do so, come what might. But still a man will do for a friend what he would not have the courage to do for himself; and so he told the Baron that, being for the moment unable to oblige him himself, he would ask Hildegard to do so, and he felt sure that she would willingly render this small service to her *protégé*. The Baron hesitated for a moment, but opined that one could not discuss such things with women; he would find help some other way. He then begged Otto to make his excuses to the ladies--who were not to be found, and promised to return, if not for dinner, at the latest before the beginning of the ball; managed to see Lydia, and so drove off.

Otto would have liked nothing better than to have gone with him. The ground beneath him seemed to be on fire. To-day the all-important debate in Parliament was coming off. If the vote was in his favour, he really might, without being too sanguine, expect his factories to rise so greatly in value as to enable him, after all, to weather the threatening storm. But, with an adverse vote, he knew he was ruined, and he kept repeating this to himself, unless he would take the extreme step of requesting Bertram's assistance. Bertram certainly would not refuse it, but, as assuredly, he could not ask for it, considering the awkward relations now subsisting between his wife and his friend.

After considerable hesitation, Hildegard had the day before yesterday communicated to him her suspicions that no one but Bertram was standing in the way of the alliance upon which she had set her heart. She wisely refrained from mentioning the impure source from which she had drawn her suspicions--though it was not of a suspicion that she spoke to her husband, but of a fact. Poor Otto naturally had to express the utmost horror, though at heart he was anything but dissatisfied. He would certainly have liked Erna to have a younger husband, but he himself loved and admired the friend of his youth sincerely, and if Erna loved him in her own way, why she had always had a taste of her own; he had never comprehended her; she would herself know best how it stood with her heart; and then if Bertram, as friend, would gladly have helped him, as son-in-law he would very surely have done so, and in that case, he too would get over the shrinking which he felt now. But it was not to be. Hildegard would never sanction it, and yet, how strange, just as he was returning to the house after seeing the Baron off, here was Hildegard coming to explain that she had been absolutely mistaken about Bertram, that Bertram was completely innocent, that she had to crave his forgiveness for much, and that she would be truly disconsolate if Bertram were to go away after all, as she concluded from some hints of Konski's. Would Otto please go up to him at once and make sure of his staying? She would do so herself, but she really had not a moment to spare, for, he could judge for himself, the Princess did not leave her alone for a minute.

Otto knew not whether to rejoice or to grieve over the new turn of events. He had, suffered intensely from the tension between his wife and his friend; and that things were right once more and better than ever, was of course very nice and pleasant. But with Hildegard's assurance that Bertram was not thinking of marrying Erna, there vanished the last ray of hope that help in his need would come from that quarter. Moreover, he said to himself that Bertram would never dream of going without speaking once more, for the last time, of his money difficulties and repeating the previous offer; and Otto was afraid of himself, afraid he might be weak enough to close with the offer. So he promised Hildegard that he would at once go to Bertram and try every means in his power to induce him to stay, but he did not go. There really seemed no need for all this hurry. Bertram could not leave without asking for a carriage too. And that had not yet been done. Perhaps it would not be done at all, and in that case, why needlessly bring such terrible excitement on one's self? And again, Herr von Busche was sure not to get on with the decoration of the portals unless he went to help him. Hildegard had been saying all along that the old Gothic structure, being the termination of the *via triumphalis*, must also be the chief point of splendour. Hildegard should be really pleased.

And five minutes later Otto was waging furious war with Herr Von Busche, who wanted the flag of the country to float from the left-hand balcony, whilst Hildegard had given express orders that it should float from the right-hand one.

Hildegard had meanwhile hurried to rejoin the Princess; she had not exaggerated,--Alexandra really would scarce leave her for a moment. She was bent upon knowing how, on such an occasion, things were managed in a German household. She could not, she said, form any idea of it, because in Russia all these things were left to the steward and other officials, and the hostess, like her guests, was simply among the spectators. It would be such a pleasure to her to be allowed to peep behind the scenes for once; if Hildegard was really fond of her, if ever so little, she should not deny her the treat. Hildegard did not find it too difficult to overcome the first shyness which she felt at such an odd request being made. The arrangements about her kitchens, pantries, and store-rooms were as splendid and in as grand a style as in any princely palace, quite in keeping with the colossal preparations for the entertainment; she could modestly accept the many exclamations of amazement and admiration which the young Princess indulged in lavishly, as a fit and proper tribute. But mere idle admiration did not satisfy Alexandra; she insisted upon lending a helping hand, and pushing back her rich lace sleeves from her fair white arms, she seized a big wooden spoon, and, to the delight of all the servants employed about the kitchen, she set to work stirring up a pudding. With all this exuberance of good-humour she was so charmingly amiable, so utterly free from all affectation, and the wildest nonsense she indulged in suited her so quaintly and funnily, that Hildegard was positively enchanted, and called upon Lydia in passing, to study in the appearance and demeanour of the Princess the mighty difference which existed between a really gifted woman and one who merely affected to be clever, and who thereby only provoked the scornful laughter of really clever people.

These cruel words were the first she had addressed to Lydia since last night.

It was impossible for the Baron to fall so suddenly into dire disgrace without involving Lydia in his fall; nay, in Hildegard's eyes she was, if possible, the guiltier of the two. Had she not been incessantly singing the Baron's praises, giving the most glowing testimony to him, been scarcely able to paint the great position he enjoyed at Court in sufficiently bright colours; and all this, of course, solely to beguile her unsuspecting hostess and to deceive her in reference to her own intentions as to Bertram. Serve her right, the story-teller, if she was completely foiled in her intentions! And now, as though the measure of her iniquity had not been already abundantly full, she must actually bring these terrible charges against poor innocent Bertram; must needs, to confirm and apparently substantiate these charges, commit a theft, and make her--a mother--an accomplice, forcing that miserable letter upon her, which, as it turned out now, had been nothing more than the harmless enough effusion of a somewhat overstrained imagination that the child had indulged in--well, well, the time would come when she could show the intriguing old maid this long list of offences; meanwhile, silent contempt should be her well-deserved, only far too lenient, chastisement.

Now, it is true she had broken through her contemptuous silence, but poor Lydia knew her friend quite well enough to be aware of the evil plight into which she had fallen. And had she been still able to have any doubt on the subject, the reproaches with which the Baron had overwhelmed her would certainly have enlightened her. Last night, even, he had ventilated his bad humour by all sorts of bitter and scornful utterances; but to-day, when he had sought Lydia in the garden after his conversation with Otto, and before he hurried off to town, his wrath knew no bounds. This, then, he sneered, was his boasted firm position in the house! A casual adventuress could come and deprive him in a moment, in the twinkling of an eye, of the good graces of the mother--in those of her daughter he had long since ceased to believe anyhow--rob him of the father's friendship, and expose him to a treatment no commercial traveller would put up with! And he would not put up with it, not he; Lydia might be sure--quite sure of that! He would prove it to the miserable toady and sycophant who changed her friends as readily as her gloves; to the poor henpecked husband, the miser who could not even spare a few dirty thousands to a friend in need of help; he would prove to them that a Lotter-Vippach was not to be insulted with impunity. And, above all, that conceited amorous old pedant should suffer for it, for he, of course, had set the whole train going against him! If Lydia,--if the others, could not or would not see, he kept his eyes open, and was not to be taken in; he knew what was what, and ... but they should see. And to-night, to the sorrow and annoyance of his so-called friends, who would wish him far enough, he would make a point of turning up in good time. Would Fräulein Lydia be gracious enough to reserve the first Lancers for her obedient servant?

So, with a mocking bow, he had hurried away, leaving Lydia in sorrow and terror. But the terror was greater than the sorrow. She had never seen the Baron like this, never dreamed that he could be like this. What if he carried out his threats! His eyes had been bloodshot and had a glassy kind of stare; and then his laugh had been awful; and he was a great strong man, assuredly in physical strength ever so much the superior of poor delicate Bertram. What if the Baron were to-night to bring about a scene, have recourse to actual violence! What will men not do in rage and despair!

Her old love for Bertram, which after all she had felt in her own way, and which long ago she had sacrificed to her vanity and worldliness, was stirring again. Lydia felt it, and was enraptured. True, she had been lying and cheating to reach a certain goal that pure calculation had fixed. Still, she was a better woman than she had thought herself. She had thought that she was following the dictates of her reason only, and lo! she had unconsciously remained faithful to her own heart. She knew it now, at the moment when a serious danger was threatening the loved one. And, curiously, although during the last few days she had positively given up all hope of regaining the loved one, and had in envy and anger seen him in the bonds of affection for a fair young rival--an affection which, moreover, was warmly reciprocated; yet she suddenly began to doubt the justice of her observations; the old dreams were coming back and asserted that they were a reality, and that everything else was but a chimera. All, all would yet come right. Falsehood and hypocrisy had been powerless; truth and love, however, would be omnipotent!

Then she began to rehearse in her mind that unfortunate letter which she had purloined in order to gain a clear insight into Erna's sentiments, now endeavouring to give the gentlest interpretation to every word that referred to Bertram; she remembered, too, the passage which seemed to refer to a former love affair of Erna's. But she and Hildegard, eager only to discover what they most, or rather what they only, feared, namely, an attachment to Bertram, had added no weight to the brief allusion in question. Some childish "dancing-lesson fondness," Hildegard had said, and she had assented to it, partly to guard against the possibility of the reproach that she, in her responsible position as Erna's educator and second mother, had overlooked or actually allowed any serious attachment on her part. "Betrayed"--that surely was plain enough, and made many things clear, even though in itself it was hard to understand, was, in fact, all but absolutely incomprehensible. Such a charming creature as Erna no one is likely to betray, no one at least who is in possession of his five senses, as young gentlemen generally are. If the thing was anything more than a passing fancy--and that one had to assume, considering how averse from anything frivolous Erna was--then her easily-wounded pride must have brought the rupture about, and it might yet be healed; and if it were healed, would turn the child from her caprice for Bertram, would set Bertram free again, if indeed he had allowed himself to be captivated by Erna's unconcealed admiration for him, set him free for herself, his first, his true, his only love!

With fancies like these, Lydia, now banished from the favour and the presence of Hildegard, was wandering along the garden-terraces, now dissolved in tears and lamenting her bitter lot, now smiling complacently and congratulating herself upon a happiness which was all the more precious the longer she had been compelled to wait for it. If she were now to meet Erna, if she could have an explanation with her, become reconciled to her, prove to her in very truth how well she meant by her! She was in the very mood for this, and here was Erna coming along! The shrinking which she often felt in the presence of the proud and self-willed girl was making itself perceptible again, but one swift glance showed her that Erna had been weeping quite recently, and that she could risk it now.

Erna had been weeping quite recently, and so indeed she had done ever since last night, whenever she felt sure that no one was looking upon her despair. For the gentle creature was in despair. All through the long sleepless night she had seemed to hear Agatha's whispered question, "What will you do if it comes out that Kurt is innocent?" She had seemed to hear it like the voice of a warning angel, and neither head nor heart had been able to reply anything but, again and again: "In that case I have betrayed him, and I have made him unhappy." Could he be innocent? She had struggled so long against the belief in Kurt's guilt, and had only accepted it when he declared that he could not explain his relations to the Russian lady; no, not even to her, from whom, for the sake of their love, he was to expect entire confidence; for confidence was the very soul and at the same time the touchstone of love. Alas, she knew yet another and a more terrible touchstone, and that was the jealousy which she had cherished in secret towards the unknown lady, and which had blazed up brightly when yesterday she beheld her, the hated temptress, in the splendour of her youth, beauty, and grace. In vain did she struggle against the charm which the lady seemed to radiate; in vain did she declare everything about her to be unreal, except her diamonds perhaps; with every furtive glance at her rival she felt herself more and more fascinated, allured, beguiled, and, in equal measure, conquered, and at last crushed.

It was a terrible state which wrapped her poor fluttering heart in absolute night, and yet even then there was something like a faint glimmering of the star of hope. If Kurt had ever loved her--and he had--he had done so once--how could he love another woman, who, however charming and seductive, was yet in all things the very opposite of herself? Kurt, who had so often assured her that he hated all display and all vanity, that he loved her because there was nothing of display, nothing, of vanity about her, because she was his own rose, which, in its dewy freshness, he would not exchange for a world of brilliant exotics!

And his large brown eyes had shone down upon her so gravely and lovingly as he spoke, and his lips had trembled with genuine emotion--and had all this been naught but lies on the part of him whom she in her turn had loved, because he had appeared to her as a lofty and lordly image of truthfulness and fidelity?

It could not be.

But then, again, what had she done? What was she to do when the other one, that good and noble man, to whom--so Agatha said, and her own heart could not but confirm it--she had given such unequivocal proof of her affection, when he came into her presence and said: "I have come to take you at your word. Not all the Flavios in the world would have kept Hilarie from loving her uncle, had she been convinced that he truly loved her. And you know it: I love you!" What could she do, but, with Hilarie, say: "I am yours for ever"? He would not fall at her feet and exclaim: "You make me the happiest man beneath the sun," but she knew,--she knew that he would be happy!

Ah me!--why had she not obeyed the voice which called to her that first evening when she met him in the wood, and he laid his heart open to her: "Open thy heart to him too," the voice had said, "tell him all." That would have been the time, the only right time. For the very next day she had read in his eyes what now made her so proud--so happy. So happy? Gracious heavens!

This was happiness, was it, that she now desired nothing better than death, swift death, to escape from the torments that tore her heart to pieces?

Did he divine nothing of these torments! Why had he not come to her last night? He might surely have spared her a minute--he had given the Princess a full hour. It was, perhaps, a relief, a sort of recreation, for him, seeing he had so long had to dispense with any intellectual conversation. Was she perchance the beautiful widow in the novelette who consoled the uncle for the loss of Hilarie? And had Hilarie already got to the point of wishing and longing for such consolation for her uncle?

Her shamefaced gaze wandered up to Bertram's windows, under which she had arrived--not quite unintentionally. What if he were to appear above--signalling: "Wait, I am coming down!"

Like a startled fawn she flitted away to one of the terrace-walks, behind whose protecting wall she could not be seen from those windows of his, and burst into tears, as she became conscious of her cowardice. Lydia appeared at the opposite entrance; she could not avoid Lydia now; she bent toward the espalier, to dry her eyes unobserved, and lo! there was Lydia at her side, at her feet, clasping Erna's knees, pressing her face against Erna's robe, sobbing.

It was a theatrical display, such as Lydia employed on all possible occasions, suitable or otherwise; Erna knew that well enough. But she had not the courage to tear herself away; never a harsh or ironical expression came forth from her to-day; nay, she all but envied a human being that found such expression for its feelings, whatever they might be. She endeavoured to raise the kneeling lady.

"I must remain on my knees until you have pardoned me," murmured Lydia.

"I'll do anything you wish--but rise, rise, I entreat you!"

She had drawn Lydia up and away into a niche in the wall, thus gaining at least some shelter from the eyes of the servants, many of whom were still busy everywhere up and down the terraces with the preparations for the illumination. There was a stone bench with a stone table in front inside the niche. Lydia sank down upon the bench, laid her face, covered by her hands, against the edge of the table, and murmured her miserable confession of guilt in a voice which was scarcely audible, owing to her constant weeping and sobbing. She had, she whined out, found out by questioning the servants that the letter had not been sent, which Erna had on the morning in question written beneath the plantain tree, and which, she assumed, was certainly addressed to Agatha; and she had, moreover, learned from Agatha--who evidently suspected nothing--that she had received no letter just before her departure from home. Then, passing through Erna's rooms, she had seen her blotting-book lying about, unlocked, as she had been astonished to notice. Then she had been unable to resist the temptation of trying if the letter was still there. The letter had been there--a sort of dizziness had come over her, and--

"I said to myself," she went on, "that you have no secrets from Agatha, that you were likely to have written to her what you felt towards Bertram, whether you loved him--I required to know it--my future, my happiness, my salvation--all, all depended upon that one question. Have pity on a poor wretched woman whom jealousy made a criminal--against her own child, too! for I have ever loved you as my own child, ever, and would gladly have sacrificed all for you, all, only not this--the trial was too much for my strength."

Then Lydia in her self-abasement and grief wept bitterly. Again Erna felt it strange that she did not spring up from her place beside the weeping old woman, did not leave her alone with her silliness and her lies; that she could listen to her exaggerated and sentimental twaddle without positive disgust. There was something stirring within her that she was frightened at herself--something almost like a wish that, this time, Lydia might not be lying.

Lydia noticed through the veil of tears in which she had wrapt herself that Erna was accepting her confession much more favourably than she had dared to hope. This gave her courage enough to pursue to the utmost the advantage thus already gained.

"I cannot and will not try to prove that I have been quite free from blame," she cried. "I have been vain and frivolous. I did yield to the temptation of becoming Countess of Finkenburg! Many more would have yielded who cannot retrace, like one of the family of von Aschhof, the long line of their ancestors to the time of the Crusaders, and who do not, as we do, have Moors' heads in their escutcheons! But vanity and frivolity alone did not make me do it. I was honestly convinced that this alliance with a poor lady of high lineage, who would bring him no other dower but her many claims and wants, could be nought but a hindrance to Bertram; that he might have made, and probably thereafter would make, a better and a more suitable choice if I released him from his engagement. Indeed, indeed; if I could but have divined how he would take it to heart, nothing in the world would have made me act as I did. And now I would give everything in the world to atone, as far as I still may, for what I did. Must it really be out of the question, dearest? Look here. He is about fifty years of age, and how long will it be before he is an old man? He is very delicate too. His servant tells me that he suffers from palpitation of the heart, and from insomnia, and that his Berlin doctor has enjoined upon him no end of precautions and care for these travels of his. Why then, he really needs some one who will nurse him and who will patiently bear with all his sickly caprices--all sick folk are capricious, don't you know? I know it but too well; I saw it in the case of my own uncle, the Minister of State, whom every one thought a very lamb in the way of kind, gentle equanimity, and who was so until one of his asthmatic attacks came upon him; and then never a living soul could bear to stay near him. Yes, yes, one must have gone through these things to know; and may God in His mercy keep you, my own dear, sweet, good child, from ever knowing it, from mourning away your sweet young life by the side of a broken-down man who has no passion left, save his books and his politics. If his politics call him he must needs follow, and poor Konski must pack the trunks. Poor fellow, Konski! I spoke to him a little while ago; he'd like to stay and see all the fun that is coming now with these manœuvres here, and what not. Besides, I rather think he is in love with Aurora. But he says there is no help for it, and off they go to-morrow, his master and he. Perhaps it is right enough, for the Baron is furious with him, and I really know not what the Baron will do, unless you convince him that he has been mistaken, like the rest of us. Oh, that we had! My own sweet child, you would be restoring peace and happiness to us all, and I would never weary of kissing your dear hands, nay, the very hem of your garment!"

She covered Erna's hands and robe with kisses. Erna let her have her way, she paid no heed to what Lydia was saying and doing; there she sat gazing fixedly across the gardens and across the village on the mountain slope, where a portion of the high road was visible which led from the north across the hills to Rinstedt. Lydia, following the direction of Erna's gaze, saw what Erna saw--a great cloud of dust, with occasional flashes of bright arms, winding down the high road, and now there came, softened by the great distance but still distinctly audible, the sound of the drum; and below, at the entrance to the village, they fired a cannon as a signal that the regiment was coming up.

Erna started as though the shot had gone through her heart!

"For goodness sake, child, what ails you?" exclaimed Lydia, terrified on noticing the pallor of her cheek and her fixed rigid look.

And again she was terrified when Erna suddenly flung herself into her arms as seeking help from a threatening danger, and then with equal suddenness tore herself away, hurried up the walk and straightway vanished behind a projecting portion of the wall.

"What does it all mean?" Lydia asked herself.

As if in answer, there came across the garden, now more distinctly, the sound of the drum.

"Ah!" said Lydia, and a meaning smile flitted over her face. "It would not be impossible," she murmured, "and if it is the case, I'll find it out!"

She turned to enter the mansion house just as the big flag was being hoisted upon the turret as a salute to "Our Regiment," at the moment when the soldiers set foot upon the village road.

CHAPTER XVIII

Bertram, too, had heard the warlike sounds. He leaned back in his writing chair and listened with bated breath.

"How her heart is sure to beat!" he said to himself.

He rose and went to the open window. From the elevation on which he was, he could see a considerable portion of the high road, could discern the flash of the bayonets through the clouds of dust which a brisk breeze was scattering at times, so that sections of the columns on the march became visible.

In the village below they were firing cannon; from the mountains yonder the echo came rolling.

"How this will resound within her heart!"

From the adjoining bedroom, where he had already begun to put up his master's things in view of their departure, fixed for the day following, Konski came hurrying in to ask, if the Herr Doctor was not going to dress? It was getting late.

"I am in no hurry," said Bertram.

"Well, sir," said Konski, "My Lady is most anxious you should be present at the reception of the officers. Aurora has twice come to the door with a message about it."

And he pointed, as he spoke, to the bedroom door and grinned.

"I do not intend to be present at the reception," Bertram said; "but I may as well dress now." And he followed Konski into the bedroom.

As Konski was assisting him, he said to him--

"Well, on what terms are you with that girl now? You will have to make haste if you wish to settle everything before we go."

"It is already settled, and settled very nicely," Konski made answer, "since last night, sir. With the like of us, such things are settled smartly, Herr Doctor, and I have a favour to ask of you in connection with it. Aurora--it's a strange name that, sir, is it not? and her two others are just as bad:

Amanda Rolline--thank you, says I. Well, it is not her fault, though, poor thing, and I won't mind re-baptizing her once we, are in Berlin. But, as I was going to say, Herr Doctor, she insists upon our getting married in the beginning of October, because at the end of October Christine is going to be married to Peter Weissenborn, and she wants to annoy Christina by being married before her, so she says; but I fancy it's meant for Peter, who used to be uncommonly sweet upon her, and, I rather think, promised to marry her at one time. And if the Herr Doctor is not going to Italy at all, or leastways not now, we thought ..."

"You know," said Bertram, "how sorry I shall be to part with you; but I will not stand in the way of your happiness."

"It would be my greatest happiness, sir," said Konski, "to remain with you as long as I live. And there's just one way, so Aurora says ..."

"Well?"

Konski hesitated a little, then took heart of grace, and said, with an embarrassed sort of smirk--

"If the Herr Doctor would be so very kind as to marry too!"

"I am afraid," said Bertram, "you will have to devise some other way out of the difficulty."

Konski was meditatively removing some specks of dust from the black waistcoat which he held in his hand, and said--

"No offence, sir! These women are always a-puzzling out something or other in their brains, and Aurora's brains are by no means bad brains. She thinks it would be uncommon nice, if I would remain the Herr Doctor's valet, and she was to be maid to your lady, sir; and then, whether you went to Italy or elsewhere, we four would always be nice and snug together."

"I have no idea what you are talking about," said Bertram. "Give me my waistcoat."

"No offence, sir," Konski repeated, as he handed his master the waistcoat and took up the dress-coat; "but she leaves me no peace, she does not, and she says that it's all up with the Baron; and from what she heard My Lady say to master this morning about the Herr Doctor, says she, the Herr Doctor need but ask and they'd give him a half dozen daughters, only they have not got more than one; and that one, dear Miss Erna--why, I knows, and no one knows better than me--how fond she is of the Herr Doctor."

As Bertram had again turned away, the poor fellow, much to his regret, could not see what impression his remarks had made upon his master; and now they heard a heavy, hurried step coming through the study. There was a knock, then Otto put in his head and asked if he might trouble Bertram for a minute. Bertram begged him to come in, and beckoned his man to leave the room.

"I have been repeatedly wishing to come up and see you," said Otto; "Hildegard is so afraid that you mean to go--and--dear me, you have really been packing."

"For to-morrow," Bertram made answer. "In no case can I remain longer. For to-day I am, as you see, already, like yourself, in evening dress. Only--you must please excuse me if I do not put in an appearance before dinner; I have not finished my letters yet, and, to say the truth, I should like to cut the reception business."

"So should I," said Otto, "if I could. They will be here in less than ten minutes now. I have not a minute to spare, not a minute."

But for all that he did not stir from the chair into which he had dropped. His mind was clearly far away. Presently he muttered--

"What if Parliament has decided against the railway!"

"We must be prepared for it," replied his friend.

"It is half-past four now, the sitting is sure to be over by this time."

"You will know the result to-morrow, and early enough, too!"

"I think that Lotter, who has had to go to town, will have waited to hear the result of the vote; I asked him to. He said he would be back in time for dinner. But I no longer believe in his influence."

"All the better."

Both were speaking in gloomy tones, as though a heavy pressure was weighing equally on either. Bertram was staring down in front of him with arms crossed behind his back, and Otto's eyes were wandering about the room--he was mechanically fingering the arms of his chair, then suddenly gave a convulsive clutch at them.

"I must go," he said.

He jumped up and was making for the door.

"Otto!"

"Are you coming too?"

"No; I have a small favour to ask which you are not to refuse me."

Bertram had meanwhile gone up to his friend, holding out his hand to him. Otto mechanically put his own into it.

"I wanted to ask you to make use of me in case you have not yet arranged about redeeming, to-morrow, that mortgage, and in the present hurry and worry, what more likely? I have not even had to write to Berlin about it. My Italian trip is given up. You know I had made arrangements for a very lengthened absence. My letter of credit is addressed to your own banker, as I had anyhow been intending to draw a large sum; I can get the money at once, and there will be just enough."

"Time enough to-morrow," murmured Otto; "however, I am much obliged to you for your kind intention. Perhaps I'll drive you to town to-morrow, if you insist upon going; we can then see about it."

His cheeks were burning; his hand, which Bertram was still holding, trembled like that of a man in great physical pain. Bertram noticed it all.

"I am very sorry," he said, "that I must thus torment you, but you left me no choice as to the time. I am sure I shall not be able to speak to you again to-day, and perhaps not to-morrow. Therefore, look here: I have made all the requisite preparations, with due despatch, to make as much of my fortune available as you will need for the settlement of your affairs. You remember our conversation when we were driving back from town last Saturday. I put no other conditions now than I did then; that you arrange the settlement with the help of your lawyer, that you leave him as free as possible in his dispositions regarding the factories, and lastly, that your wife is taken into your confidence--these are not so much conditions, as necessities. And of the last, and doubtless the most painful one, I am willing to relieve you."

Otto flushed to the roots of his hair.

"It is impossible!" he ejaculated. "I cannot take it."

"I am not making you a present of the money, man!"

"The money--the money--but Hildegard! To-day all this display--the Princess--all those officers--a huge party--covers for a hundred or so; and then to-morrow the most awful wretchedness--it is quite impossible. And even if you had the courage--if you were to speak to her, I mean--you are on such good terms again, she had intended to come herself and see you, and I had thought--but that, that she would never forgive you--never!"

"I am prepared for that," replied Bertram. "To be quite frank, I care infinitely more for your welfare than for your wife's favour. Otto, these is no time for long debating. A plain yes from you, and the thing is settled--now or never--do you hear me?"

From the great courtyard there came the sound of merry military music; many voices, too, were heard. Otto was still standing by the door irresolute.

He suddenly seized Bertram's other hand and exclaimed-- "Then marry Erna at least! Hildegard will get reconciled to it, once she knows all. Erna is fond of you--let me talk to her!"

"One word from you, and--I shall not alter my resolve, it is fixed for good; but you and I will never meet again."

Bertram had torn himself away and was striding along the chamber. Now he came back to Otto who was standing there in utter helplessness, laid his hand on his shoulder, and said to him--

"Otto, remember what we vowed to each other in the dear old student days in Bonn: to be and to remain friends in gladness or sadness, friends to the death! This surely is sufficient. Let us not speak of Erna, or, at least, let us not connect her name with this business; such a connection is an insult to me, because it is casting doubt upon the purity of my motives. I can tell you something else, in reference to which I must, in the meantime, request your discreet silence. I have good reasons for assuming that Erna has already disposed of her heart, and this may explain certain oddities in her demeanour which have struck us both. I believe I shall soon know if I am right. In warning you, and your wife against Lotter, I gave you a proof of my careful observation and of my faithful friendship. Confide in me further: you will not repent of it. And now, old boy, go with a lighter heart than you came, and receive your guests, or else the great event will come off without you, and for that Hildegard would never forgive you, and she would be right."

He was almost pushing poor helpless Otto out of the door, when Konski came hurrying up with an impatient message from My Lady.

"Would Otto come at once? The military were just marching up the courtyard."

Otto hurried away. Bertram was still standing near the door, his eye rigidly fixed upon it.

He was murmuring to himself: "That was the first step. I should not have thought, after all I have already endured, that it would prove so hard. But it had to be done!"

He walked slowly up and down, and paused again.

"Had it to be done? And thus? Would it not have been better if I had not absolutely denied it? Anyhow, I have not resigned in every case; only, in case it is as I fear. Supposing it is not? What if the young man who has gone through the schooling of a Princess Volinzov, is not one whom our Erna can and should love? What if the Princess is mistaken in this part of the story, or if she has been deceived by the man who may have, had good reasons of his own? What if the whole thing has been a little gentle dallying which Erna has all but forgotten, and I were, with my diplomatic wiles, to fan again into life and light the almost extinguished flame, were to repel her from me and push her into his arms, which will be willing enough to open?"

He stretched out his hands, as though he wished to ward off something. They were all assailing him again now in the broad light of the day, those dread phantoms with which he had wrestled in the awful darkness of the night. Then he had conquered them. Was he to be vanquished now? Was his strength exhausted?

No, no; the worst had yet to come. Though he had persuaded himself that it would be only fair and proper not to be a witness of their first meeting, yet he would have to see them together, perhaps learn at the first glance that they had already made it up, and that the great sacrifice, which the beautiful Princess was making for her darling, had been wholly unnecessary. All the better! In that case the torture of uncertainty would be over all the sooner, and he would at least be spared the humiliation of pushing Quixotic generosity to its utmost limits, and of acting the part of an obtrusive mediator, who clears away all obstacles and ultimately joins the lovers' hands with a "Bless you, my children!"

He sat down at the writing-table to complete his election address. But he could not write, could not think. Pen in hand he sat, hearkening to all the confused sounds which came up and across him from courtyard, garden, and mansion house. The music, after some little pause, is now playing again in long-drawn triumphant strains--representing the salute of the regiment to the house that now guarded its colours; the fair mistress appears on the threshold, surrounded by the other ladies, and the tall and gallant-looking Colonel, hastening up, followed by his officers, bows deferentially and kisses her hand. And lo! from the circle around the mistress of the house, there steps forth another lady, at whose sight the gallant soldier starts. But she smiles, and signals with those mobile orbs of hers--

"Be calm, my friend, be calm! I shall explain all as soon as we are alone for a minute, or, if not all--that being contrary to my habit--as much as you need know. It is a matter concerning these people."

And she points aside to another pair, bowing to each other and presumably renewing--a casual acquaintance, shall we say?

"I hardly know, my gracious Fräulein, whether I still have the honour..."

What a farce it all was!

And what a ghastly tragedy too--its silent scene his heart--forsaken, lonely as he was.

So he sat on, brooding gloomily, musing dismally, he knew not how long. Silence now reigned around without. Had they forgotten him? Oh, that they had! and that he could steal away from the house--from the farce--from life!

But no, they would not be so pitiful. Hearken!--yes, this is Konski's swift step.

"I beg your pardon, sir, but My Lady bade me urge you to come. They are just going to dinner, and are only waiting for the Herr Doctor!"

CHAPTER XIX

It was a princely banquet that Hildegard had prepared for her guests in the dining-hall of the whilom princely abode. The closed curtains had excluded the daylight from the beginning, and the light of innumerable candles fell upon the table from the three great chandeliers and from a number of candelabras fixed to the wall. The table shone and sparkled with crystal and silver, was decked with a profusion of the choicest flowers, and surrounded by a most brilliant company. There were five and twenty officers in their uniforms--and the general *coup d'œ il* was truly enchanting. Everything went off well. Hildegard herself could scarcely distinguish from her own serving-men the extra waiters ordered from town, and put into liveries; in the adjoining hall the band of the 99th was playing, for Colonel von Waldor had insisted upon My Lady thus honouring his regiment, although she had a band from town in readiness. The toasts, in reference to which she had been somewhat uneasy, had been a wonderful success. Otto had not blundered or stopped short in the first toast--His Majesty the Emperor, of course; then Bertram, whom she had, at dinner, by means of a pencilled note, asked to do so, had in the name of the host, and as the oldest friend of the family present, welcomed the guests and proposed the health of the 99th. Thereupon Colonel von Waldor returned thanks in a really capital speech, abounding in merry quips and happy inspirations. He called the brilliant reception given to the regiment, a posthumous celebration of their doings in the last war, and a lordly payment "on account" for what they were destined to do in the campaigns of the future. He then proceeded to describe the reception in detail, and added that to him, personally, it had been the most charming of all the charming surprises of the day, to find in the gentleman who had so cordially welcomed them all to this most hospitable house, an old and dear friend from whom he had been separated for years; and at last, passing adroitly from the host's representative to the host himself, he proposed the health of "their far too generous entertainer, and of the kind, gracious, and beauteous lady of the manor, by whose side, he had the rare happiness of being seated."

And the other officers--four and-twenty in number--had started from their seats like one man, and had three times shouted their *Hoch* in singularly sharp and definite intervals, overpowering the *Hoch* of the other guests as the roar of cannon drowns the sound of musket firing, and the band had joined in the celebration; and they had all crowded around Hildegard, with their champagne-goblets held on high; and as she received all these homages, she looked radiantly, superbly beautiful, and so the Colonel had told her, adding that she was by far the fairest of all the fair ladies there; and as they settled in their places again, he had kissed her hand in eager gallantry.

Hildegard thanked the enchanted Colonel with a gracious smile for his flattery, and thanked him warmly, too, for his excellent toast, in which she had missed but one thing, to wit, some clever allusion, some dainty reference to her illustrious guest, the Princess, who, from her place of honour next to Otto, on the opposite side of the banqueting-table, had, followed the speaker with the greatest attention, and had evidently expected something of the kind.

The Colonel smiled and shrugged his shoulders.

"I had thought of it, too, My Lady," he said; "but, upon honour, it could not be done."

"Why not?

"I have already told My Lady that the Princess and I met last year in Teplitz. Since My Lady--and I must express my sincere gratitude for the condescension--did me last night repeatedly the honour of mentioning my name to her, without, it would appear, recalling any reminiscence on her part, I surely could not indulge in reminiscences. My wounded vanity peremptorily forbade any such thing. And, moreover, it was wounded ere then. It is no joke for a Colonel who has been somewhat spoiled, to see a young officer, and particularly one belonging to his own regiment, preferred to himself, and such, was then undoubtedly the case. The young gentleman suffering, like myself, from a severe wound received during the '70 campaign, had accompanied me to Teplitz, and was my constant companion, so that he can bear witness to everything. The reminiscence of that wound inflicted upon my vanity is at this moment the more vivid, because the young gentleman is here."

The Colonel pointed, as he spoke, to a slender young officer, dark of eye and hair, who was sitting between Agatha and Augusta, and who was conversing eagerly with the former, while Augusta, a coquettish beauty, looked supremely bored.

Upon Hildegard the young man's appearance had already made so pleasing an impression after he had been introduced to her, that she had actually remembered his name and rank--Premier-Lieutenant and Adjutant

Ringberg. But she thought she was acting prudently in saying that she saw nothing remarkable in the young gentleman. Much to her amazement, the Colonel seemed almost offended at this; Ringberg, he said, was really in every way a remarkable man, the most studious, and at the same time the smartest officer in his regiment, a man of excellent character; and a jolly companion, for whom he himself had a sort of paternal fondness; indeed, Ringberg was the son of a dear friend of his own, left early an orphan, and he, the Colonel, had acted for him *in loco parentis*, and wished him every happiness under the sun, including the conquest of the beautiful Russian and her millions.

"But there seems little prospect of that," Hildegard said, smilingly interrupting the Colonel in his eager talk; "as far as I have been able to observe, your *protégé* does not exist for our beautiful friend."

"That may be one of her masks," replied the Colonel. "I think the lady has a great many."

"You must not talk like this to me; I adore Alexandra."

"But, My Lady, so do I too, otherwise I should never dream of abusing her."

"That, too, I must forbid."

"Then I will swear that she does not even know what a mask is, and I am ready to face a world in arms in proof of the assertion," laughed the Colonel, and Hildegard laughed too, and kissed her hand to the Princess across the table, a compliment which the fair Russian returned eagerly.

Hildegard felt so happy by the side of her brilliant cavalier, that she could scarcely make up her mind to give the signal for rising from the table. But at last it had to be done, after she had exchanged a few hurried words with Herr von Busche, who had quietly come up behind her chair. When, a few minutes later, she rose from her seat, the curtains were suddenly and simultaneously withdrawn from the windows and doors, the glass doors flew wide open, and before the amazed eyes of the company lay the garden in fairy-like illumined splendour. Rows of coloured balloons were drawn like garlands along and adown the terraces; and every prominent point-- and there were many of them--had been utilised for some effective purpose of decoration: a pyramid of stars, a wreath of light, or a radiant crown. And the guests, now hurrying away from the tables, had scarcely all gathered upon the verandah before they found themselves enveloped in the dazzling brilliancy of coloured lights; the magnificent façade of the mansion-house, wrapt in a glorious purple glow, stood out with wonderful effect against the darkening sky, and a deep green flame sent a soft and tender light along the terraces and mingled on the great grass plot in front of the verandah with the red light, the combination yielding a dim, mysterious kind of magic dawn. And before the glow had faded away, and before the admiring and wondering exclamations of the delighted and surprised guests had ceased, there was the thunder of cannon, a signal, and lo! from the wide common below, a rocket winged its shining flight upwards, followed by another and yet another, in such swift succession that the fiery missiles bursting anon high, high up in the air, seemed to fill the dark sky with a galaxy of glowing stars, whilst below squibs and crackers were exploding and wheels of fire were whirling round in all directions.

But now the younger members of the company could be restrained no longer. In vain did anxious mammas preach patience and caution and call for shawls and cloaks, the young ladies would not wait, and fortunately the night was so calm and warm that they could really dispense with wrappings; the officers had, anyhow, to remain bare-headed unless they cared to put on the spiked helmets with which they had appeared at the banquet. So they all danced merrily down the wide steps; and were soon scattered over the terraces; and from all sides there came the laughing shouts of those who were looking for each other, who perhaps met unexpectedly at some turn in the labyrinth, or who were pretending to escape, a merry game in which the young ladies, whether staying in the house or belonging to the neighbourhood, being familiar with the locality, gladly assumed the leadership, adroitly using their knowledge to their own advantage.

Meanwhile the greater part of the guests had gradually withdrawn to the chambers on either side of the great banqueting-hall, the ladies to the music-rooms and tea-rooms on the left, the gentlemen mostly to the billiard-room, which opened into the smoking- and card-rooms. Some still went in and out at the great French windows, all of which opened on the verandah, but on the verandah itself there were now comparatively few people, so that Bertram had but now and again to exhort the Colonel to lower his sonorous voice a little. The friends were pacing up and down arm in arm; the Colonel's uniform was all but entirely unbuttoned, he was puffing vigorously at his cigar, and his handsome, gallant features were aglow with the after-effect of the champagne, and with the excitement which increased with every word which he was rapidly uttering.

"Believe me," he cried, "my good fellow, if anything could still increase my feeling of absolute worship for this unique woman, it would be the pluck with which she went into action for young Ringberg. But unfortunately with all those fair and adorable creatures, intention and execution never correspond. A masterly outflanking of the foe, an assault *comme il faut*, and then at once this ludicrous mistake! I could have died with laughter! Not the slightest idea on her part that you are such a very special and intimate friend of mine! And so she goes and tells you all the minutest details of our story, as to an absolute stranger, supposed to be quite incapable of translating it back into German from the French, because he can have no idea as to the identity of the real persons involved! And why this stupendous want of caution? To frighten you away! From what? From falling in love with the little damsel, or to induce you, in case you had already done so, to be kind enough to retire immediately! As though the like of us were to be rightened away from our purpose by a reconnoitring like this, however forced! 'You may thank your stars,' I said to her 'that Doctor Bertram has better things to occupy himself with than the childishness which you impute to him!' To be sure she swears that she became convinced of it last night, for you remained perfectly calm and self-possessed, and had the contrary been the case, it would certainly not have escaped her, as she was scrutinising your every mien with the upmost care; but then her own mien, as she was telling me all this, proved how pleased and relieved she felt that all had gone off so happily!"

"And what," asked; Bertram, "have you decided in Ringberg's affair? Will you not at least take Erna, and, of course, her parents, into the secret?"

"The deuce I will!" cried Waldor. "I surely should not hesitate to rescue Ringberg at any cost from some position of great danger, but this is, not a question of my making a sacrifice, but of Alexandra making one that she cannot make, unless she wishes to give up half her fortune, which goes to the deuce as soon as our engagement gets known. But I want the whole fortune and not the half! When I was but a lieutenant I swore a great oath to myself that I would die a Field-Marshal, and would live like a Prince until I got to be one! Now you surely cannot expect that I should break my oath, and, to myself too?"

Bertram did not think it advisable to point out to his friend, the contradictions he was guilty of in one breath. He only said--

"I should think the sacrifice might be avoided, if you made the people who are interested pledge themselves to secrecy. None of them would hesitate to accept that objection."

"In such things," replied the Colonel, "one should not trust any one's promise of secrecy. Why, every thing would already be betrayed, if Alexandra had honoured any one but yourself with her indiscretions!"

"But if the Princess absolutely insists upon making the sacrifice?"

"Then I shall as absolutely forbid her doing anything of the kind! The services which Kurt has rendered us are considerable, I admit; but then, in the first case, they were rendered to me. How can I ask her to act such a generous part? Nay, what does she mean by wishing to do it? One would not, one could not, do more for one's lover! And, to the best of my knowledge, she is in love with me, and not with Ringberg!"

His cigar had gone out and he flung it away, turning to light a new one at one of the lights placed along the verandah. Thus he did not see the smile which Bertram--though his heart was little attuned to mirth--had not been able to repress at the words which his not over-modest friend had been uttering.

"In that case the Princess will have to say, like the priest Domingo, in Schiller's 'Don Carlos:' 'We have been here in vain,'" he resumed, as the Colonel took his arm again.

"To be sure," was the calm reply; "and I have strongly urged her to leave to-morrow. Surrounded as we are here by my officers, one or two of whom are already likely enough to know more than I care for, we are not for a single moment safe from startling disclosures. I think I have as strong nerves as most people, but to be seated upon a powder-barrel when there is a conflagration raging all round, is uncomfortable for the most courageous."

"What is uncomfortable, Colonel?" asked Alexandra's voice behind them.

The Colonel turned on his heels; and quickly buttoning his uniform, exclaimed--

"Ah, most gracious Princess!"

"Let us call each other by our names before this good friend," said Alexandra. "Give me your arm, dear Doctor Bertram; and you, my friend, please to come to the other side. So now we can talk confidentially."

"May I go on with my cigar?"

"I should like to smoke one myself, if I dared! But now to the point. What have you decided?"

"That is the very question," Bertram said, "which I was just submitting to Waldor."

"I have decided, that the young people are to see how they can best settle things for themselves!"

"That is an abominable decision!"

"It is necessary."

"Not for me! I shall speak to the young lady."

"You will not do so if you value my advice ever so little. Moreover, if you felt so sure of this, why did you not do so yesterday?"

"Because I require your co-operation."

"Which I refuse!"

They were talking excitedly, almost vehemently now. Then, there was a pause, a very uncomfortable one for Bertram, although he said to himself that discord between the two ought to be welcome to him. He had closely watched Erna and Ringberg. At dinner, where they had been seated almost directly opposite to each other, they had not exchanged a single word; and just now, whilst Erna had followed the other young ladies into the garden, Ringberg had remained on the verandah and had subsequently gone into the billiard-room. As Erna was so very proud, a meeting of the two seemed difficult, almost impossible, without kind and skilful mediation, and there would be little time or opportunity for it now. To-morrow the regiment was again to leave its quarters. They would again be separated for long--for ever, if he chose to avail himself of the influence which he doubtless had over Erna; and if he could only bring into play something of the robust egotism, with which the handsome soldier by his side was smoothing his own way to rank and unlimited riches.

"Then I only know one way to achieve our object," the Princess said at last, speaking somewhat huskily.

"I knew you would find something," said Waldor; "but what is it?"

"It is this ..."

Alexandra paused abruptly, for as they reached the end of the verandah, and were turning round, the very man of whom they were all thinking was approaching them.

"Anything for me, my dear Ringberg?" exclaimed the Colonel.

"Yes, Colonel; an orderly from the General in command ..."

"May the ..." muttered the Colonel through his teeth.

He went up to the young officer, who made his report in a low voice, whilst the Princess and Bertram remained standing at some little distance. They saw the Colonel angrily fling away his cigar, and draw himself up.

"Thank you, my dear Ringberg; you need not come with me. It is bad enough if one of us has to lose all the fun. No remonstrance, sir! I shall want an orderly to go with me, and, perhaps, you will, in passing, kindly bid them saddle Almansor."

"Yes, Colonel," said the young officer, saluting.

Ringberg had gone. Waldor turned round.

"It seems," he said, "that the soldiers have taken a different position from what His Excellency had expected, and now he is getting all the officers in command of regiments together, to get things done as noisily as possible. The old owl! Upon my word, I would let him have a bit of my mind, if he did this in actual war, and summoned me at such a time two or three miles off from a position where we may be 'alarmed' at any moment. However, there is no help for it. I shall not spare the horse, but I am afraid I shall not be back before one o'clock. My officers must be in their quarters by twelve o'clock precisely, and the rest of the party are likely to vanish too. I presume that we shall be attacked between two and three o'clock. If, then, I do not see you again, dearest Alexandra, the arrangement is this: you drive to town to-morrow and remain there until I can look in for a moment, as I hope to be able to do the day after, or else until I send word. Farewell, dearest! And you, my good friend, will probably not have gone to bed before I return. I will come to your room, and learn what the best and cleverest of women will have planned in the interest of our *protégés*."

The Colonel kissed her hand again, and hurried away. Alexandra looked gloomily after him, standing with her hands crossed over her bosom, until he had vanished through the door of the billiard-room; where several of the senior officers were advancing to meet him. Then, with a passionate gesture, she turned to Bertram.

"He is mistaken! Alexandra Volinzov is not to be ordered about like a pack of recruits. I shall not leave to-morrow! I shall not leave at all, until I have achieved my object; and you, friend, you must help me to achieve it."

She flung the end of her shawl impatiently across her shoulder, and took Bertram's arm, drawing him away from the verandah down into the garden, whence the young people, in pairs and in groups, were now hurrying merrily back to the mansion-house, attracted by the sound of the band striking up a polka in the banqueting-hall, which had been cleared in the interval.

"And what is my help to consist in?" asked Bertram.

"You must speak to Erna. You must explain all to her. I am powerless without Waldor's co-operation, and you have heard how he refuses it? Nay, more; I have learned from Hildegard, that he has definitely denied standing in any special relation to me, and as he could not disown me altogether, has accounted for it all by talking of a casual watering-place acquaintance; nay he has actually gone the length, of reviving the old suspicion of there being something between Kurt and myself; in a word, he has done his utmost to shake my credibility with the parents, and with Erna; and to make my interference, if I dared interfere, appear a ridiculous and hideous farce. You are the intimate friend of the parents; you are Erna's natural protector and guardian--you are more to her than her own father. The foolish dread of the mother, that you loved the dear child in a different way, I have absolutely put an end to; you will be met on all sides with the utmost confidence, and if any doubt still existed, if any objections were still raised, why, you are so clever, so wise, so eloquent, that you will with ease remove every objection, that you will with a sure hand bring all things to a good end, be the saviour of those two poor dear souls, and rescue them from the infernal torments of jealousy, doubt, and despair. I shall not be found wanting; I shall confirm everything that you say; I shall take the full responsibility of it all, of course. I am firmly resolved upon this; it is simply my duty, and I shall do it, and Waldor may put up with it or not, as he pleases."

Alexandra had been saying all this with hurried breath and heaving bosom. Bertram's own excitement was intense, too, but he managed to reply in calmer accents--

"You ask much, My Lady. You call me Erna's guardian, her second father. I accept these titles; now, will you please and try to fancy yourself in the position of a guardian, a father, under these circumstances. In the story of Claudine you have told me your own, striving, I do not doubt for a moment, to be strictly truthful, seeing no danger in this, when speaking to a stranger, and being, moreover, impelled to do so, both by your quick temperament and by your passionate sympathy. But now comes the question: Has your truthfulness really brought out the truth? Not the truth of yesterday and to-day, but of to-morrow. The truth, the truthful picture of the future, when you will be constantly and closely brought into contact with the former object of your ardent love, when you will be ever seeing him by the side of a woman who is not much younger than yourself, who is not as beautiful as you, not as clever as you; who, however graceful, lacks that nameless charm which is radiated by a beautiful and clever woman of the great world, and which is so apt to beguile the hearts of men; can you then--I am now speaking of yourself only, My Lady, only of what is in your power--can you, for your part, for your own heart, undertake the guarantee for the future? I conjure you, by all you hold sacred, can you conscientiously give the guardian, the father, this assurance?"

"By all I hold sacred," replied. Alexandra, "yes! And I will rather die than break my oath!"

She had stooped suddenly, and was about to draw Bertram's hand to her lips, but he prevented her with gentle force.

"We must not soften each other's hearts," said he, his own voice quivering with emotion, "must not dim the clearness of our vision by tears of emotion. I accept your vow. And now I crave but one boon from Fate, to wit, that I be permitted one look, one deep, searching look into the young man's heart,--and into Erna's heart!"

He had been murmuring the last words in a scarcely audible tone; his lips were trembling; Alexandra also was too much moved to be able to speak. Thus they had silently reascended the verandah-steps and moved on--unintentionally--to the open door which led to the card-room. Alexandra paused, uttering a slight exclamation.

"What is it, My Lady?"

She made no answer, but drew her arm swiftly out of his, and hurried away from him into the card-room. Bertram did not follow her; amazed and hurt that she could so suddenly leave him, attracted it would seem by the large oval table, around which there stood a fairly large group of gentlemen, either staking money themselves or watching the progress of the game which was evidently some game of chance, with Lotter acting as banker. Bertram anyhow saw that hated person sitting at the head of the table and dealing the cards, and next moment he heard that loud voice of his, which he disliked so much, exclaiming: "*Faites votre jeu, messieurs!*" Alexandra had advanced to the table as though she meant to join in the game, and Bertram turned away in grave displeasure. How could he have full confidence in a being, who was accustomed to obey every movement of a restless heart, every temptation of a light-winged fancy? No, no! If he was to resign, Erna's happiness must be anchored in firmer ground!

He leaned against the door of the hall in which the couples were taking their places for the Lancers. Erna and her partner were standing but a few yards off. She was conversing with him in her usual, measured way; he could watch every movement of those beloved lips, when she spoke or when, with a fleeting smile, she answered a jesting word of her partner's. Her face was partly turned in his direction; he thought every moment that she would turn round completely and look at him. I "felt that some one was looking at me," she had said on that memorable morning, when he found her writing beneath the plantain-tree. Now she did not feel it. What had broken the magic spell of his glance? Was it because his love was no longer unselfish? Because a fierce wild longing seized him to press the slender white-robed form in his arms, to cover the sweet lips with wild kisses? No, no--it was not that! It was this! her heart no longer knew anything of him. It was this: new and younger gods had moved inside the temple, and the old one's might now depart ingloriously and hide their disgrace in the darkness of night!

The music struck up, Erna held out her hand to her partner and floated across to the other side of the hall; and Bertram hurried away, down the verandah steps, away into the garden.

Then he wandered about aimlessly, muttering wild words, wringing his hands despairingly. The deserted garden, with the coloured lamps swinging in the night wind, some dead, some dying, seemed a fit image of his wasted and desolate life; whilst the strains of mirthful music wafted across to him in mighty volumes from the brightly illumined mansion-house, and the sounds of singing and rejoicing that came up to him from the village below, seemed to mock the solitary self-tormentor. He felt that this could not go on, if he did not wish to go mad; he asked himself, pressing his hands to his throbbing temples, whether he was not mad already? Whether he was not the ill-omened victim, pursued by the relentless furies of jealousy, pursued until he breaks down--and to be spared only by voluntary resignation? Yet you surely can but resign what you own, what--if need be--you could defend; the possession of which you could dispute anyhow with your adversary to the last gasp. Despair does not resign, it only lets go what can no longer be held. What had he done to hold Erna? What was he doing at this very moment, except again making room for a rival, for whom, as it was, the stars in their courses were fighting, one who had youth and the privilege of an earlier attachment on his side? No, he deserved to be conquered, he who neither had the strength to conquer himself, nor the courage to join issue with the rival. Let the decision come then!

CHAPTER XX

Bertram stood on the lowest step of the terrace when this decision struggled forth from his tempest-tossed soul, that could no longer bear the torment. A small steep stair led upward from this place, at the very extremity of the garden, without any landing-places; he hurried up, taking two and three steps at a time. He had reached the top; next he turned to the right, across the lawn, in the direction of the verandah, when suddenly the music was silent within the hall, and instantly the dancers came forth from the many doors to cool and refresh themselves in the balmy night air. He did not care to meet the merry, motley multitude. Here and there isolated couples were descending the stairs. He withdrew into the darkness of the shrubberies surrounding the winter garden. It was lighted up; and, as far as he could judge by a glance through the windows, was deserted; he would pass through it, and so regain, unseen and undisturbed, the rooms where the others were.

He entered. Between palm-trees and many broad-leaved plants there was a narrow passage, bisected in the centre by a shorter and broader one. Where the two passages met, towered a huge palm, set in a tub of mighty dimensions, and all but touching the glass-dome above. Behind, within the enclosure of the wall, was a small recess, furnished with dainty iron garden-chairs and with a table.

This, he knew, was a favourite spot of Erna's, where, on rainy days, she was wont to spend hours. He could not resist the temptation of visiting the spot which on her account was sacred to him. He sank into one of the chairs, put his folded hands to his head, and let it rest upon the little table. As he sat thus in the attitude of one praying, his thoughts became a prayer: and he prayed that Fate would now determine his lot, now and here, be it bliss or be it--death. He was willing to submit to either, in all humility, knowing himself subject to the heavenly powers that would deal with him by their own inscrutable will.

He lifted his head and rose slowly, hesitatingly, from his stooping, position. Was his prayer not heard? Could love not work a miracle, like faith, which was less strong? Surely, she would come, for whom he was longing with all the force of his heart!

And lo!--as he turned his gaze to the door, the velvet curtain which draped it was drawn aside, and she appeared on the threshold, a slender, white-robed figure, bending forward, gazing into the silent green wilderness before her, listening! And now she was descending the stairs with lightsome step, moving along the passage that led to the tall palm-trees, and again she paused, leaning one hand against the edge of the tub, pressing the other against her bosom.

"Erna!"

He had, for fear of frightening her, uttered her name in a very low voice; yet she started where she stood, but did not turn to him who was so near, but stooped, listening, towards the other side; and at the same moment he heard, the little door open, by which he had himself entered the winter garden; and now some one was hurrying along the passage, towards Erna, who made a movement as though she would escape, but could not.

"Miss Erna!"

She made no answer, and Lieutenant Ringberg seemed to have exhausted his strength and his presence of mind with these two words, which he had uttered in a very diffident tone of voice. For a few seconds they both stood motionless. Then Erna said--

"Fräulein von Aschhof has told me that you wished to speak to me. I only came to request you not to honour Fräulein von Aschhof any longer with your confidence. I--I am indignant that you could do so at all."

"By Heaven! there is some misunderstanding here. I should never have dared to apply to Fräulein von Aschhof. She began, and spoke so confidently that no doubt ever arose in me. I could not but believe that you--that yourself, Miss Erna...."

"This is too much!"

The breathless listener heard the rustling of her robe, and then some hurried words of entreaty which again chained her to the spot. Meanwhile they had somewhat changed their position; the dense foliage of some shrubs now intervened between himself and them, and he could now scarcely see anything of them, but he could hear every word even better than before.

"You must not let me suffer for a misunderstanding of which--I swear it--I am so innocent, that I cannot even guess how it has come about. But be this as it may, I bless it as a heavenly favour, for surely Heaven would not have me condemned unheard. I pray and entreat you: listen!"

"What have you to say?"

"What I wrote in my last letter. If you will not believe in my assurances--and indeed I can understand that, as things are, appearances are against me--give me time--only a little time, until these unfortunate circumstances have become clearer, and those appearances will dissolve themselves into nothing. Only this much I can, I must say, I am not in love with the Princess, and I never have been, I have never felt anything for her but sympathy, respect,--and friendship, if you will,--feelings which that rarely-gifted woman will awaken in all who come to know her intimately. She is here for no other purpose but to plead for me, to clear up this wretched mystery which condemns me to silence, at the sacrifice of considerable personal advantages to herself. But she has met with resistance which she cannot overcome, and which compels her, and compels me also, to remain in this miserably odd position. Therefore, once more, give me time--give me a respite. A criminal gets that, and I am free from guilt, unless it be a crime that I look upon those duties which gratitude and the friendship of years impose upon me as sacred, even now, when it is so unspeakably hard for me, and when it puts me to the risk of forfeiting the happiness of my life!"

"Is this all you have to say to me?"

"All; for what else. I might say would find no credence, if your faith in my veracity does not go even this length."

"Good-bye."

"Erna! is it possible? Is every voice silent in your heart? Does nothing stir, nothing plead for one whom once you--I dare not say the word any longer, for I must fear to offend you again if I remind you of what once was? Great heavens! and I had thought, that if my pen were powerless, and my pleading on paper appeared clumsy and lifeless, I should but require to be once more face to face with you, looking into your loved eyes whilst you looked into mine, and that then you would believe me even before I uttered a word. And now, now, my glance is powerless, my words are mere sound. I no longer know what to say; I am standing here like a beggar who has been telling his story of bitter woe, and in whose face people close the door at which he has knocked with trembling hand. Have I become so poor? Well, I am most unwilling to appeal to a friend for help, but you leave me no choice. There is, living in your own circle, a gentleman who is in the secret, to whom the Princess has told it, half involuntarily; drawn on by the vivacity of her temperament, which she has never learned to control, half voluntarily, hoping that she was not betraying anything which all, or at least all concerned, would not know to-day. Well, this hope of hers has not been fulfilled. The gentleman in question knows it; and not deeming himself, under the circumstances, justified in speaking, he will, if I judge him correctly, be silent, although the Princess has already given him full liberty, nay, has entreated him to tell you all. I must confess, I was much taken aback when, a little time ago, she came and told me this; apart from other considerations, it was painful to me to know that the key to the fatal enigma was in the hands of a third person. But now, when, to my sorrow, I realise my impotence, let him plead for me, if he will. He will do it, if I, too, entreat him. I have barely exchanged three words with him, but looks like his, so imbued with the true nobility of the soul, cannot lie. Ask him--you will believe him!"

"Never!"

"You will not believe him?"

"I will die rather than hear from him, speak to him of ... It is a shame, a shame! This is going too far. What happened before was ... but this, this ..."

"How now? By the heavens above us, what is the meaning of this?"

"The meaning is this: my last word to you is, Begone!"

"I go. But one thing more, and let it be my last word. It is very bitter to have to say it. There is one greater misfortune yet than to see one's love misjudged, scorned, rejected, and that is, to have to say to one's self that she whom one had loved more,--a thousand times more than one's self,--is surpassed by other women, whom one had never dared to put on the same level as her, had barely dared to compare with her, in kindness and in generosity."

There was a quick step passing away over the tiled passage, then the sound of the little garden-door being opened and closed, and then a cry of anguish, half suppressed, and all the more terrible on that account, the cry of one who had met with a deadly hurt.

Bertram hurried round the intervening shrubs to where Erna stood with her arms raised on high, with wild staring eyes.

And then she gave another cry, and the next moment she lay in his arms, clutching him, clinging to him, as a drowning man would clutch, would cling to, a rock.

"Uncle Bertram! dear, dear Uncle Bertram!"

"My sweet child!"

"Save me! save me!!"

A great gush of tears relieved her. She was now sobbing aloud, bending over his shoulder. Thus had come to pass that for which, but a brief time before, he had longed as the greatest bliss; a bliss he would fain taste for a moment, and for which he would willingly die, after having tasted it. He held her close to his heart, held the slender maiden's frame, the tender, heaving bosom; her sweet breath was floating around his heated cheek, and he knew she was his, was in his keeping; he had the power to hold her now, and it would cost him but one word. And yet it was all a dream-gift, which one may retain for a second or two by keeping one's eyes closed, but which fades away, to return no more, as soon as the eyes re-open.

"Yes, I will save you, save you from yourself; you have lost yourself, and I will restore you."

She lifted her head and looked at him, confused, questioning.

"Not to-day, my sweet child, to-morrow; but you must be a good and obedient girl."

"I will do all that you wish, that you command, dear one, beloved one! For there is none as good, as noble as you, not one, and I love no one as I love you!"

Again she clasped him, more violently even than before, and pressed her hot, quivering lips, to his.

But he did not return her kiss, and a gentle, melancholy smile played about his mouth as he said, putting her gently from him, and stroking her dark hair--

"And never did father love his dearest child better than I love you."

And again she gazed up to him with a strange expression of fear and shame.

"Now go, my child; to-morrow we will talk together. I shall not leave to-morrow. I shall not go until you need me no longer. Good-bye till then. And then your dear eyes are to weep no more."

She clung to him still, but hesitatingly, shyly now; he disengaged himself gently, and repeated--

"Go, my child, go."

She went, slowly, reluctantly, holding her head very low. On the topmost step, in the doorway leading to the tea-room, she paused and turned, as though expecting that he would summon her back.

But he beckoned with eye and hand: "Go!"

She vanished behind the velvet curtain. He was alone!

CHAPTER XXI

The mirth and fun of the feast were at their height now. The commander-in-chief had ordered that at twelve o'clock all officers should be in their respective quarters, including those who had been told off to the houses of the ranger, the mayor, and the other chief denizens of the village. It was past eleven o'clock already. No time was to be lost, if the guests wished to drain the cup of delight which the hospitable mansion-house proffered in such abundance.

"Vivat Champagne!" exclaimed one of the young officers, taking a glass of the foaming wine from the salver which a footman offered him.

"And pretty girls!" returned his friend von Köppingen, emptying his goblet at one draught, replacing it on the salver, and turning upon his heel to hurry to the fair Augusta, with whom he was engaged to dance the *Rheinländer*, the music of which the orchestra was just playing.

"And where have you been, Ringberg?" asked another comrade, Herr von Rollintz; "been gambling a little?"

"You know I never play," replied Kurt, who was leaning against the door.

"Nor dance? Well, well, you are always so sensible; I feel half dead already, upon my honour! And yet I have to dance this *Rheinländer* with the belle of the ball. I am looking for her everywhere; have you seen her, perchance? Ah, there she is!"

Von Rollintz flew right across the room to meet Erna, who was just entering from the tea-room. A minute later the pair whirled past Kurt; von Rollintz, with radiant and glowing face, chattering even during the dance, Erna still and pale, the long dark eyelashes lowered.

Kurt gazed gloomily after them; then he turned away and began pacing the verandah. After a little while he saw, at the end opposite to him, a gentleman ascending the steps, in whom, as soon as the bright light fell upon him, he recognised Bertram. The young man advanced rapidly two or three steps, then paused hesitatingly.

"Why, after all!" he murmured, "everything now would be in vain."

Bertram, who had gone up to one of the windows of the ball-room, was now slowly coming along the verandah. It was painful to Kurt to meet the man to whom, but a minute ago, he had been willing to apply for help. So, happening to be just in front of the card-room, he slipped in.

"He avoids me," said Bertram to himself. "In that case the mountain will indeed have to go to Mahomet!"

As he was about to look for Kurt in the card-room, he saw, on his way past the open doors of the ball room, Lydia in conversation with one of the older officers, a conversation carried on by Lydia with her customary abundance of gesture and the frequent use of her fan. He drew nearer, and, as he had hoped, her ever-roving glance had soon lighted upon him. A slight movement of his eyes was sufficient for the highly experienced lady, who left the Major with a jesting word, and tripped up to Bertram.

"You have something to tell me, dear friend?"

"Can you spare me one minute?"

"One minute? For you?"

She gave a sentimental glance at Bertram and started.

"Merciful Heaven!" she exclaimed, "you are ill. You wish the doctor sent for; but there is one here, nay, there are two,--pray let me...."

"Pray remain here," said Bertram, seizing her by the hand as she was hastening away. "It is true that I feel rather worn out--a consequence of the unrest and noise to which I am not accustomed--but otherwise perfectly well. Let us sit down there!"

He pointed, to a couch near, and sat down; Lydia followed him with trembling knees, shaking all over, feeling her heart rising to her throat. The whole unusual approach of Bertram who was generally so reserved, his pallor, his solemn manner--all this could have but one reason, one meaning--and what was she to reply? Act surprise and terror, of course! But not too long, just a few moments of half fainting, with her head leaning back against the wall and her eyes turned rapturously towards the chandelier.

"My dear friend--for I must appeal to your friendship--to your love...."

"Good Heavens!" murmured Lydia.

"To the love which you doubtless cherish for Erna, and which has, I assume, misled you to this last extremely equivocal step of yours."

"Good Heavens!" murmured Lydia again, but this time with accents of the greatest terror, as of some one who suddenly feels the ground beneath him giving way.

"I will not reproach you," continued Bertram, "which indeed I have no right to do. I was wrong myself in not taking you into my confidence in reference to Erna, in wrapping myself in secrecy and silence, and thus all but compelling you to act alone and independently in order to help our dear child to what, let us trust, will prove her lasting happiness. But the remedy which you applied came too soon and was too strong; it has not had the desired effect, at least not in the meantime; indeed, at present things look desperately bad. Do not ask me how I have learned this, I may tell you later on, when perhaps you will tell me, too, how you discovered the secret which both guarded so carefully. All this does not matter just now; but one thing is of the greatest importance, and this I heartily beg you will grant me. We must henceforth act in common, take no one into our confidence of whom we cannot be sure that he aims at the same thing as we do--namely, at Erna's happiness. And I think you will do best if you leave me to judge when this is the case. Are you agreed?"

Poor Lydia was sadly embarrassed. For her terrible disappointment it was some compensation that Bertram himself had evidently no matrimonial intentions with reference to Erna, and that he was offering Lydia his alliance and friendship. How gladly would she have agreed! How gladly said yes to everything, averring that she would blindly obey his behests. But alas, in addition to her first indiscretion which he had so kindly pardoned, she had meanwhile committed another which he would scarcely pardon.

"It is too late, I see," said Bertram, who had not failed to notice the terribly anxious expression of her mobile countenance. "You have already told Hildegard."

"No, no--not Hildegard--worse! far worse!" murmured Lydia, wringing her hands and casting down her eyes. "In my anxiety, my--ye Heavens! I cannot excuse myself on any other ground--in my tender anxiety, for you ... the Baron ... you ..."

"Pray speak distinctly," said Bertram, repressing his anger. "I must know all. The Baron ..."

"He was so angry with you ever since that miserable letter--no, I cannot tell you that; I am too much ashamed of myself--but Erna has already pardoned me, and so will you. We had all lost our heads. He asserted that you alone were to blame for his failure with Erna. And that Otto had not given him the money--a great big sum--three thousand thalers--was your doing too, he said. This morning already, before he drove away, he vowed in my presence that he would inflict a terrible vengeance upon you; and at dinner, when he sat next to me, he talked dreadfully, and drank ever so much champagne--and I knew--I thought I knew--I saw that Erna and Ringberg--Erna had denied him altogether; and the girls--Augusta, you know, and Louise--told me that Ringberg used constantly to meet her at their house ...! Erna was so excited when the regiment came, and ..."

"Go on!" cried Bertram.

"And now the Baron wanted to make you suffer for it. And I really could not tolerate it, seeing that perhaps I had contributed to the Baron's wrath against you."

"And so you told the Baron all?"

Lydia was sitting with rigid, tearful eyes, and started in terror as Bertram quickly rose.

"What would you do?"

"Try if I can repair the mischief a little."

"Let me go, I entreat you! and I will tell the Baron ..."

"And I wish you to tell him nothing. I wish you to remain where you are, and to appear as unconcerned as possible to all, specially to Erna, if she should come to you, which, however, I doubt; and mind that you do not betray one word of what we have been discussing here. Will you promise that?"

"I promise everything you wish."

"I shall not be ungrateful."

Lydia gazed after him with tears in her eyes as he hurried away. "I shall not be ungrateful," he had said; and saying that, he had pressed her hand--for the first time since they had met--and supposing, supposing that it came to pass after all!

Major von Keberstein approached her again, and said laughingly-- "You seem to have had quite a long confidential conversation with the gentleman who carried you off so abruptly from my side. And then a poor old bachelor like me is not to get jealous!"

"I will do my best now to make up for it."

"It will take you all your time, we shall have to tramp back to our quarters in ten minutes."

"Can you not throw in half an hour?"

"Not for worlds!" exclaimed the major, replacing his watch which he had been consulting. "My orders are very strict."

"Then I must claim the ten minutes at least," she rejoined, gathering her robe together and making way for the stout old gentleman by her side on the couch.

In the adjoining card-room, too, the guests were bent upon making the most of the last few minutes by doubling and trebling their high stakes. All the players now were civilians, chiefly neighbouring proprietors, who could afford to lose a few hundreds. Some of the officers had at first joined in the game, but only at first, and with very small stakes, as if to show that, so far as they were concerned, the whole thing was a little harmless social amusement--nothing more. When heavier sums began to be staked, they had at once ceased playing, and had gradually melted away. The *Oberförster*, or ranger, who was only looking on, thought that this had been done in obedience to a signal from the Colonel himself, who had passed through the card-room on his way out.

"All the better," the Baron had sneered; "then we shall remain snugly among ourselves. *Faites votre jeu, Messieurs!*"

And indeed the Baron, so the gentlemen present thought, had good reason to find his position a snug one. He was winning almost without interruption. The heap of bank-notes and gold coins by his side was ever increasing; among the bank-notes were already a good few slips, on which the players had written their names and the amount of their stakes; his gains were said to be several thousands. He asserted that it was nothing like that sum, and repeatedly offered to let some one else take the bank; but no one cared to accept his offer; and thus the losers had no right to grumble, although for some time now they had been, as one of them said, hurrying in pursuit of their own money. They had need to hurry if they would overtake the money which was ever fleeting. The Baron's proposal that the game should cease punctually at half-past eleven, the time fixed for the conclusion of the ball, had been agreed to, and it was now almost a quarter past. The Baron saw already, from the large stakes which the players were venturing, that, as the cards were more than ever in his favour, his gains would be doubled; his jubilant mirth proved the excitement he was labouring under; he had some funny word for every card he dealt, every deal he scored, and all the while his eyes were glowing, and his busy hands were twitching nervously. Suddenly there was a change. One of the players had staked a sum equivalent to the total of his losses during the evening--and had won! This daring play, and the success which had crowned it, stimulated the others; and now everything went against the banker. In a few minutes his heap had dwindled down to less than half, and it became evident that if, during the remaining quarter of an hour, the bank were pursued by the same bad luck, it must needs end with a considerable balance the wrong way. The jests of the Baron became more and more bitter; presently he took to whistling savagely through his closed teeth, interspersing this with muttered curses; his eyes, now roving restlessly around the room, seemed repeatedly to be fixing themselves upon same one within the room. Suddenly he stopped in the middle of a deal, and exclaimed, with a semi-audible curse-- "You are bringing me bad luck, sir! You are in my way, sir!"

These words, which he had uttered in the most violent way, were accompanied by a fierce look at Kurt, who, to avoid meeting Bertram, had entered the room a few minutes ago, and had since been standing with folded arms among the spectators, who, attracted and enchained by the sight of the maddening game, had, in ever-increasing numbers, grouped themselves around the board of green cloth. The scene had not had any attraction for him; his mind was far away; he had stared mechanically before him without seeing anything; nor had he heard the Baron's words; he only felt it disagreeable that several gentlemen near him were looking hard at him. One of them thought it incumbent upon himself to whisper to Kurt that the Baron had meant his remarks for him. Kurt, under the impression that Lotter had been asking him to join in the game, and not wishing to say it aloud, replied in a courteous whisper to the gentleman who had called his attention to the fact that the Baron had meant his remarks for him--

"I am sorry, but I never play."

He accompanied this by an apologetic shrug of the shoulders towards the Baron, and turned upon his heel. As soon as he was free of the crowd surging around him, he made for the door leading to the verandah, hoping that there he would be left to himself and to his own sad thoughts.

The Baron burst into a hoarse, mocking laughter when he saw Kurt turn; he went on dealing, with trembling hands, then jumped suddenly to his feet, exclaiming--

"Excuse me, but I must ask the gentleman, what he means by shrugging his shoulders."

He flung the remaining cards upon the table, and was rushing towards the door through the crowd of amazed and excited spectators, whom he pushed rudely aside if they did not make way quickly enough. Before he reached the door, however, Bertram faced him, barring the way.

"What do you want?" the Baron hissed through his teeth.

"I want to call your attention to the fact that you are the guest of this house, and that you are on the point of basely violating its proffered hospitality."

Bertram had spoken firmly, but in so low a voice that the Baron alone could hear him. His look, too, was perfectly calm; even those next to him, who saw but his face, whilst the Baron was turning his broad back upon them, could not but think that it was simply some indifferent communication.

The Baron was speechless with wrath. Bertram gave him no time to break out. He continued in the same low, incisive tone--

"I see that you quite understand me. I need scarcely add that I am at any time at your service, should you consider yourself in need of a comment upon the lesson which I have given you."

"You shall hear from me, and forthwith!"

"The sooner the better!"

He bowed slightly; then, raising his voice as he turned to the others, he said--

"A thousand pardons, gentlemen; but I was commissioned by our amiable host to remind you that his military-guests have, alas! to retire already; and that they will be wishing to bid you farewell."

As if in confirmation of Bertram's words, the music just then broke off in the adjoining ball-room, the door flew open, and quite a host of officers came rushing in. There could no longer be any question of resuming the game, even if the players had been willing, which they, however, certainly seemed not to be. Some of the older ladies had come in, looking for their husbands; some others, young ones, followed; the room was overflowing with guests; the players had difficulty in getting back to the table to pocket their stakes. Not a few of them had yet to square accounts with the Baron; they crowded round him, but he was shoving the remnant of his gains--gold coins, bank-notes, I.O.U.s--higgledy-piggledy into his pockets, and when questioned, as he constantly was, replied with surly mien and in briefest words, and repelled rather than answered their questions--muttering that they might apply to-morrow; and that, in this confusion to-night, the devil himself could neither hear nor impart information.

Bertram had eagerly watched, this scene, keeping close to the door which led to the verandah. He made sure that the Baron's time was meanwhile absolutely taken up, and that he would, not be able to think of following Kurt and inventing some new reason for a quarrel, since the first attempt had failed. Under any circumstances, the Baron would have to settle with him first; and then he saw how, breaking away from the players who were still surrounding him, the Baron hurried up to meet Herr von Busche, who, looking very heated and flushed, was just coming from the ball-room. The two gentlemen Bertram knew to be, as shooting companions, on good, though not on specially friendly terms; anyhow, there could be no doubt as to the subject of their present discussion in yonder far-away corner, where the Baron was gesticulating, while Herr von Busche, the young gentleman from the Woods and Forests' Office, listened intently, now and again shaking his head, and at last nodding it, more, it seemed, in courtesy than in assent. Then Bertram remembered that it was time for him also to look out for a second.

Looking for Ringberg, he saw him on the verandah, which now was filled by the guests, among a small group of officers, already with helmets and overcoats on, who were bidding him good-bye. These departing heroes had their quarters in the village; they were in a mighty hurry; a couple of servants were in readiness with lanterns to light up the shorter way to the village, down the terraces; fair Hildegard had, indeed, been mindful of everything needed. As the other officers were hastening down the steps, Bertram stepped up to Kurt.

"Can you spare me a minute, Lieutenant Ringberg?"

Kurt was evidently very much surprised, but he at once bowed his assent.

"To be sure, a minute will not suffice, if, as I hope, you will grant my request."

The young man's bronzed cheeks assumed a yet deeper hue, as he said--

"Pray, speak; and be assured beforehand that it will be a pleasure and an honour to me to be of use to you in any way."

"Then have the kindness to give me your arm and to accompany me into the garden, that I may tell you uninterruptedly what is the matter. Well, it is briefly this: Baron Lotter--I do not know whether you have had the doubtful pleasure of making his acquaintance--a friend of our host's, by the way, with whom he and I have been staying here for the past week,-- thinks himself insulted by me, and, according to the usual code and my own conviction, he has good cause for it. It is an old feud resulting from a certain mutual rivalry as to the respective consideration and influence which he and I claim, or think we may claim, in this house, an old feud about to be ultimately settled. The actual occasion of the quarrel is merely accidental, and, as such, absolutely irrelevant. I mention this particularly to enable me to add the request that in the subsequent negotiations, supposing that you are willing--well, very well, then, and I am really obliged to you--that in these negotiations you may lay absolutely no stress upon that occasion, nay, that you may avoid touching upon it at all. You will please accept the conditions for the hostile meeting exactly as they may be proposed by the other side; I have my own reasons for wishing to be particularly obliging in that respect. Only the fixing of time and place troubles me. Here of course the duel cannot take place. I should therefore propose some spot near town. This would suit me all the better, as I have, anyhow, announced my intention of leaving this place to-morrow, and could, therefore, remain in town for a short while without attention being called to it; and as the Baron also was to leave to-morrow too, and as he also must pass through town, the delay will be very brief for him. The only question now is: Whether and when do you think you can be free yourself?"

"In no case," replied Kurt, "before to-morrow afternoon, but then for certain, because, if circumstances were less favourable, I could then get leave of absence from the Colonel--without, of course, mentioning the special reason why I needed it. Circumstances are, however, favourable, and, if our suppositions are at all correct, and if the big sham-fight is once over, the regiment will, sometime to-morrow afternoon, be somewhere between this and town, and may even have to bivouack there. Under any circumstances, I shall be able to attend punctually at the time required.

"This," said Bertram, "will do excellently. So we are now free from this trouble; and this, I think, is all that we need settle in the meantime. Now it may be as well if I put you in communication with Herr von Busche. I have no doubt that he is to be the Baron's second. If required, a question from you, as to whether he chanced to have a commission, a message, for me, would at once settle things."

They had meanwhile come again near the verandah, and just then Herr von Busche was coming out of the card-room, looking round apparently in search of some one. Bertram and Kurt hurried their advancing steps, and he again turned swiftly round, to speak to Bertram, the moment he had recognised him, saying--

"I am so glad, Herr Doctor, to have met you at last, since I was about to do myself the honour of bringing you a message of some importance. I have already been looking, and looking in vain for you, in all the rooms."

"A thousand pardons," replied Bertram; "but I, myself, have not in the meantime been idle in this affair. May I now have the pleasure of introducing to you the Premier-Lieutenant Ringberg, who ..."

"I have already had the honour," said Herr von Busche with a bow.

"All the better. Then I will no longer disturb you, gentlemen. You will find me in my rooms. Good-bye till then."

He shook hands with Kurt, bowed to Herr von Busche, and left them both, as they retreated into the semi-obscurity of the shrubbery, until, passing along the verandah and the side building, he reached a postern, from which a stair led, straight from the garden, to his rooms.

CHAPTER XXII

Even on this stirring evening Konski had not been oblivious of his duty. He knew from experience that his master was wont to retire from festivities before their actual close, and thus Bertram, on entering his rooms, found his candles duly lighted, and all preparations made for the night. He praised his faithful servant for his careful attention, but told him he was not in a hurry to go to bed, as he was expecting a visit from Lieutenant Ringberg, and that Konski might hurry back to his sweetheart, as no doubt he would like.

This he said in his wonted playful tone, to Konski's intense delight, for the servant gathered from this that his fear, lest his master should again be the worse for all the noise and excitement of the big entertainment, had been uncalled-for. He even ventured upon a remark on the subject.

"I am astonished myself," Bertram said in reply. "I think you must be right; we both had put ourselves down too soon as old fogies."

Bertram smiled as he spoke, and Konski thought that his hint had fallen upon fruitful soil, and that his own favourite wish would, after all, be fulfilled. Perhaps his Aurora might know some details. To be sure, My Lady had given strict orders that within ten minutes after the departure of the last carriage no soul was to stir about the mansion-house, lest any of the officers billeted there should be disturbed in their brief slumbers. But Aurora would surely find out some place where they could quietly converse.

So the faithful servant left Bertram, and instantly the master's serene mien changed, and assumed a look of great anxiety. He listened: perhaps his expected visitor was even now crossing the servant's path. No; the noise died away in the corridor and on the stair. Konski had vanished somewhere in the court-yard, and all now was silent. Bertram began to pace softly up and down his room, then paused again, listening. What if Kurt were to learn that the duel was to be fought for his sake? In that case, the chances were everything to nothing that he would insist upon precedence, and would himself challenge the Baron. Bertram, anyhow, had some scruples as to whether he should not have told the young man the true state of affairs, because he had now exposed Kurt to the possibility of one or other of the witnesses of the scene in the card-room misinterpreting Kurt's action, and asserting that he had simply been unwilling to understand Lotter's insulting remarks; and this would, of course, according to the military code of honour, have been identical with a reproach of downright cowardice.

But, then, it might be hoped that in the wild confusion and frantic excitement of the moment, no one had been at leisure to observe the little incident minutely enough to be able to give a clear account of it either to himself or to any one else. On such occasions a dispute or wrangle was by no means of rare occurrence, and none of the spectators had looked as though they were in the habit of attaching much importance to such scenes; and it certainly would be foreign to the good, easy-going Thuringians to have done so. Fortunately, not one of Kurt's fellow-officers had been present at the time; and even Herr von Busche, the young gentleman from the Woods and Forests, had only come in at the last moment. The question was simply whether the Baron would subsequently try to pick a quarrel with Kurt, seeing his first attempt had clearly failed through no fault of Kurt's; and now, of course, the Baron would have a capital chance of doing so. The pity of it, thought Bertram; why had he blindly followed that inner voice which bade him choose Kurt for his second? Why? It had been Bertram's only chance of getting one deep, searching look into the young man's heart? But was not the fulfilment of his ardent prayer purchased all too dear, if it led the way to the very thing which he was desirous of preventing at the sacrifice of his own life?

And yet, he said to himself, he need not quite despair. Lotter, to be sure, now knew who was his real rival. And the desire to wreak his vengeance upon that rival, to annihilate him, if possible, was very sure to become overpowering in the heart of a hot-blooded, terribly angered, absolutely unscrupulous man, one never at a loss, and one passionately in love with Erna. But was this really the case? No, and again, no! That man never had loved Erna. His whole suit had, from beginning to end, been nothing but a vulgar speculation upon Erna's presumably colossal fortune, by means of which he hoped to free himself from disagreeable temporary embarrassments, and to continue his good-for-nothing life of self-indulgent ease. Even before Kurt had appeared upon the scene, those dreams of a brilliant future had become greatly obscured; he had, it was clear, been virtually dropped; and he was surely quick enough to have found out speedily to whom he was indebted for this fate. His savage utterances to Lydia were sufficient proof that he knew quite well who, from the very beginning, had stood between Erna and him, who afterwards had delayed the decision, prevented any further approach, roused the distrust of the parents, turned the daughter's thoughts away, and ultimately had done the very worst for him. If there was any one who had deserved the Baron's wrath and hatred, on whom his vengeance was certain to fall, surely it was himself. Why pick a quarrel with any one else as well? The Baron was no coward, far from it; yet, being a perfect shot, he would have it all his own way with an opponent like Bertram, who had hardly ever hit the target when they practised together. Why then should the Baron not play a trump card when lie had one in his hands?

Thus cudgelling his brain, carefully weighing every reason for and against it, Bertram kept viewing his position, and all the while the weary moments seemed to creep slowly, slowly by, and each succeeding one weighed more and more heavily upon his soul. And yet, would he not perchance learn all too soon, that his bold attempt to take the place of Erna's lover, and thus to guard their new-born happiness, which was already so much endangered, against a new and most serious peril, had failed, and that he himself had missed this most excellent opportunity of dying? He was doomed to go on living this life of his, which had lost its savour and had no longer any meaning for him! Half an hour had already gone by; they might have finished their consultation long ere this, for there was little enough to consult about--unless it was the other duel!

In the court-yard, whence the noise of the departing carriages and divers shouts had been ascending, silence began to prevail. Bertram could master his impatience no longer; he stepped across the corridor and went to one of the windows looking out upon the court-yard which the expected lieutenant would have to cross. Presently he heard a swift, elastic step upon the stairs; he hastened to meet his hurrying visitor, and cried, holding out his hand to him--

"Is everything settled?"

"Everything."

"Thank Heaven!" Bertram had all but said; he just managed to change it into a polite, "Thank, you so much!"

He kept Kurt's hand in his own as he led him into his room. He made him sit upon the sofa, and seated himself by his side. Kurt thought that one could not welcome a dear friend, the bringer of the most pleasant news, with greater warmth and delight. This feeling was still more strengthened when his singular host presently sprang up again, and fetched from his stock of provisions for the journey a bottle of wine, which he proceeded to uncork; next he brought some glasses, and even a small box of cigars. Although no smoker himself, he said, he always had some cigars by him for his friends.

He filled the glasses, and held out his own to Kurt.

"May everything turn out as we wish!"

"With all my heart!" replied the young officer.

Kurt said these words with a deep, almost melancholy gravity; which contrasted strangely with the gladsome excitement of the older man; Kurt's lips barely touched the wine, whilst Bertram drained his glass hurriedly, greedily, and instantly refilled it.

"I have fasted almost all day," he said, as if by way of excuse. "A festive entertainment always puts me out and takes away my appetite. But now, please, tell me--do they agree to everything?"

Kurt reported with military brevity and precision. The only difficulty had been to fix the time, as the Baron had at first asserted that he could not delay his departure beyond noon on the following day at the latest; ultimately, however, he had agreed to the meeting coming off at six o'clock in the afternoon. The place was to be a certain spot in the great forest, almost exactly midway between Rinstedt and the town, by the banks of a little lake. It would be easy to move thence to a still more remote portion of the wood, in case the manœuvres should have brought any one to the neighbourhood, which, in its normal state, is absolutely deserted.

"I remember the place exactly from former walks," Bertram said.

"Capital," replied the young man, "for that removes another difficulty--namely, how you were to find your way to it from the town. The spot suits me singularly well, because we shall probably bivouac not a mile from it. I forgot to mention that I have already secured the services of our very skilful staff-surgeon, and that Herr von Busche will provide a carriage. Lastly, for the sake of keeping the whole affair secret, it seemed desirable that the Herr Baron should not go straight from here to the meeting. So, under pretext of wishing to make to-morrow an excursion to the scene of the manœuvres in company with Herr von Busche, of returning here at night, and leaving definitely on the day following, he has sent word asking his host and hostess to excuse him until to-morrow evening, and even now he is driving with Herr von Busche to the ranger's house, where he is to pass the night."

"Excellent! excellent!" exclaimed Bertram. "Everything is arranged most thoughtfully and carefully. I thank you very much. Herr von Busche appears to have been perfectly willing to facilitate all arrangements?"

"He was charming," replied Kurt; "nay, more, he told me quite openly that he was doing the Herr Baron this service most reluctantly, very much against his own will indeed, and only in deference to the traditional courtesy in such matters, and that he would give a good deal, if it lay in his power to settle the whole affair amicably. I confess I fully sympathise with him in the last point. It was a most painful thought for us both that a man like you should risk his life against a Baron Lotter, who, it seems, does not enjoy any one's special sympathy; and all the chances are against you, too."

"Why all the chances?"

"Herr von Busche said that your opponent was one of the best pistol-shots that he knew, unerring of aim, and steady of eye and hand. Herr von Busche, of course, has never seen you practise, but he fears, and so do I, that ..."

"That I am a miserable shot?" exclaimed Bertram smilingly. "Out with it! Yes, yes, you gentlemen have little confidence in us bookworms for this sort of thing. But fortunately you are mistaken. I am more or less out of practice, I admit; but I can shoot a little, and at such a short distance too!"

"I am delighted to hear you say so," replied Kurt. "And yet I would like to ask you if there is no possibility of bringing about an amicable settlement. It is not by any means too late yet. Herr von Busche quite agrees with me in this. Only, as we are both absolutely ignorant of the real cause ..."

"But I have already told you that an old feud is about to be settled," Bertram interrupted him somewhat impatiently. "The momentary cause--by the way, a small lesson in good manners which I gave the Baron--is of no consequence at all."

"So Herr von Busche, too, had been told by his client, and we agreed to accept this as sufficient, considering that a man like you would not act in such an affair except with due deliberation, and that we younger men must respect your motives, even if we regret that they are not communicated to us."

"I thank you both all the more for the sacrifice which you are making for me," exclaimed Bertram, holding out his hand to Kurt.

"Then I will say good-bye; you will be in need of rest."

Kurt had risen; Bertram retained him.

"Stay a little longer," he said, "if you are not too tired. I am not fatigued at all. To-morrow's meeting is not weighing upon my mind in the slightest; nay, more, I am as sure of my good fortune as ever Cæsar was of his; and I hope, confidently, that we two shall meet many a time again in the land of the living. Yet one should not claim from the future what the present offers, and therefore let me, at this present moment, touch upon a matter which concerns you very specially, and which I have, Heaven knows, much more at heart than this wretched business over which we have already wasted far too much precious time."

A deep blush burned upon the young officer's cheeks; his dark eyes now evaded the bright light of those great blue orbs, whose extraordinary brilliancy and beauty he had already repeatedly admired in the course of their previous conversation.

"You know what I wish to speak about?" Bertram asked next; and again the young man was struck by the complete harmony of the ring of that voice and of the radiance of those eyes.

"I think I do," he replied, almost in a whisper.

"Then you will know, too, the sort of relation in which I stand to Erna?"

Kurt still dared not look up. He nodded his assent.

"But you cannot know," continued Bertram, "how very intimate this relation is--so much so, that I cannot find quite an appropriate name for it. I should say that of a father towards a most beloved child, if there did not mingle with my feelings for her a touch which--perhaps you will understand me--I would call chivalrous tenderness. This touch may perhaps occur in other cases too, I mean between a real father and daughter--I am sorry to say I never had a daughter of my own--and I only mention this element, because it helps me to understand why Erna, who otherwise confides in me unconditionally, has kept her love a secret from me. Perhaps it was solely an outcome of the long interval of time during which we had not met; in such cases a kind of estrangement is apt to occur, which, to be sure, once overcome, is wont to be followed by a greater cordiality. But above all, the poor darling deemed herself rejected, betrayed. Her happiness she would gladly have let her paternal friend share; unhappiness always seals the lips of the proud; and yet I know that more than once the secret was trembling upon those sweet lips of hers, and that had she overcome her shy shrinking, she would have spared herself--and spared you, my friend--much suffering; and the palms in the winter garden would, an hour ago, have waved their magnificent heads above two happy, blissful souls, and not above two young fools who, from sheer love, were tearing each other's hearts to pieces!"

Kurt gave a quick quiver, and all but jumped from the sofa; but Bertram's eyes shone forth in glorious radiance, and a smile of infinite tenderness played about his mouth. A strange thrill passed through the young man's heart, as though he were in the presence of something unapproachably lofty, something which imperatively demanded humble submission and confiding obedience. So he lowered his eyes, which had flashed indignantly for a moment, and said, scarcely above his breath--

"I thank Heaven that He led you to that spot."

"And I," replied Bertram, taking both the young man's hands and pressing them heartily, "I thank you for that word which sets me free from all restraint, and takes away the last remnant of shrinking shyness. Who, indeed, would not shrink, feel awe-struck, when it comes to touching those tender threads that spin themselves from heart to heart, until, God willing, they become united in a woof so strong that death itself cannot rend, it? What God joins, let no man put asunder; what God puts asunder, let no man try to join! What has come between you two is sheer misunderstanding, provoked by extraordinary circumstances, which would have puzzled even older and more experienced people, and in which you young, passionate, inconsiderate folk knew not what to do. And being so thoughtless and helpless, you have assuredly committed mistakes, mistakes on either side, and the demon of pride--'by that sin fell the angels'--will have gloated over it all. Not to enable me to register and chronicle your mutual faults, but only in order that, being taught by the past, we may look the future more clearly in the face, just tell me how it all came about? When did you make Erna's acquaintance? Was it not in her aunt's house in Erfurt?"

"Yes," replied Kurt; "and to know her and love her was one and the same thing; nay, I may say, without the slightest exaggeration, that she was one 'whom to look at was to love.' One evening, I saw her at a party. I had been visiting at the house for some time, and I think I was rather fond of Augusta von Palm, who is staying here now, and with dear Agatha I was on terms of heartiest friendship; but Agatha; wishing to give me a surprise, had not told me of Erna's visit. So I saw her quite unexpectedly among the other young ladies. It would be quite bootless for me to try and describe what went on in my heart. So, I thought afterwards, the men must have felt of whom the Bible tells us that they were held worthy of beholding some divine apparition. My breath failed me; all the others present seemed to vanish from my sight; I saw only her, or, properly speaking, not her, only her eyes. It seemed like a double stream of unearthly, transcendent light; and again it was a stream which bore me resistlessly onward and upward into realms of bliss, whereof but an hour before I had known nought, divined nought, and which yet were, I felt clearly, my true home, to which I was soon returning after much aimless wandering in far off regions."

The young man's voice quivered. He drained the glass which, before, his lips had scarcely touched. Bertram filled it afresh. Kurt never saw how his hand shook as he poured out the wine, nor observed how curiously veiled the voice was in which Bertram, breaking the pause, said--

"Strange, or perhaps less strange than highly gratifying, that at least for once I find, this kindling effect of Love's divine flash confirmed in reality, of which the poets of all times and in all climes have sung in praise. I am almost ashamed to confess that although I do not think I am a hopelessly prosaic individual, I have always thought this but a fond and fair dream."

"And it is a dream," Kurt made answer, "inasmuch as things real are most curiously shifted and changed in it, and as one can give scarcely a clearer account than a somnambulist, of what occurs and of what one does one's self. I do not remember how I got home that night; I have no idea whether it was several days after, or really on the day following, that, during a picnic in the country, I was strolling apart from the rest by her side through a leafy grove. The light of the dying sun was trembling among the trees, and a few subdued notes of birds' song were heard. Silence was all around; and in silence we passed on, side by side. Sometimes she stooped to gather a flower for the tiny bunch which she held in her hand, and once, as she stooped again, and I wished to anticipate her, our hands touched; and, startled, we both looked up, looked into each other's eyes, and the flowers dropped from her hands, and--well, it was just a dream, a brief and blissful dream. Who can tell the story of a dream?"

The young man had risen and gone to the window. Bertram kept his seat, leaning his head on his hands. When Kurt turned back to the table, he thought that the noble countenance which now looked up with a very sweet smile was paler than before.

"Pardon me," he said, "but I think I see that you are in need of rest; let me pause here. You know what happened next."

"Yes, but not quite how it happened," said Bertram in reply. "Please sit down by my side again, unless you are tired yourself. As for me, I am a regular old night-owl. How it happened, yes--how did Erna come to hear of your connection with the Princess? Some malevolent traitor must have been at work there."

"Would that it had been the case!" answered Kurt. "A traitor Erna's clear eyes would have speedily recognised as such. But the one who told her of it was a dear friend of my own, a fellow-officer, who in the course of a visit to our former garrison--our own regiment had meanwhile been transferred to Magdeburg--made Erna's acquaintance, without having the slightest conception of our relations. And as the conversation chanced to turn upon me, he babbled, under a promise of discretion, of the secret; and probably adorned and amplified matters, so as to let the enormous stroke of good luck which was supposed to be in store for me appear in its greatest splendour. As he was known to be on very intimate terms with me, as I had myself given him an introduction to the von Palms, and specially commended him to Erna, she had to believe that his romantic story was sheer truth; nay, the awful thought came to her that I had myself authorised my friend to make these communications, or, if this had been quite too infamous, she assumed at least that he had been commissioned by me to prepare her, and had solely blundered over his commission, so that I was personally responsible, if not for the manner, certainly for the matter. We corresponded, and with the connivance of Agatha, under cover of a correspondence of hers with an old school-friend in my present garrison; but Erna's next letter contained nothing but the question whether it was true that I had some relations or other with the Princess? The question thus put, I could not but answer in the affirmative, begging her at the same time, in connection with the subject, not to believe in what any one, except myself, might say. My request came somewhat late, but still did not fail to have its effect upon Erna's heart, which had assuredly opened with the greatest reluctance to the terrible suspicion, and which was now jubilant at being freed from it. She teased my friend about his fertile fancy which invented stories devoid of a particle of foundation, as she had since learned from a trustworthy source. Thus challenged, and piqued at being declared undeserving of credit, my friend stated that he had the knowledge, if not at first, at least at second hand, for his authority was my own Colonel, whose testimony Erna would surely not reject. Again he begged her to be discreet, but hinted pretty plainly that other fellow-officers were aware of it too, and had likewise learned it from the Colonel. And now for Erna the doubts which she thought she had vanquished turned to despair. She knew through me the very intimate terms on which Herr von Waldor and I stood, and indeed many a time I had called him to her my best and kindest friend, my protector and second father. Erna wrote another question. Did Herr von Waldor know my relations to the Princess? And again I had to answer in the affirmative, without being able to mention the suspicion which now--and now for the first time--rose within me, that Herr von Waldor might have purposely misrepresented those relations in his own interest--you know why. What need to continue to describe the wretched position in which I now was placed; how the net was tightened more closely and more fatally round me, so that I at last had given up all hope of ever being freed from it; all the more because Erna--as you heard yourself--repelled with such passionate indignation your mediation, which I was about to claim. I must confess, I cannot even guess why."

The dark eyes of the young man were raised inquiringly to Bertram, who did not at once reply to the questioning look. He had turned aside a little, and was busied refilling the glasses; he did not seem to notice that he was filling the second to overflowing, and that the wine was saturating the table-cloth.

"Dear me," he said, presently, "I beg your pardon; I was--thinking. Why, did you ask? Well, we settled already that, according to all experience, girls are not fond of confiding to their fathers the secrets of their hearts. They dread paternal jealousies, a paternal prejudice against the one who ventures to claim the little hand, which, as a matter of course, is far too precious even for the best of the best. But fear not! Erna shall find in me a friend, protector, and counsellor, who hopes to give the proof that one may love like a father without being blinded by a father's prejudices, and, above all, one who means more honestly by her than, I am sorry to say, Herr von Waldor does by you."

A dark shadow flitted over the young man's open countenance.

"I thank you," he said very gently, "I thank you from the bottom of my heart for so much goodness, and to deserve it will be the fairest task of my life. But pray do not condemn Herr von Waldor. It is impossible to measure him by the common standard. Contempt of death and greed of life, princely generosity and petty egotism, tenderest love and bitterest hatred--all these things lie side by side in his soul, and cross and re-cross each other in such a way that even to me (and I think I know him better than any one else) it is a perfect enigma. But if at times I cannot solve it all, if in this present case I cannot but see that he is willing--I must not say to sacrifice, but to stake--me and my happiness in the hope of gaining his own great stakes, then I need only remember what he has been to the orphaned boy, after he had carried my father, fatally wounded, upon his own shoulders out of the bloody struggle around the fortifications of Düppel; how he, of all men the most impatient, has watched over me with a mother's loving patience when I have been ill; how he resumed his studies in order to be able to supervise and guide mine; how he paid my expenses when I was a cadet; how he equipped and helped the ensign, the young officer; how he pressed upon the poor young man of *bourgeois* birth abundant help to enable him to hold his own in an expensive and aristocratic regiment; and how he thundered in his wrath when I refused to accept it any longer, as I had learned that he had himself to borrow the needful money at usurer's interest. Surely you will admit that one so deeply indebted to Herr von Waldor as I am, has lost the right, nay, more, the ability to struggle and resist, even if the hand which has done so much in the way of kindness weighs heavily, terribly so, upon him."

"I think I can follow you in your feelings," replied Bertram, "although Waldor is by no means thereby excused in my eyes; on the contrary, I adhere firmly to the Scriptural saying, that the right hand should not know what the left does; and I hold that he who claims gratitude has already his reward. Moreover, was the sacrifice really requisite, which Waldor expected from you, when he put you into this ominous position? From a moral point of view it is a matter of indifference; but I should like, if possible, to be enlightened on this point, which I have not hitherto understood."

"How things stand exactly," Kurt replied, "I can hardly say myself. I assume that the marriage-contract of the Princess contains certain conditions which deprive her of the greater part of her present fortune, if she contracts a new matrimonial alliance; or rather, would seem to deprive her, for a judicial interpretation of this dubious point is to be the result of the law-suit which is now reaching its final stage. Further, it may be assumed that the view of the Princess herself is the only correct one by all the laws of sound logic; but she fears--whether rightly or wrongly I know not--that the decision will be adverse to her if the authorities learn that her choice has fallen upon an alien."

"But you are an alien, too," objected Bertram.

Kurt shrugged his shoulders.

"An obscure lieutenant, not of noble birth, and Princess Volinzov! No one need imagine that they would have taken this *au sérieux*, any more than a dozen other *liaisons....*"

He paused abruptly, blushing to the very roots of his hair.

"For shame!" he cried, "that was basely said. Let others sit in judgment upon the poor victim of a most abominable bad education and of most wretched circumstances. I dare not, I dare not feel for her aught, but admiration and gratitude, and renewed gratitude, for I know and have experienced in my own person that, through all the badness and baseness that have been crowding around her from her childhood, she has preserved the capacity for a great and heroic love, a love of which we men are scarcely ever, and of which among women only the best and noblest are, capable."

Only at the last words Kurt had again ventured to look up, and he swiftly lowered his eyes again. Bertram's great eyes shone in wondrous radiance, and a curious smile, half melancholy, half ironical, was hovering about his lips, as he slowly answered--

"To be sure! you are quite right. Only the noblest women! We men are egotistical scoundrels; that is our lordly privilege; and he who resigns it, deserves to be crucified with malefactors on either side."

He had risen and was now pacing up and down the room; then he stepped to the open window. Kurt had kept his seat, thinking that Bertram would turn to him again. But he did not. The young man grew embarrassed. Reverence forbade him to disturb the dreamer. Never before had Kurt met one whose presence had thus thrilled him as with a breath of highest, purest vitality. And to this consciousness, which seemed to lift him out of and above himself, was joined the painful feeling which humiliated him in his own sight: that he had but just now been petty enough to say a bitter word about the woman of whom he yet knew, that she had come here to bring the greatest of all sacrifices that a loving heart can bring. And he, Bertram, knew this too; for Alexandra had said to Kurt: I have confessed all to Bertram! What a painful discord his own evil words must have been in the pure and high-souled Bertram's ear! And now Bertram, who had in all good faith shown him so much sympathy, had found him ungrateful, had turned from him, now and for ever.

He would, he must go!

But invisible fetters seemed to chain him to the spot; and as he sat there, angry with himself, in gloomy thought, it was no longer only the heavy, weary limbs that refused to obey him. His thoughts, too, flitted and wandered beyond his control. Something like a dense veil sunk upon his eyelids, and he saw surrounding objects but momentarily, indistinctly; the lighted candles upon the table seemed to be far-off bivouac fires, then they turned to dim and distant stars, then were lost in night and darkness.

Bertram had carried the candles to the writing-table, and shadows now rested upon the weary sleeper. Then he returned to the sofa and spread a coverlet over him.

"Poor lad! I saw how you were struggling against your sleepiness. The examination was a long one. But I could not spare you, and you have done well!"

He stood gazing upon him.

"And, like this, his head will rest by the side of hers--on one pillow!"

He drew his hand over his eyes, stepped noiselessly back to the writing-table, and presently his pen was gliding lightly and gently over the paper.

"My dear child,--I may henceforth with good right call you so, since Fate gives me one opportunity after another, to prove myself a good, and, I hope, also a thoughtful, father to you. But an hour ago I had to calm and comfort my beloved child, and yet dared not give her true comfort, dared not express my full and firm conviction that a good, upright heart always makes choice of the right thing at once. For good and upright as my dear child's heart is, yet it is a very defiant heart too, and would rather be miserable in its own way, than happy and blessed in other people's way; and it would have steeled itself against my persuasion and against my testimony, and would again and again have reverted to this: You do not know him! But now I say to you: I do know him; and you must accept my testimony as that of a man of great experience and knowledge of the human heart, of a man whose eyes--sharp as human eyes go--love for you and care for your welfare have filled with divine perspicuity. I know him now, after one hour spent here in my room in confidential conversation, as though I had known him from childhood, stalwart young man as he is; and even as I sit writing this, he is sleeping, under my watchful care, the sweet sleep of exhausted youthful vigour, notwithstanding his painful anxieties and the bitter sorrow of his heart. I have been watching him in his sleep. Sleep is a terrible betrayer of narrow minds and feeble hearts. Here there is nothing to betray, and sleep can but put its soft yet sure seal upon the beauteous image of a great and noble soul. And even as this soul, helpless and resistless as it were, is in my keeping, receive it, loved one, from my hands, as a great and glorious gift of the gods on high, who have deemed me worthy to be their envoy and the executor of their sacred decision.

"I promised you not to leave as long as you had need of me. You need me no longer, and I shall leave in the morning without bidding you farewell. From your mother, too, I shall take leave in writing; she knows my weakness for vanishing noiselessly from society. It is a long journey that lies before me, and we shall not soon meet again. Separation is death for a time, and time, again, is nought but a tiny speck, and its complement is eternity. A noble human being should plan his thoughts and action not in reference to the former, but the latter. Let, therefore, what I now say to you, for the brief space wherein we shall not behold one another, be said for evermore: Fare thee well, *Lebe wohl!* that is, live according to the bidding of your heart, as you hear it when you listen to it in secret silence and reverence! Howsoever this our life may be shaped, it is no longer our concern, but that of the powers on high, over whom we have no influence, and therefore it matters nothing to us. Once more then: *Lebe wohl!*

"My kindliest greetings to sweet Agatha! She is your true friend. I always felt that she would counsel nothing that I would not counsel myself.

"And another is your friend, too, though you do not think her to be one. You know I am speaking of the Princess. She also will leave your house to-morrow, not without making an attempt to prove to you that she is your friend. Be good to her for my sake; in that case I feel convinced that you will part from her with kind and grateful feelings, and that she herself will have inspired them. Whatever she may say to you, I guarantee its truth. Hers is one of those natures that may go astray, but that can never be untrue.

"Should you have a message to send me, send if through your father, whom I shall see in W---- tomorrow. Should I have anything else to say to you, I will send my message through Kurt, whom also I shall meet again to-morrow.

"And now remember your promise to be my good and obedient child; and again, and for the last time: *Lebe wohl!*"

He had put the letter into an envelope, and now turned in his chair, looking towards the sofa. His young guest was still lying in the same position, only his head had fallen back a little. Perhaps deeper shadows were now falling on the forehead and on the closed, eyes, whilst chin and lips stood out in brighter light and bolder relief; anyhow, the features that appeared so soft awhile ago seemed sharper, and the expression of almost feminine gentleness was turned to one of manly resolution, nay, of angry indignation.

"Thus Simon Peter may have contracted his brows, thus his lips may have quivered that night! And yet he could sleep, although he knew what was to happen. Even as this one, knowing, yet sleepeth!"

Again he stood by the open window, leaning against it.

A dead silence; only at times the night wind came rushing past, and there was rustling and roaring among trees and shrubs. In the village, veiled in mist, a dim red light gleamed faintly here and there. At times confused sounds, as of far-off horses' tramp and the measured step of soldiers on the march, with clashing of arms. Then deep, dead silence again, and then, piercing the deep silence, the half-smothered crow of a cock. Over the edge of yonder mountains the moon--almost at the full--hung, bloody-red, in the vapour which came steaming up from the woods.

"Did you look so mournfully up to it that night? And had all the heavenly stars to expire for Him too, that He might remember the heaven within His heart?

"Alas! He knew that He was dying for the world. I humbly claim but to die for her,--she is my world.

"One cannot choose one's own Gethsemane. One must take it as it comes, whether to the sound of the last trump on the Day of Judgment, ringing through the hearts of all the generations of men, or in deep and world-forgotten loneliness and secrecy, whither human eye shall never penetrate, any more than it penetrates into the nethermost depths of the sea.

"And this is my silent Gethsemane!"

The moon had sunk behind the hills, and the cool morning breeze came floating along. Bertram was about to close the window when he heard from afar a short, sharp sound, soon succeeded by other similar sounds, succeeding each other so swiftly that the echo could clearly continue the scattered noises and reverberate them as thunder. And now shrill, long-drawn trumpet-blasts were heard, mingling with the beat of the drum.

Bertram quickly turned to the sleeper, who was not, for his sake, to neglect his military duties. But already Kurt had staggered up from his sofa-corner, his eyes wide open, though still veiled by slumber, and his arms stretched out, clutching the air, as though in search of some weapon.

"I--I--not you! I will fight him! Give me the pistol!"

Bertram touched his shoulder.

"They are sounding the assembly in the village!"

"Oh! I thought ..."

He brushed his hand across his eyes.

"I have been asleep! Pardon me. How good you are! You have been watching for me. Is it long since ...?" and he pointed to the window.

"Not half a minute."

"Then I am in good time!"

He had already fastened his sword, and seized his helmet.

"Excuse my hurry. You know ..."

"No excuses! A matter of course. *Au revoir.*"

He held out his hand to the young man, in whose fine features, now full of life again, he noticed a strange quiver. Kurt evidently wanted to say something, and could not hit upon the right word. So he only pressed Bertram's hand vigorously.

"Well, *au revoir!*"

He hurried away. Bertram stood gazing at the door through which the slender young figure had vanished.

"Heaven be thanked! It is at least no disgrace to yield to him. He is thoroughly sound and sweet,--mind and body alike!"

CHAPTER XXIII

In the mansion-house which had until now been hushed in slumber, many voices were heard shouting, and the tramp of horses came echoing from the court-yard. A smart, heavy step was heard below in the passage.

"Which door?"

"The second, Colonel. Allow me, Colonel."

But Bertram had already opened the door, and Colonel von Waldor came rushing in.

"Good evening, friend, or rather good morning. A good thing that I met your servant at once--otherwise I might have been hunting for you ever so long--I have only one minute to spare--where is Ringberg? Your servant said he was here."

"He left five minutes ago, when they were sounding the assembly."

"That came unexpectedly, eh?" cried the Colonel. "An hour before the time--I did it on my own responsibility. His Excellency will be furious--wait for the attack, forsooth!--in such an exposed situation--not if I know it!--we shall have to retreat ultimately as it is--so I'll give them some trouble first. But that does not concern you. Here is something that does, a little, and which will greatly please you. Read this!"

Waldor drew a folded paper from between a couple of buttons in his uniform and handed it to Bertram. The telegram was in French, and in the following! words:--

"I sincerely congratulate Madame la Princesse. Lawsuit definitely gained.

Your obedient servant, Odintzov."

"Odintzov," Waldor explained, "is our Petersburg lawyer and business-man, a most trustworthy fellow. What do you say now?"

"That I do congratulate you heartily. How did you get hold of this?"

"See what it is to be in luck! I knew that the lawsuit would soon be decided, though Alexandra refused to believe it. So I gave orders that any telegram arriving, by day or by night, was to be straightway sent here by mounted express. Returning just now from the outposts, close to Rinstedt, I overtook on the high-road a fellow trotting along in front of me. 'Telegram from Rinstedt?' 'Yes, sir.' 'Princess Volinzov?' 'Yes, sir.' 'Give it to me.' The beggar had got rid of the telegram before he knew what was up. I read it by the light of my cigar; hence this stain. May I trouble you for an envelope? Or perhaps you would be so kind as to hand it to the Princess with my respectful compliments? It would give her double pleasure. I can assure you that you are still as fortunate as ever with the sex! Alexandra quite raves about you. Good! Now, you may both put your wise heads together and settle how and when the battle, which is won, is to be utilised for the benefit of our young *protégés*. I give you two *plein pouvoir*. I should say, let them dangle a little longer. I could come over with Kurt, never saying a word of this to him. We would have a nice little supper. 'Ladies and gentlemen, I have the exquisite pleasure of presenting my future wife to you--the Princess Alexandra Paulovna.' Capital! The amazed look in the eyes of our beautiful hostess is worth doing it for. And then the young ones immediately afterwards--only, of course, you must first pitch into the little girl properly; she seems to have a bit of a will of her own. All right, you'll see to it all between you, no doubt. Good-bye, *mon cher*! You are looking deucedly fagged. That's the result of being so much indoors. I have been on my legs since four o'clock yesterday morning, and feel as fresh as paint. Is this Kurt's glass? Oh, bother all ceremony! It is not the first that he and I have been using the same glass."

He filled the glass and drained it at one draught.

"Capital wine that! Well, good-bye, and *au revoir!*"

The Colonel had rushed off again.

"And thus," said Bertram with a smile, "one conquers the world. Perhaps it looks harder than it really is."

He again sat down at the writing-table and took up a fresh sheet of paper.

"Gracious Princess,--Waldor has just left me, after handing me, for transmission to you, the enclosed telegram, on the contents of which I beg to offer my hearty congratulations. I am sorry I must do so in writing, for a few hours hence I shall leave this--secretly--not to return. Business that will brook no delay makes this imperative, and I have not told Waldor of it. He hopes to find me here this evening, that I may be a witness to the amazement which the announcement of your engagement will cause in this friendly circle, as all obstacles to it are now removed. I am sincerely sorry that I cannot afford him that pleasure--for to him it would really be a pleasure.

"I regret it the more, because I must prepare a worse disappointment for him. For I consider it, in the interest of our *protégés*, to be desirable-- necessary, if you wish--that you, My Lady, should also leave to-morrow; without waiting for Waldor's evening visit. The communication which you were resolved to make to our fair young friend Erna, before Waldor had given you *plein pouvoir* (which he now begs to do through me), will only have the right calming effect if you strike the proper note on Erna's heart, and then let it ring out full and clear. In life, as on the stage, a good ending has to be provided for. This is missed if one lingers on the stage, when once the decisive word has been spoken.

"And what about the communication itself?

"I should deem it presumptuous on my part, were I to venture to advise Claudine's clever friend on this point. She knows that one is compelled to say the whole truth only in a court of law. In life it is sufficient, nay, it is often requisite in the interest of humanity, to say nothing but the truth, to be sure, but, of the truth, only what is needful and useful--to use the words which Lessing puts into the mouth of his wise Jew Nathan.

"And, now, let me add to my requests, a word of deep and sincere gratitude that you deemed me worthy to make the acquaintance of Claudine and of yourself. Your friend is perhaps more interesting and intellectual--at least you said so--but your heart is a thousand times more noble.

"I have always paid due respect to intellectual capacity; but before a noble heart I gladly and reverently bend my knee."

Silence had for a long time been reigning again in the mansion-house. The combat, too, though it had commenced in the immediate vicinity, was now being continued a long way off, and one only heard something like the rumbling of a distant thunder-storm. The candles on Bertram's writing-table had all but burned down to the sockets; he turned his wearied eyes towards the window, through which the dull grey morning light was coming. Konski came into the room.

"What time is it?"

"Just five, sir."

"So late? Well, I am ready. Did you get hold of a carriage?"

"It is waiting at the bridge below."

"Did you get if from the mayor?"

"Yes, Herr Doctor. At first he was making no end of excuses; for they all want to drive to the manœuvres, every man of them; and Herr von Busche has ordered a trap, too, for the afternoon. He'll have to be content with a common cart and a sack. Never mind that, though!"

"Why should you look so miserable about that?"

"It isn't about that at all, Herr Doctor."

"Well?"

"It is because I do not like to let the Herr Doctor drive away like this. Can you not take me with you?"

"Impossible! You see yourself that you have a couple of hours' work before you yet. These sealed packets are to go into the small portmanteau which you keep by you. These letters you will deliver, when the ladies have risen. This money is for the servants. Do not forget any one, and do not be stingy, Konski! And remember me kindly to your Aurora. And now my cloak, please, and so good-bye, Konski."

"Am I not at least to see the Herr Doctor to the carriage?"

"No."

"Herr Doctor, do not be angry; I really mean so well by you, and Aurora does too. We have been speaking of nothing else. And she swears that the Herr Doctor, if he wished it, could have Miss Erna for the asking."

"Then tell your Aurora that the Herr Doctor does not wish it, and that the Herr Doctor has better things to do than to spoon and fool about, like you and her."

He had held out his hand to the faithful servant, and now he was gone. A minute later, Konski, standing mournfully by the window, saw the dark figure striding swiftly past the lawn, and vanish behind the terrace-wall. He closed the window with a sigh.

Bertram lessened his pace, as soon as he knew himself unobserved. Slowly he descended the steps to the second terrace. Here was the leafy grove which, on the left, led to the platform beneath the plantain-tree. He glanced timidly that way. His foot had already touched the next step, he wanted to get down,--to get away,--but something like a magic spell drew him to the spot.

There, in this chair, she had sat; he was facing her; and the golden sunbeams had flitted through the dense foliage, and the birds had been holding a gleeful festival in the branches, and from the gardens below fairest fragrance of flowers had been wafted up, and his heart had been full of light and joy, and of all the blissfulness of spring. And now! and now!

"Thou sacred dawn of early morn, forgive me! You quiet trees and bushes, tell it not! I have borne what man can bear; more, I cannot."

And pressing his hand to his face, he wept.

CHAPTER XXIV

In the little-garden, under wide-spreading chestnut-trees, the lawyer and Bertram were sitting, about four o'clock in the afternoon, at a table covered with books, documents, and papers. From, the small garden one could look across a narrow court-yard, at the windows of the office, where they had just begun to make a fair copy of the will, which had been settled after long deliberation.

"And now, most grave and most conscientious of men, seeing that you go into this election campaign as into actual war, let us drink that victory may be on your side--that is, on ours, on the side of liberty, and right--and that the victor be granted, over and above his allotted time, as special allowance for special services rendered, a respectable series of not inglorious years, at least as many as this '68 Rüdesheimer wine numbers!"

The lawyer took a venerable-looking bottle, from a side table, filled a couple of green goblets, and touched Bertram's with his own.

"I thank you for the kindly wish, and drink to its fulfilment, although as you know, I have well-founded reasons for assuming that it will not occur."

"Nonsense!" cried the lawyer. "I am not a giant either, but I confidently expect to outlive all the giants among my contemporaries. What does Wallenstein say?--'Es ist der Geist der sich den Körper bauet' (It is the mind that builds, this frame of ours). And I would add, that also keeps the building together, even if it were shaky in every joint; and that is assuredly far from being the case with you."

Bertram smiled absently. His looks were wandering away to the garden gate.

"I wonder where Otto can be?" he said. "I urgently asked him to be here at four o'clock at the latest."

"I am in no hurry at all," replied the lawyer. "After having had to keep you waiting the whole forenoon, my entire evening is at your disposal instead; or, if you insist upon leaving at five, we can have another second witness in, and you can communicate to our friend in writing those points which have special reference to him."

"I am most anxious to do so by word of mouth."

Upon the wretched pavement of the narrow street which lay behind the garden wall, a carriage came hurriedly thundering along.

"*Lupus in fabula!*" exclaimed the lawyer. "Any one coming from Rinstedt would have to pass this way."

As he spoke, Otto's broad-shouldered figure appeared in the little yard.

The two men had meanwhile risen from their seats below the chestnut-trees, and had gone to meet the newcomer.

"What tricks are these of yours?" Otto was saying, "to cut away from the village in the middle of the night in a trap? What will people think? Why, that I am driving my guests from my house! But, of course, you intellectual people never can do things like the rest of us mortals; always something out of the way! Eh, old fellow?"

He brought his hand with a laugh down upon Bertram's shoulders; but the laugh was forced, and, indeed, in all his look and manner there was painful unrest.

"I am sorry that I must leave you gentlemen alone for a little," said the lawyer, with a meaning look at Bertram; "but you can call me at any time from the office. By the way, there is an empty glass here, Bermer. You must be thirsty after your drive along the hot road, and you have not in your own cellars at Rinstedt a better Rüdesheimer than this."

He turned his back upon the friends now, and forthwith the last trace of forced mirth vanished from Otto's face. He had flung himself into a garden chair, and there he sat, his elbows leaning on his knees, his hands put to his full round cheeks, staring fixedly in front of him.

"This has been a day which I shall remember!" he said.

"You have spoken to your wife?"

Otto nodded.

"In detail?"

"Well, yes; that is to say ..."

"That you might have spoken in greater detail. It does not matter, however, as long as you have informed her of your situation in the main. That has surely been done?"

"Been done!" exclaimed Otto. "Great Heavens! it was fearful! At first she seemed to think that I had gone mad; at least she looked so ... so frightened at me, don't you know, and wanted to ring the bell. But I told her that I was, unfortunately, still quite in my right mind, and perfectly sober, although yesterday I did perhaps, in my despair, drink a little too much. And then, I do not know how it came about, but one word led to another; and when she told me that the whole thing was my own fault, and the outcome of my bad economy and my costly foibles,--she could not mean anything more by this, than that I like to drink a good glass of wine and to smoke a decent cigar;--why, then, something passed within me that I cannot describe. I felt as though my very heart were turning, and as though I had never loved her in all my life. And then there was no longer any need to hunt for appropriate words; they came fast enough, and harder, too, than I liked at last. It was horrible!"

Otto gave a deep sigh and drained his glass.

"This is really good wine," he said, taking up the bottle and looking at the mouldy label. "I wonder where he got hold of it. But what does it matter to me? All grapes are sour for me henceforth."

"I hope not," said Bertram. "Anyhow, I thank you for having taken to heart and faithfully carried out what I wrote to you last night. This was indeed the first needful step, if the execution of my plan, the details of which I will immediately communicate to you, was to be possible. But one question first: you have not let Erna hear anything of the subject of the conversation between you and your wife? And, as I know your wife, she will surely keep as long as possible from Erna, what she considers less a misfortune than a disgrace?"

"You can rely on that," replied Otto; "she would rather bite her tongue off. But how long will it be before Erna has to learn all?"

"I hope that will never be the case!" replied Bertram. "Now, to come to the point. I have asked you to come here to-day to be a witness to my last will and testament. I might have told you its contents yesterday, but I did not do so, because--to speak quite frankly--I was afraid you would not keep the secret entirely, and thus the impression upon your wife, on learning the whole truth, might have been considerably lessened. If, after all, things come round again and change for the better, then--for she is not bad, your wife, only spoiled and not given to looking beneath the surface-- then something like gratitude will stir within her. And should this really not be the case, then I am, as it were, master of the situation and you will both yield; you willingly, she, because she must. Well then: in this will of mine, of which they are now making a fair copy in the office, I have made Erna my residuary legatee, except some smaller legacies, among which there is a suitable annuity for Lydia. From her future inheritance, there will at once be taken and made immediately available the sum which you require to set your affairs thoroughly right again, with our legal friend's help. He guarantee's that with this sum the greater part of your fortune may yet be saved, if you agree to his arrangements, above all about the factories. This sum will be advanced as a mortgage on your estates--our friend will explain to you how it can be done--at a moderate percentage, and the total revenue accruing from it is to be Erna's from the day of her marriage. Concerning that marriage, Erna has of course absolute freedom of choice, although I for my part hope that she will fall in with the wishes which I have expressed to her on this subject. And now shake hands, old man, and pardon me if I have had to add another unpleasant hour to the one which I already caused you to-day. *Tu l'as voulu!* From me you would not accept anything; with your own child you will, I trust, stand upon less ceremony."

"It is your money for all that," murmured Otto.

"As long as I live; who knows how long that will be! And there is our legal friend coming, bringing the document in question with him, which you are now to hear read, and which afterwards you are to adorn with your signature, as one of the two witnesses."

"The other," said the lawyer, now approaching the group with his chief clerk, "will be Mr. Kasper here. Sit down, Kasper, and read away."

During the reading of the somewhat lengthy document Otto's countenance kept changing colour; his eyes were very wet, and he repressed his tears with difficulty. When the lawyer handed him a pen for signature, his big powerful hand trembled to such an extent, that he could scarcely produce a few strokes in lieu of writing his name.

The document in question was now legally completed, and the lawyer had left the friends, to put it himself into a safe place of keeping. He came back at once. Would the gentlemen kindly excuse him? His Excellency the Herr Oberhofmarshal von Dirnitz had just appeared in the office, and desired to see him on business of importance.

"It probably will not be so very important, after all," said the lawyer, "I hope to settle, it in a very few minutes, and then we can talk at our ease."

Again the friends were alone. Otto seemed to have paid no heed to the lawyer's coming or going. He sat still at the table, supporting his head upon it, and staring gloomily before him. Bertram bent over him, and said, laying his hand upon his friend's shoulder--

"Otto, old man, you must not view the matter in too tragic a light."

"Perhaps I ought to look upon it as a joke having signed my own death-warrant," murmured Otto, without stirring from his position.

"You have done nothing of the kind," replied Bertram. "I should rather say, that now a new life was beginning for you; a life of purpose, sobriety, energy, independence, however strange the last word may sound to you. Until this day you were not living an independent life; nothing but a sham existence, in slavish subjection to the caprices of your wife, to whom you sacrificed your fortune, and, worse than that, your own better judgment. Now, having come to see this, you are enabled, by means of some assistance, to re-conquer your fortune, or at least the greater part of it; and this surely is no alms, but a mere loan, for which you are responsible in every respect; and, perhaps, in addition, you may conquer what you never possessed before--I mean, the love, or, at the very least, the respect of your wife, which she only denied to the husband who had no will of his own, but which she will not refuse to grant to the husband who is strong, determined, and who respects himself."

"Yes, yes," Said Otto; "it all sounds very well, and I surely mean to try to atone for my miserable shortcomings; but this I know already to-day, it will not do. I mean, I shall not have the energy you speak of, nay, I shall look upon myself as a downright scamp, and I shall not dare look my wife or any one else in the face, far less confront them energetically, as long as I see no chance of paying off my whole stupendous debt to you. Not to the uttermost farthing, that may perhaps be made possible--but in my heart. I do not know how to express it aright, but you will understand my meaning--by giving you in exchange something that no one else could give you."

He lifted his eyes to Bertram in anxious inquiry. Bertram shook his head.

"I thought we were not to mention it again," he said.

"Nor should I, to be sure, have done so," replied Otto; "however fond one may be of a man, and however indebted to him, one's only child is of course one's only child; and just now, above all, to have to give her up, to live in the big house alone with--but I cannot give up the thought that now, after all, nothing is to come of it, after they, Lydia and my wife, have tried to prove to me in writing--in black and white, don't you know--that you loved each other, and that at least Erna ..."

"I hardly know what you are talking about," Bertram impatiently interrupted his friend; "and what do you mean by 'in black and white'?"

"A stupid story," Otto made answer, embarrassed, "in which those women have got me involved, and which; yesterday, I did not wish to refer to, as I was desirous of sparing Hildegard. But now let the whole thing come out; it may as well. Listen, then!"

So he told him of the letter which Erna had written to Agatha, and which Lydia had purloined for a few hours. Hildegard had read the letter to him, and his excellent memory enabled him to reproduce it now, if not literally, at least in its general bearings. He also had remembered well the passage referring to some *liaison* which Erna would seem to have had, and to which the ladies had not attributed any special significance.

"Now," he concluded his report, "you see why my wife, who was so bent upon having Lotter for a son-in-law, was so annoyed with you during the last few days; nor do I know what would have come of it all, if the Princess had not yesterday brought, her round to reason: how she managed it is a riddle to me, but it is a fact, there, is an end of Lotter, for good and all. This morning Hildegard went the length of saying that it had been I who had favoured Lotter, and--for I may as well tell you all now--you suddenly appeared to her not only as an acceptable husband for Erna, but rather she saw in your union the only possibility--if my carelessness had really wrought our ruin--to save Erna at least, and to preserve for her such a position in society as she was born for. Well, old man, it's off my mind at last, and for all that, and, all that, it would be the grandest day in my whole life if you were able to say to me: 'Well, better late than never!'"

"It is too late!" Bertram replied.

He had ejaculated those words, in intensest excitement, bounding from his chair as he did so, and now he was, with uneven step, pacing up and down beneath the chestnut-trees. But presently he returned to Otto, who, frightened, had not stirred from his seat, and said in his usual calm tone--

"It would be too late, even if everything were--as it is not. I did not mean to speak about it, because I am not commissioned to do so, and because, therefore, those interested might have had good reason to be annoyed, if I told you before they themselves thought the time had come for doing so. I meant to rest satisfied with paving the way, so that there should be no obstacle to the fulfilment of their wishes. But now, since you seem unable to rid yourself of the curious idea of an alliance between Erna and myself; since, oddly enough, your wife finds pleasure therein; and since now, perhaps the fact of my making Erna my heiress, might seem to both of you an indirect confirmation of your opinion, I had better tell you this. I know that Erna has already given away her heart, that for more than a year she has loved Lieutenant Ringberg, and has been loved by him. It is my most earnest wish that the union of the lovers may meet with no obstacle, and I firmly believe that this marriage will lead to Erna's supreme happiness. And now let me confess one thing more, so that I may have nothing whatever on my conscience with regard to you. It was not for nothing that I have thus hastened to put order into my own, and, I trust, into your affairs, and to secure Erna's future. In the very next hour I have to go forth on an errand from which, in all human probability, I shall not return with my limbs whole, and where, very possibly, I may lose my life."

Then he briefly told his friend of his quarrel with the Baron last night and of its consequences. The true reason he did not refer to any more than he had to Kurt.

Otto was quite beside himself when he heard of it.

"It must not be, it shall not be!" he cried again and again. "It is sheer madness. How can you go and fight a duel with pistols when you scarcely know how to fire one? And with Lotter, of all men, who hits an ace at twenty paces. This is no duel, it is downright murder. I will not allow it!"

"Please do not speak so loud, anyhow," said Bertram; "they can hear you in the office."

"All the better!" cried Otto; "every one may hear that you cannot fight the fellow. Why, Ringberg is far more sensible than you, for he pretended last night not to notice the fellow's impertinence, and left the card table without replying a word."

"Who told you that?" cried Bertram, terrified.

"The forest-ranger," replied Otto, "He came over to breakfast this morning. Yesterday's events were discussed; I did not pay much attention to the talk, for the scene which I expected to have with Hildegard was weighing upon my mind; but I remember now. The ladies were discussing, whether Ringberg had done right in ignoring Lotter's impertinence. Lydia thought yes, but the Princess declared that it could not be thus, because ... I cannot remember why not; it had no interest for me. If I had been able to divine that Ringberg and Erna--that you ..."

"Was Erna present?"

"Erna? No. That is to say, I do not know--I was very absent--she went out riding afterwards with the Princess, who sent me word that I had better drive to town alone. Confound the fellow! Picking quarrels with everybody! And we are to blame; good Heaven, it is my fault that you ... I thought the worst had already come, but this is far worse than anything. But I cannot allow it, and I will not. Never! When did you say it was to come off? And where?"

"I shall tell you nothing more, and I am sorry I told you anything at all."

Bertram rose swiftly, Otto sprang up too, exclaiming as he did so--

"I shall go with you."

"You are about to leave, gentlemen?" a thin voice behind them was asking.

In their excitement neither had noticed that the lawyer and the Herr Oberhofmarshal had entered the garden, and had already approached within a few yards of them.

"Will you very kindly introduce me to the Herr Doctor?" said the Marshal, after he had courteously tendered his hand to Otto.

The introduction was made.

"It is not quite right," said the Marshal, "that only now I have the honour ... I hear you have been for more than a week at Rinstedt, and yet you have not had a minute to spare for us! Not for our theatre, our school of art, our museum! Not to mention my humble self, although I have for years been accustomed to no stranger of distinction passing my threshold. You must make up for this yet, you really must."

Bertram answered the old gentleman in a few courteous words, looking at the same time entreatingly at the lawyer.

"Your Excellency will excuse me," said the lawyer, "if, considering how pressed the Herr Doctor is for time, I venture ..."

"Quite right, quite right," said the old gentleman. "Indeed, I already noticed myself that the gentlemen were leaving. Let us come to the point--a very, very disagreeable point, in reference to which, acting on the advice of our common legal friend, with whom I originally intended only to discuss the judicial bearings of the case, I should now like to be allowed to claim also your assistance, my dear Mr. Bermer."

"In that case," said Bertram, who in his impatience almost felt the ground burn beneath his feet, and who also thought this a splendid opportunity for getting rid of Otto Bermer, "you will perhaps allow me to take my departure."

"Pray remain, Herr Doctor, I entreat you!" exclaimed the Marshal eagerly. "Quite apart from the painful interest which the matter will have on psychological grounds for such a profound student of human nature, I feel a moral necessity to have an affair, which it is desirable to withdraw from the cognisance of the judge, adjudicated upon by a forum of men of enlightened intelligence and honourable character--adjudicated upon and,--alas, alas!--condemned. The case is this ..."

"If your Excellency will allow me?" said the lawyer, in response to another still more entreating glance of Bertram's.

"Please, please," replied, the Marshal, conveying the pinch of snuff, which he had just, taken from his box, somewhat abruptly to his nose.

"The case is this," the lawyer went on, without heeding the old gentleman's annoyance: "your friend Baron Lotter, my dear Burner, has been guilty of an action which amounts to fraud and forgery. He had been commissioned to, buy a couple of race-horses for the Court during the summer, somewhere in Bavaria, and had drawn the money for them-- three thousand thalers--from the Grand Duke's privy purse, upon an order signed by His Excellency; but he appears not to have paid the money, but to have given a bill of exchange instead, with the forged signature of His Excellency, as representing the Marshal's office."

"Is not this monstrous?" cried the old gentleman, "as if the Upper Court Marshal's office ever paid, with bills of exchange!"

"The daring of the deed is indeed tremendous," continued the lawyer, "considering the fact which His Excellency has stated just now, and which was also known to the Herr Baron. And indeed he had taken the precaution to inform the clerk of the privy purse--into whose hands the bill of exchange would necessarily come first--when presented for payment, that the affair was all right; that he would hand him the money a week before it was due; the little service would not remain without its reward, as soon as the Baron had got his foot in the stirrup, in other words, as soon as he was Chamberlain. The poor fellow was weak enough ..."

"It is incredible!" murmured the Oberhofmarshal; "quite incredible!"

"To be sure, your Excellency," said the lawyer; "nevertheless, he was weak enough to consent to what was evidently a fraud, until to-day, two days before the bill was due, and when the money promised by the Baron had not appeared, his terror compelled him to make a clean breast of it to His Excellency. Meanwhile the bill had, yesterday, been sent to a local banker for collection. This banker, who, of course, had never seen anything of the kind occur in business, thought it advisable to make private and confidential inquiries of His Excellency as to the state of affairs, just before the clerk made his confession, and now His Excellency has the proof in his own hands."

The little old gentleman, who accompanied the lawyer's report with many a nod and with eager play of features, was opening his mouth, but the lawyer continued swiftly--

"His Excellency at once went to His Highness ..."

"I beg your pardon!" cried the Marshal. "I struggled for an hour as to whether I could not spare His Highness this grief. Moreover the young man's father was my dear old friend, who would turn in his grave if he could hear that a Lotter, his own son--it is terrible! And be assured, gentlemen, if I were a rich man--every one knows I am not--I ..."

"Your Excellency would in that case not have gone to Serenissimus," the lawyer went on; "but it was not to be avoided. His Highness, with his customary generosity, resolved at once ..."

"That is," the Marshal interrupted him, "in consequence of my report and recommendation."

"Of course, in consequence of His Excellency's report and recommendation, resolved at once that the bill was to be paid as if everything were in perfect order, under the condition that the Herr Baron should never show his face at Court again, and depart straightway. This latter point, the Grand Duke declared with very natural anger ..."

"I really must beg ..." objected the Marshal.

"Declared with considerable emphasis to be the *conditio sine quâ non*, if he were to show a merciful forbearance, in lieu of allowing the law to take its course. And now we come to the point when ..."

"When," the Marshal said, turning to Otto, "I must claim your kind services. You have the ... I can only say the great misfortune to be a friend ... I mean an acquaintance of the Herr Baron, who is at present a guest in your house. My appearance there, however greatly I should esteem such an honour, would perhaps cause some sensation, the very thing His Highness wishes to avoid at any cost. Serenissimus himself suggested and our common friend here ventures to propose directly, that ..."

"That you, my dear Bermer," resumed the lawyer, "might give the young gentleman the requisite strong hint, to which a letter which His Excellency has just drawn up in my office ..."

"And which I beg herewith to produce," said the Marshal.

"Would give additional emphasis," concluded the lawyer.

"I would beg your Excellency to intrust the letter to me," said Bertram. "I chance to know where the Herr Baron, who left my friend's house last night, is to be found at this present moment. To be sure I must leave at once, lest I miss him. You are coming with me, Otto?"

"Of course," cried Otto; "my carriage is at the door."

"And your horses are swifter than the hired ones, which I had ordered to be here at five. It is a quarter to five now. We have not a moment to lose."

"But tell him it as gently as possible, I entreat you," the Marshal called out after the two friends, who were already crossing the little courtyard.

Bertram waved his hand in assent.

A minute later the carriage was rattling along the narrow lane behind the lawyer's garden towards the broad street leading to the town gates.

CHAPTER XXV

Bertram, on entering the carriage, at once told Otto of the place in the wood where, by the shore of the little lake, the meeting was to take place, and Otto replied that they could easily reach it in half an hour, going first along the high-road, then turning off to the right and driving along some country lanes, and at last, for a brief stretch, through the forest.

But they had scarcely left the gates when unexpected obstacles intervened. The high-road, which had been perfectly free and clear a little while ago, when Otto was driving to town, now swarmed with troops belonging to the corps which had made a victorious advance; they were now utilising this convenient road for taking up their position for the sham-fight which was to be resumed tomorrow. This was the gist of the information conveyed to the friends, with due military politeness, by an officer who had hurriedly ridden up to their carriage, whilst Otto was vainly storming at some artillerymen in charge of a gun which they had managed to upset in a ditch, and of which the horses were blocking the road. The officer pointed out that the gentlemen would do better to deviate from the high-road than to try and force their way, and he said that, farther on it was occupied in even greater strength, and was likely to be absolutely impassable for the next half hour.

The advice seemed very sensible, and it was possible to follow it at once, for there was a country lane branching off to the right in that very spot.

"It is a deuced deal farther," said Otto. "We shall have to drive by way of Neuenhof and Viehburg; however, there is no help for it now, and after all we shall be in good time."

"We have already lost a quarter of an hour," said Bertram.

"We'll easily make up for that," replied Otto; "you see the road is in good condition and quite clear. Make haste, John--as quick as the horses can go!"

Otto was very far from really feeling the energy which he was displaying. On the contrary, he was cherishing the hope that the round-about way would ultimately prove too long; and that, even if they were to arrive in time, this insane duel should not come off. Thus the one care which had still been weighing somewhat upon his elastic temperament was gone. As for the rest, why all had come about as nicely as possible. Could he have anticipated anything of the kind when, an hour ago, he was driving to town in his despair, with the remembrance of that awful scene with his wife upon him like a nightmare? What would she say now? How would she take it? Not well, of course. She would call it a terrible humiliation--disgraceful. Nonsense! It was the simplest and most loyal arrangement in the world. Why should not Bertram make Erna his heiress, for he had neither kith nor kin, and had always been so fond of her? Hildegard had never liked Erna to call Bertram uncle. In future, perhaps, she would not object to it. And what about the big loan? Well, the bigness was its chief merit. A few thousand thalers here, a few thousand thalers there, how ignoble, how mean! But a hundred thousand thalers, that was decent; there was nothing derogatory about that. Hildegard would herself see that; and moreover, if Erna was to inherit the money anyhow, it remained, as it were, in the family. Then he wondered how his wife would get on with the young lieutenant, whom yesterday they had both seen for the first time. Only yesterday! But a man must see his son-in-law once for the first time. And he seemed to be such a charming fellow! What a pity that he was not of noble birth, for that had, after all, been Lotter's chief merit in Hildegard's eyes. Poor beggar! he really was sorry for him. That is what a man may come to when he is seriously embarrassed! Awful! And all for a mere trifle--those dirty three thousand thalers! If he had given him the money yesterday, or if Lotter had won them at play, the whole business might have been hushed up, and the beggar would not have run a-muck at everybody. The fellow was not a bad sort, hang it, quite a jolly fellow to get on with! Now, what fiend had possessed Bertram on this occasion; Bertram, who, on principle, made a point of avoiding all social conflicts, or, if the worst came to the worst, always knew how to make a courteous and clever diversion; Bertram who, even as a student, had never fought a duel, and had never concealed his aversion on the subject? And where on earth was, in this case, the necessity for fighting the man? Bertram must have known that Lotter's farce at Rinstedt was played out, that Hildegard had given him up for good and all. The foe who is running away should have golden bridges built him, not be impeded in his retreat. Well, well, it was to be hoped that Lotter at least had meanwhile come to his senses and gone away. To be sure, this was the most likely thing to have happened. Lotter, cunning fellow, had set all this duel business a-going, by way of putting them on the wrong scent, knowing that his pursuers would presently be on the alert, and now, whilst he was being looked for in the wood, he had most probably decamped altogether.

If Otto, good easy-going fellow, on arriving at this comforting conclusion, did not actually rub his hands in sheer glee, he refrained solely out of regard for his companion, who was sitting by his side in silent gloom, as though he were most terribly grieved at the prospect of the duel not taking place after all.

And so it was. Bertram felt like a man wearied to death, drawing his blankets around him and preparing for the greatly-desired rest, and abruptly startled by the alarm of fire. He had, indeed, been longing for death, but, of course, could not accept it from a dishonoured hand, neither for his own sake nor for that of the others who had agreed to act in what they thought an honourable cause, but which now was irrevocably stained with dishonour. Thus he would have to live on, on, nor might he let any one see what a torment this life was and would be to him; no one, and least of all Erna. She was even never to guess that he had been willing to sacrifice himself. But how was she to be kept from this conjecture, when gradually it would appear that there had been a connection between the Baron's insult to Kurt and his own intervention, which occurred in the same place and the very next minute? The remark of the Herr Oberförster at the breakfast table proved that the right scent had been discovered. Had he not thought of it at all? Or had he done so, and then quieted his scruples by assuming that his death would spread an impenetrable veil over the real circumstances of the case? And if that veil were really ever lifted in Erna's sight, and if she had to say to herself that he had died for her, it would be but as one note of melancholy, dissolving anon in the pure and full harmony of her own firm happiness. Was this certain? Or had he been playing a comedy after all, and assumed the easiest and most grateful part himself? Had he but draped himself as a dying hero, in order to hurt his rival, who might thereafter see how best to get on with an uncomfortable part? And now the piece was not to end, and he would have to remain upon the stage in the attitude of a hero, and Erna would have ample time to make comparisons; and they must needs all tell against Kurt! And would proud Erna forgive her lover this? And was this to be the result of his own unselfish devotion for Erna's sake?

Thus tormenting himself, he groaned aloud under the weight of the reproach which he was heaping upon his conscience.

"Yes," remarked Otto prosaically, "that comes from driving so fast. However, we shall again be delayed, and no mistake!"

After a short quick drive they reached the first village, and came upon the rearguard of corps number two retreating towards the shelter of the woods. In the narrow village lane a very compact mass of men and horses had accumulated, and a forward movement was quite impossible, because those marching on in front had not yet cleared the line. The men had stacked their rifles; by the roadside, on the road itself, weary men were crouching; others were crowding round the different house-doors, whence compassionate hands were holding out water in every possible and impossible sort of vessel. In front of the little inn had gathered an absolutely impenetrable knot of human beings. The driver was compelled to branch off again, this time into a very narrow little lane, thence he had to work his way with the greatest difficulty into the open, then drive across stubble-fields, and so back to the road, frequently alongside of columns of soldiers on the march, who made way with the greatest reluctance; and thus they made but slow progress.

Slow, far too slow for Bertram, whose feverish impatience was increasing every minute, although he knew not what to reply to Otto when he argued that it really did not matter much, even if they arrived a quarter of an hour or so too late. And what did too late mean in a case like this? They would arrive in ample time for the awkward explanation to the Baron.

"Well, and I might as well admit," said Otto, "that personally I hope we shall not find him at all."

"I think we shall, though," replied Bertram; "for in spite of his having morally gone so much astray, he is no coward. A man with weaker nerves would not have so long borne the danger of being discovered. And he must assume that he will be left alone until the day after to-morrow."

"In any case," said Otto, shrugging those broad shoulders of his, "we cannot advance any faster."

They had meanwhile passed the second village, and the troops on the march were behind them, and as the road was now both smooth and clear, the horses were really doing their best. They had by this time reached the border of the forest, and again they were obliged to proceed at a walking pace, for the road, which was old and ill-kept, had been made much worse by the foot-deep furrows which the pressure of the cannons had produced upon the soft soil. There were many traces of a hot combat having been waged here; cartridge-cases abounded, being scattered all over the place; there were plenty of broken branches, moreover, and now they actually came upon a kind of barricade; and it was impossible to drive round it, since on either side great trees skirted the road.

"Confound those soldiers!" said Otto; "they carry on as though they were in the enemy's country. We shall have to get out and walk whilst John clears away this obstacle, so as to enable him to pass; fortunately, it does not seem to be very firmly built. The lake is within a hundred yards of this."

The wood did indeed form a kind of glade, and in this spot a fairly broad one; and the road now lay between the sedge-grown banks of the little lake on the left and the edge of the forest on the right. This was close to the very place chosen for the hostile meeting. At first the sedge prevented a clear view, but, hurrying along, the friends soon discovered the centre, and thence they could see the rest of the ground, up to the spot where the wood came closing in again. All was deserted and silent.

Otto said--

"When they came, they probably found too much company hereabouts. Rely upon it, they have passed along the cutting, and are now in glade number two. Come along, I know every inch of the ground. Look,--a carriage has stopped here, and has then gone on through the cutting. And here is no end of traces of horses' hoofs. I have no idea where, they can all come from!"

The tracks of carriage-wheels and traces of horses' hoofs continued all along the cutting; but the friends had only advanced a few yards in the same direction when it occurred to Otto that his coachman, on finding nobody on the appointed spot, would probably drive straight ahead, possibly all the way to Rinstedt. The man was quite fool enough to do so, he said; so perhaps he had better turn back and instruct him, whilst Bertram went on. It was impossible, he added, for Bertram to miss the place now.

So Otto turned and Bertram hurried on. Already a certain gathering brightness indicated the whereabouts of the glade which Otto had spoken of, and to which the slope was now leading, but leading so gradually that Bertram could not yet get a glimpse of it, although he surely must be very near it, for he heard human voices and the neighing of a horse. And now he saw at least a portion of the glade, and there were several horses on the spot--as he perceived to his amazement--and grooms were holding the horses. Looking again, and more carefully, he noticed that several of the horses had side-saddles. An abrupt thought flashed across him. He recoiled involuntarily somewhat to the left, and then, standing behind some broad-stemmed fir-trees at the very edge of the glade, he saw before him a scene which for a moment held him spell-bound with terror.

Four or five men, Colonel von Waldor and Herr von Busche among them, were lifting a wounded man or a dead man upon a low country cart filled with straw, and then the doctor and his assistant received their charge and laid him carefully down, raising his head as they did so. The evening light shone brightly on the pallid face--Kurt's face; but, Heaven be thanked, Kurt wounded, but not dead! His eyes were open, and a smile flitted across his pallid features as Erna bent over him where he lay. Her fair countenance, darkened by the riding-hat which she wore, was as pale as his own, but she, too, was smiling, and she bent lower and lower still, and closed those lips of his that would speak and that were not to speak, with a kiss; and then she leapt down from the cart and bounded straightway, with Herr von Busche's help, into the saddle, her horse having meanwhile been brought to her. The Colonel, too, had mounted by this time, and the cart now set off, the wounded man being supported by the doctor's assistant; the doctor had also mounted his horse and joined the procession, which, following the cutting in the opposite direction, soon vanished within the glade. There remained but Herr von Busche and Alexandra, whom Bertram only saw after the cart had disappeared; there were two grooms, too, and they were now bringing up the horses; one of them a spare one, probably the one which poor Kurt had been riding.

The whole scene only occupied a few minutes, during which Bertram just had time to overcome the first paralysing feelings of horror. What subsequently retained and restrained him in the sheltering darkness of the trees, was a flood of curiously mingled feelings, out of which there emerged with potent forces the warning: They have found each other for life and death; step not again between them; touch not again with clumsy hands the dainty and complicated wheels of a fate which laughs your calculations to scorn!

He would have liked best to creep away unseen by any one, but here was Otto ascending the cutting, and loudly calling Bertram's name. Alexandra, who was just about to let Herr von Busche help her into the saddle, started; Herr von Busche sang out in reply to Otto; Bertram stepped forth from under the trees, and the Princess hurried up to him, gathering her riding-habit with one hand, and holding out the other to him.

"My dear friend! you here? Thank Heaven! I was just debating whether I had not better wait for you, rather than leave a servant with a message."

"Is Kurt badly wounded?"

"How do you know? but never mind! No; not badly. That is to say, it will be a tedious affair, but the surgeon guarantees a complete cure, and states that his life is in no danger. He found the ball at once; we were already on the spot--and, great Heaven, what a splendid, heroic creature Erna is!"

Otto had meanwhile come up. There was much cross-questioning, of course; and the friends speedily gathered at least the main facts of the occurrence. Herr von Busche was naturally best qualified to give all the information required. He had heard from the Oberförster, upon that gentleman's return from Rinstedt, of the scene in which Kurt, evidently without knowing it, had acted a singular part--one quite incompatible with the traditional honour of an officer--of a man who is grossly insulted in the presence of many others, and who withdraws without replying. The Oberförster had been quite excited on the subject which he had been discussing with the ladies at the breakfast-table; he had added that other gentlemen, who had also been present last night, had expressed their amazement at the young' officer's conduct.

"I am myself an officer in the *Landwehr*." continued Herr von Busche, "and my duty was clear. I was bound to communicate as quickly as possible to Ringberg the insulting suspicion to which he had made himself liable. To apply to the Baron for information was out of the question. He had left the ranger's house some hours before, to pay, he said, some farewell-calls in the neighbourhood; besides, I think, he wanted to procure the horse on which he afterwards came to the meeting. We had agreed to meet here. Herr Ringberg was also to be here, of course, but then it would have been too late; there would have been two duels in lieu of one; and Ringberg's was bound to have precedence. Then there was no second provided for Ringberg, unless the Herr Doctor had acted as such, and that was not exactly feasible. Well, in a word, I got on horseback, and searched the length and breadth of the ground employed for the manœuvres, until at last, when I had given up all hope, I found Ringberg at the moment when the regiment were stacking their rifles. This was at five. The original hostile meeting was fixed for half-past. Ringberg was on the point of leaving, having previously, under some pretext or other, obtained two hours' leave of absence from the Colonel. I told Ringberg what I had heard. He requested me to accompany him to Colonel von Waldor to whom he would have to report the case. You know the Colonel. 'I am your second,' he cried; 'we'll teach the Baron a lesson in good manners.' A minute or two afterwards we were in the saddle, accompanied by the staff-surgeon and an assistant, and galloped here. The carriage was waiting by the side of the lake, and at the same moment the Baron appeared. I must do him the justice to say that he not only did not deny having made the insulting remarks, but declared his perfect readiness to give instant satisfaction for them. The issue unhappily was what, knowing the Baron's wonderful skill, I expected it to be; or rather, it would probably have been even more unfortunate, if, at the moment of firing, the ladies had not appeared. I am sure that the Baron, who stood facing the cutting, must have seen them coming, before the rest of us heard the sound of the horses' hoofs upon the soft turf, and that the unexpected sight robbed him of his usual unfailing aim. I find it natural enough that, under the circumstances, he preferred to vanish immediately, and I expect that he will be waiting for me at the Oberförster's now. To say the truth, I am not particularly anxious to meet him again."

Whilst the young man was relating this in his wonted vivacious style, and whilst Otto briefly explained how Bertram and he had been detained upon the road, they reached the end of the cutting, and had come to the place where Otto's carriage was waiting.

"How right we were to divide," said Herr von Busche. "The escort of the wounded man would have been really too numerous. As it is, it will cause a certain amount of sensation, although fortunately it will not have to leave the wood till it is close to Rinstedt."

"It might be as well to divide once more," said Alexandra. "I feel, to say the truth, somewhat shaken, and would like to await in town news about the sufferer; for his state inspires me with no alarm now, and I am expected to appear at Court to-night. I know you will very kindly let me use your carriage, and mount Lieutenant Ringberg's horse instead. You will be glad to get home as speedily as possible, although we sent word to your wife so as to prepare her."

"But," remonstrated Otto, "most gracious Princess, you cannot go alone...."

"I hope the Herr Doctor will be so good as to accompany me."

Alexandra turned, as she spoke, to Bertram who was standing silent, evidently in deep thought, and who had scarcely joined in the previous conversation. Now he looked up, and their eyes met.

"I was just going to request that honour," he said.

Otto looked amazed, but ventured upon no remonstrance. A shrug of the shoulder behind Alexandra's back, seemed to imply that he considered Bertram the lamentable victim of a lady's caprice. He instructed the coachman to regain as quickly as possible the high-road, which was now likely to be clear of troops, for this would enable the Princess to be driven with greater ease and quickness. He pointed out to her that there were plenty of wrappers in the carriage, and begged her to make use of them in the cool of the evening. The Princess thanked him for his attentions, and added that she would not fail to inquire personally at Rinstedt on the following day.

"And you too, of course, Charles," said Otto.

Bertram nodded—

"Then I will not detain you any longer."'

They shook hands; the gentlemen mounted their horses and galloped away, followed by the grooms, and the carriage set off more slowly in the opposite direction.

CHAPTER XXVI

For a little while Alexandra and Bertram sat silently side by side; then Alexandra said--

"We are at one in the conviction that it will be in the interest of our *protégés* if we vanish from the scene?"

"Absolutely," replied Bertram. "I suffer acutely already, and recognise the outrage that man is guilty of who would play Providence for others."

"In that case I should have been guilty too," said Alexandra, "but I am by no means dissatisfied with myself; on the contrary, I believe it is good that things have happened thus; it was necessary. And when you know all, you will admit that I am right. You must know it, for the sake of the future, which will still claim much from us. Listen in patience.

"I have rigidly adhered to your advice. I announced my departure for noon to-day; my maid was despatched with the luggage a little before ten; our host insisted upon escorting me in person to the town. Then I went to see Erna. We had a memorable conversation which I cannot reproduce to you in all its details, but the result was that Erna no longer doubted the sincerity of my desire for her happiness; but her pride revolted against receiving this happiness at my hands, or, if that be saying too much, she had the painful impression that her happiness could only be brought about at the cost of my own, in other words, that I was still in love with Kurt, and that my marriage to Herr von Waldor, which I announced to her as impending, was an act of resignation, if not of despair. Of course she did not give utterance to all this, nor did she even hint at it; these things one simply feels. And there was another thing that came between her and the prospect of calm happiness by Kurt's side. Dear friend, do not deny it any longer--not to me, even if to all the world besides--you are in love with Erna! Thank you for this pressure of the hand. It does not reveal a secret to me, and yet I thank you for it with all my heart. You owed me this satisfaction, as I have told you Claudine's story; and even as Claudine's story is buried in your bosom, so the story of a noble human heart shall be buried in mine."

Alexandra withdrew her hand with a cordial pressure from Bertram's. They were both too much moved to be able to speak for some time. At last Bertram said--

"And does Erna believe me to be in love with her, after all I have done to shake her conviction?"

"I should not assert that her faith has not been shaken," Alexandra replied, "but she was still under the sway of that intuitive feeling which guides us women wellnigh always aright, and which in her case betrayed itself in a hundred turns, every one of which had for its object your future welfare and happiness. And then, my friend, you did at last the very opposite of what you should have done to calm Erna, and to brighten her future. You may thank Heaven that Erna does not divine the real motive which influenced you; that between the two duels she sees a sort of mechanical connection of time and place, if I may say so, and not the real one. But for all that, if you had fallen in this duel, Erna would never have consented to an alliance with Kurt, and she would never in her heart have forgiven him for not being the first on the ground. Whether it was within the limits of possibility to have forestalled you, the woman's heart does not stop to inquire. The loved one must be not only the best and noblest and bravest of men, but the cleverest too; how he sets about it is his own concern! Dozens of duels have been fought in my immediate neighbourhood, and, I am sorry to say, I have been the direct cause more than once, so I had no difficulty in understanding the whole business. That old chatterbox, the ranger, was relating the circumstances to us at breakfast; I then sent for your servant, and, examining him, found out that you had held a long conversation with Kurt, which had been preceded by negotiations between Kurt and Herr von Busche; and last of all came that crackbrained person Fräulein von Aschhof, and confessed her horribly indiscreet statement to the Baron, and your remark, my friend, that you would try to settle the matter. I saw it all as clearly as though it had been acted before me. Then I knew, too, what I should have to do. Again I sought Erna, and told her that your life and Kurt's honour were both at stake; of course I took care to represent matters in such a way that the idea could not well occur to her of your having wished to sacrifice yourself directly for Kurt. She spurned with contumely the idea that Kurt had only pretended not to hear the Baron's insulting remarks; no need for me to tell her, she said, that Kurt must be instantly informed of it. I am convinced that she felt that her fate was about to be decided, that now once more she became fully and thoroughly conscious of her love for Kurt. The great, strong, energetic nature of the glorious girl shone forth in mighty radiance. I could have knelt at her feet and worshipped her! I may say that I forgot completely my own self, forgot that he for whom this passion was flaming heaven-high had been the object of my own mad love. I even concealed what I knew--that I had distinctly recognised the Baron, when I saw him at the card-table last night, as the man who also, at a card-table, had cheated my mother out of a hundred thousand francs--that the Baron was not a fit man for an officer and a gentleman to fight. I dreaded lest that objection should destroy what I saw coming. How we hurried all over the ground in search of Kurt; how we came upon his regiment when he had just ridden off; how a surgeon's assistant who had been sent back to fetch some forgotten bandages or instruments helped us to find his track; how we followed up that track at the utmost speed of which our horses were capable; how we reached the goal just in time to see Kurt fall, whilst his miserable opponent flung the pistol to the ground and fled when he beheld me--all this you know, or may easily picture for yourself. But I picture to myself how Erna will now be leading her love to her parental abode, to keep and to hold him there for her very own;--for what is more, what becomes more a woman's very own than the man whom she loves, if she has to tend him and wrestle with death for his possession;--and I picture to myself how now only she recognises with a shudder what a lordly treasure she had all but forfeited through exaggerated pride and obstinacy; and I think of, all the wealth of love and bliss which is in store for them both! And then I look at us both, at us who have opened for them the gates of their paradise driving away into darkness like two exiles; and I ask you, friend, have we really need to be ashamed of the part which we have played? Or, rather, are we not fully and fairly entitled to rejoice in our success and to be proud of it? Yes, friend, we must be glad, we must be proud. Where else shall we, who are sick unto death, gain the strength to get well again? For we must not, dare not die; but we must live and be happy, to prove to those two that they may be happy on our account. I, my friend, mean to live on; I will and shall recover. I shall appear at Court to-night, and be beautiful and witty if I can, or at least serene and in good-humour. And not to-day alone, but to-morrow too, and every day, and most so by Waldor's side, for he very surely does not marry the Princess Alexandra for the sake of getting a moody, melancholy wife. Some secret corner somewhere will surely be found where now and again one may weep in peace, and let the grievous wound bleed. And you, dear friend? What shall you do? How will you set about recovering? I should not have an hour's quiet if I had to think you could not. Give me your word that you will recover, give me your hand on it."

Bertram's answer did not come at once. He raised his eyes and saw the beacon-fees blazing on the mountain tops and far away in the plains. He heard the calls of the patrols, the neighing of many horses, the talk and laughter of the men round the bivouac-fires, the dull thud of marching columns. It was but a mimic warfare, but it spoke to him of a true and earnest fight in which he was called upon to take his place in the ranks as a good and true soldier, to do his duty as long as strength was granted him- -it might be for years, or for a few days only. And he held out his hand to Alexandra, and said--

"Whether I shall recover, I know not. But I swear to you that I will try!"

CHAPTER XXVII

"Then you insist upon joining in to-morrow's debate?" the doctor was saying.

"I flatter myself that it is necessary!" replied Bertram.

"As a political partisan I admit it; as your medical adviser I repeat, it is impossible."

"Come, my good friend, you said just now, it is undesirable; now, from that to impossible is rather a bold step. We had better stick to the first statement."

The doctor, who had taken up his hat and stick a few minutes before, laid both down again, pushed Bertram into the chair before his writing-table, sat down again facing him, and said--

"Judging from your momentary condition it is merely desirable that you should have at present absolute repose for at least a few days. But I very much fear that to-morrow's inevitable excitement will make you worse, and then the downright necessity for rest will arise, and that not only for a few days. Let me speak quite frankly, Bertram. I know that I shall not frighten you, although I should rather like to do so. You are causing me real anxiety. I greatly regret that I kept you last autumn from your projected Italian trip, and that I pushed and urged you into the fatigues of an election campaign and into the harassing anxieties of parliamentary life. I assumed that this energetic activity would contribute to your complete restoration to health, and I find that I made a grievous mistake. And yet I am not aware where exactly the mistake was made. You mastered your parliamentary duties with such perfect ease, you entered the arena so well prepared and armed from top to toe, you used your weapons with all the skill of a past master, and you were borne along by such an ample measure of success--and that of course has its great value. Well, according to all human understanding and experience, the splendid and relatively easy discharge of duties for which you are so eminently fitted, should contribute to your well-being, and yet the very opposite is occurring. In spite of all my cogitations I can find but one theory to account for it. In spite of the admirable equanimity which you always preserve, in spite of the undimmed serenity of your disposition and appearance, by which you charm your friends, whilst you frequently disarm your foes, there must be a hidden something in your soul that gnaws away at your vitals, a deep, dark under-current of grief and pain. Am I right? You know that I am not asking the question from idle curiosity."

"I know it," replied Bertram; "and therefore I answer: you are right and yet not right, or right only if you hold me responsible for the effect of a cause I was guiltless of."

"You answer in enigmas, my friend."

"Let me try a metaphor. Say, somebody is compelled to live in a house, in which the architect made some grave mistake at the laying of the foundations, or at some important period or other of its erection. The tenant is a quiet, steady man, who keeps the house in good order; then comes a storm, and the ill-constructed building is terribly shaken and strained. The steady-going tenant repairs the damage as best he can, and things go on fairly enough for a time, a long time, until there comes another and a worse storm, which makes the whole house topple together over his head."

The doctor's dark eyes had been dwelling searchingly and sympathisingly upon the speaker. Now he said--

"I think I understand your metaphor. Of course, it only meets a portion of the case. I happen to know the house in question extremely well. True there was one weak point in it from the beginning, in spite of its general excellent construction, but ..."

"But me no buts," interrupted Bertram eagerly. "Given the one weak point, and all the rest naturally follows. I surely need not point out to such a faithful disciple of Spinoza's, that thought and expansion are but attributes of one and the same substance, that there is no physiological case that does not, rightly viewed, turn to a psychological one; that so excitable a heart as mine must needs be impressed by things more than other hearts whose bands do not snap, happen what may, and notwithstanding all the storms of Fate. Or are you not sure that, if you had had to examine the hearts of Werther or of Eduard in the 'Elective Affinities,' you would have found things undreamed of by æsthetic philosophers? I belong to the same race.

I neither glory in this, nor do I blush for it; I simply state a fact, a fact which embodies my fate, before whose power I bow, or rather whose power bows me down in spite of my resistance. For, however much I may by disposition belong to the last century, yet I am also a citizen of our own time; nor can I be deaf to its bidding. I know full well that modern man can no longer live and die exclusively for his private joys and sorrows; I know full well that I have a fatherland whose fame, honour, and greatness I am bound to hold sacred, and to which I am indebted as long as a breath stirs within me. I know it, and I believe that I have proved it according to my strength, both formerly and again now, when ..."

He covered forehead and eyes with his hands, and so sat for a while in deep emotion, which his medical friend respected by keeping perfectly silent. Then, looking up again, Bertram went on in a hushed voice--

"My friend, that last storm was very, very strong. It shook the feeble building to its very foundation. What is now causing your anxiety is indeed but a consequence of that awful tempest. The terribly entrancing details no one as yet knows except one woman, whom an almost identical fate made my confidante, and who will keep my secret absolutely. So would you, I know. You have been before this my counsellor and my father-confessor. And so you will be another time, perhaps, if you desire it and deem it necessary.--To-day only this one remark more, for your own satisfaction; for I read in your grave countenance the same momentous question which my confidante put to me: Whether I am willing to recover? I answered to the best of my knowledge and belief: Yes! I consider it my duty to be willing. It is a duty simply towards my electors, who have not honoured me with their votes that I may lie me down and die of an unhappy and unrequited attachment. If the latter does happen--I mean my dying--you will bear witness that it was done against my will, solely in consequence of that mistake in the original construction which the architect was guilty of. But, in order that it may not happen, or may at least not happen so soon, you, my friend, must allow me to do the very thing which you have forbidden. The dream I dreamed was infinitely beautiful, and, to speak quite frankly, real life seems barren and dreary in comparison with it. The contrast is too great, and I can only efface it somewhat by mixing with the insipid food a strong spice of excitement, such as our parliamentary kitchen is just now supplying in the best quality, and of which our head-cook is sure to give us an extra dose to-morrow. And, therefore, I must be in my place at the table tomorrow and make my dinner-speech. *Quod erat demonstrandum.*"

He held out his hand with a smile. His friend smiled too. It was a very melancholy smile, and vanished again forthwith.

"What a pity," he said, "that the cleverest patients are the most intractable. But I have vowed I will never have a clever one again, after you."

"In truth," replied Bertram, "I am giving you far too much trouble. In your great kindness and friendship you come to me almost in the middle of the night, when you ought to be resting from your day's heavy toil; you come of your own accord, simply impelled by a faithful care for my well-being; and, finally, you have to return with ingratitude and disobedience for your reward. Well, well--let us hope for better things, and let me have the pleasure of seeing you again to-morrow."

Konski came in with a candle to show the doctor the way down, for the lights in the house had long since been extinguished. The gentlemen were once more shaking hands, and the physician slipped his on to Bertram's wrist Then he shook his head.

"Konski," he said, turning to the servant, "if your master has a fancy one of these days to drink a glass of champagne, you may give him one, as an exception; but only one."

"Now remember that, Konski!" said Bertram.

"It is not likely that it will happen," grumbled Konski.

"Konski will leave me to-morrow," explained Bertram.

"Will, is it? No, I won't, but ..."

"All right!" said his master, "we must not bother the doctor with our private affairs. Good-bye, my friend! With your leave I will dine with you to-morrow."

The physician left; Bertram immediately again sat down at the writing-table, and resumed the work which this late visit had interrupted. It was a disputed election case, and he would have to report upon it to the House. There had been some irregularities, and it was in the interest of his own party that the election should be declared null and void; he had been examining the somewhat complicated data with all the greater conscientiousness and care. But now he lost the thread, and was turning over the voluminous page of the evidence, when, lo! a daintily-folded sheet of paper--a letter--fell out.

"Good heavens! how came this here?"

He seized upon it with eagerness, as a wandering beggar might seize upon a gold coin which he saw glittering among the dust on the road. The hot blood surged to the temples from the sick and sore heart; the hand that held the slight paper trembled violently.

"Now he would not be grumbling at my slow pulse!"

Yesterday morning he had received this letter, but had not succeeded in composing himself sufficiently to read more than a few lines. He thought that, perhaps, on his return from the *Reichstag* he might have been in a more settled frame of mind. Then he had not been able to find again the letter which had been laid aside, although he had searched for hours, first alone, then with Konski.

And now--after all those documents were pushed aside--he was again, as yesterday, staring hard at the page, and again, as yesterday, the different lines ran into each other; but he shook his head angrily, drew his hand over his eyes, and then read:--

"Capri, *April* 24.

"Dearest Uncle Bertram,--If to-day for the first time, in our travels I write to you, take this as a gentle punishment for not having come to our wedding. Take it--no, I must not tell you a falsehood, not even in jest. We--I mean Kurt and myself--regretted your absence greatly, but were angry only with those wretched politics which would not release you just at a time, when, as Kurt explained to me, such important matters were at stake. Take, then, I pray you, my prolonged silence as a proof of the confusion under which I labour, amidst the thousand new impressions of travel, and through the hurry with which we have travelled. Kurt has just four weeks' leave, so we had indeed to make, haste; and, therefore, we steamed direct from Genoa to Naples, calling at Leghorn only, and yesterday evening we arrived there only to leave this morning, and to sail to Capri, favoured by a lively *tramontane*.

"I am writing this my first letter upon the balcony of a house in Capri.

"Dearest Uncle Bertram, do you know such a house which 'stands amidst orange groves, with sublimest view of the blue infinity of the ocean, a fair, white hostelry embowered in roses'?

"The words are your own, and do you know when you spoke them to me? On that first night when I met you in the forest on the Hirschstein hill. You have probably forgotten it, but I remember it well, and all through the journey your words were ever before me; and of all the glories of Italy, I wanted first to see the house which had, since then, remained in your fond remembrance, where you 'ever since longed to be back again,' and the very name of which was always to you 'a sound of comfort, of promise: *Qui si sana!'*

"And now we are here--we who need no comfort, we to whom all promise of earthly bliss has been fulfilled, and so drink in the blue air of heaven, and inhale the sweet fragrance of roses and oranges.

"And you, dearest Uncle Bertram, you dwell--your heart full of longing for fair Quisisana--yonder in the dull grey North, buried beneath parliamentary papers, wearied and worn--and, uncle, that thought is the one grey cloud, the only one in the wide blue vault of heaven, like the one floating yonder above the rugged rocky front of Monte Solaro, of which our young landlord, Federigo, foretells that it will bring us a *burrasca*. I gave him a good scolding, and told him I wanted sunshine, plenty of sunshine, and nothing but sunshine, but I thought of you only, and not of us. And surely for you too, who are so noble and good, the sun does shine, and you walk in its light, in the sunny light of great fame! Yes, Uncle Bertram, however modest you are, you must yet be glad and proud to learn how your greatness is recognised and admired. I am not speaking of your friends, for that is a matter of course, but of your political opponents. In Genoa, at the table d'hôte, we made the acquaintance of some Count from Pomerania--I have forgotten his name--with whom Kurt talked politics a good deal. In the evening the Count brought us a Berlin paper, which contained your last great speech. 'Look here,' he said, 'there is a man from whom all can learn, one of whom each party should be proud.' He had no idea why Kurt looked so pleased and proud, nor why I burst into tears when I read your splendid speech.

"Only fancy, Uncle Bertram! Signor Federigo has just brought me, at my request, an old visitors' book--the one for the year 1859, the year in which I knew you had been here. Many leaves had been torn out, but the one upon which you had written your name was preserved, and the date turns out to be that of the very day on which I, was born! Is not this passing strange? Signor Federigo has, of course, had to present the precious leaf to me, which he did with a most graceful bow--the paper in one hand and the other laid upon his heart--and we have resolved to celebrate here the day of your arrival in Capri and of my arrival in the world. Why, indeed, should we travel on so swiftly? There can be no fairer scene than this anywhere. Sunshine, the fragrance of roses, the bright blue sky; the everlasting sea, my Kurt, and the recollection of you, whose dear image every rock, every palm tree, everything I see brings as if by magic before my inner eye! No, no; we surely will stay here until my birthday.

"Signor Federigo is calling from the verandah that 'Madama' has only five minutes more for writing if the letter is to leave to-day. Of course it is to leave to-day; but I have the terrible conviction of having written nothing so far. It cannot now be helped. So next time I will tell you everything that I could not do to-day: about my parents, who are writing letters full of happiness--papa, in particular, who seems delighted that he has given up his factories--which surprised me greatly; about Agatha's engagement to Herr von Busche, which did not surprise me, for I saw it coming during the merrymakings previous to my wedding; about ...

"Signor Federigo, you are intolerable!

"Dear Kurt, I cannot let you have the remaining space of two lines, for I absolutely require it myself to send my beloved Uncle Bertram a most hearty greeting and kiss from Quisisana."

Bertram laid the paper very gently down upon the table; he was stooping to imprint a kiss upon it, but before his lips touched the letter, he drew himself up abruptly.

"No; she knows not what she does, but you know it, and she is your neighbour's wife! Shame upon you! Pluck it out, the eye that offends you, and the base, criminal heart as well!"

He seized the parliamentary papers, then paused.

"Until her birthday! Well, she will assuredly expect a few kind words, and has a right to expect them; nay, more, she would interpret my silence wrongly. I wonder whether there is yet time? When is her birthday? She has not mentioned the date; I think somewhere in the beginning of May. Now, on what day did I arrive there?"

He had not long to seek in the old diaries, which he kept methodically, and preserved with care. There was the entry: "May 1.--Arrived in Capri, and put up at a house which I found it hard to climb up to; the name had an irresistible attraction for me: Quisisana--*Sit omen in nomine!*"

The first of May! Why, to-morrow is the first. It is too late for a letter, of course, but a telegram will do, if despatched at once.

"Konski!"

The faithful servant entered.

"My good Konski, I am very sorry, but you must be off to the telegraph-office at once. To-morrow is the birthday of Miss Erna--well, well, you know! Of course she must hear from me."

He had written a few lines in German, then it occurred, to him that it might be, safer to write them in Italian. So he re-wrote them.

Kanski, who had meanwhile got himself ready, entered the room.

"You will scarcely be back before midnight. And, Konski, we must begin the morrow cheerfully. So put the key of the cellar into your pocket, and bring a bottle of champagne with you when you return. No remonstrance, otherwise I shall put into your character tomorrow, 'Dismissed for disobedience'!"

CHAPTER XXVIII

It was nearly three o'clock when the doctor came hurrying in. Konski would not leave the master, and had despatched the porter. Konski took the doctor's hat and stick, and pointed in silence--he could not speak--to the big couch at the bottom of the room. The doctor took the lamp from the writing-table, and held it to the pale face. Konski followed and relieved him of the lamp, whilst the doctor made his investigation.

"He must have been dead an hour and more," he said, looking up. "Why did you not send sooner? Put the lamp back upon the writing-table, and tell me all you know."

He had sat down in Bertram's chair. "Take a chair," he went on, "and tell me all."

Then Konski told.

He had come back at a quarter-past twelve from the telegraph-office, and had found his master writing away busily, when he brought in the bottle of champagne which he had been ordered to fetch from the cellar. His master had scolded him for bringing only one glass, and made him fetch another, for they must both drink and clink glasses to the health of the young lady.

"Then," the servant went on, "I sat opposite to him, for the first time in my life, in that corner, at the small round table, he in the one chair and I in the other. And he chatted with me, not like a master with his servant, no; exactly--well, I cannot describe it, sir; but you know how good and kind he always was. I never heard an unkind word from him all these ten years I have been with him, and if ever he was a bit angry, he always made up for it afterwards. And, to-morrow I was to leave for Rinstedt to get married, and he had given us our furniture and all, and fitted up a new shop for us into the bargain. Then we talked a good deal of Rinstedt, and of the manœuvres last year, and of Miss Erna that was, and of Italy, where, as you know, sir, I was with the master two years ago. Well, I mean, it was not I who was talking so much, but master, and I could have gone on listening, listening for ever, when he was telling of Capri, where we did not get that time, and where Mrs. Ringberg is staying now--Miss Erna as was. And then his eyes shone and sparkled splendidly, but he hardly drank any wine, just enough to pledge the young lady's health with, and the rest is in his glass still. But he made me fill up mine again and again, for I could stand it, said he, and he could not, he said, and he would presently finish his work; and there are the papers on the table in front of you, sir, that he had been looking at. And then, of a sudden like, he says, 'Konski, I am getting tired; I shall lie down for half an hour. You just finish the bottle meanwhile, and call me at half-past one sharp.' It was just striking one o'clock then.

"So he lay down, and I put the rug over him, sir, and, oh--I'll never forgive myself for it; but all day long I had been running backward and forward about these things of mine, and then at last the long walk at night to the telegraph-office, and perhaps the champagne had gone to my head a bit, since I am sure, that I had not sat for five minutes before I was asleep. And when I woke it was not half-past one, but half-past two, so that I was regular frightened like. But as the master was a-sleeping calm and steady, I thought, even as I was standing quite close to him, that it was a pity to wake him, even though he was lying on his left side again, which formerly he could not bear at all, and which you, sir, had forbidden so particularly. I mind of our first evening in Rinstedt, sir, but then he did wake up again ... and now he is dead."

Konski was crying bitterly. The doctor held out his hand to him.

"It is no fault of yours. Neither you nor I could have kept him alive. Now, leave me here alone; you may wait in the next room."

After Konski had left, the doctor went to the little round table on which the empty bottle and two glasses were standing, one empty, one half-full. Above the sofa, to the right and left, were gas-brackets, with one lighted jet on either side. He held the half-full glass to the light and shook it. Bright beads were rising from the clear, liquid.

He put the glass down again, and murmured--

"He never spoke an untruth! It was in any case solely a question of time. He drank his death-draught six months ago. The only wonder is that he bore it so long."

Erna's letter was lying upon the table. The doctor read it almost mechanically.

"Pretty much as I thought!" he muttered. "Such a clever and, as it would seem, large-hearted girl, and yet--but they are all alike!"

A scrap of paper, with something in Bertram's hand writing caught his eye. It was the German telegram.

"All hail--happiness and blessing--to-day and for ever--for my darling child in Quisisana."

The doctor rose, and was now pacing up and down the chamber with folded arms. From the adjoining room, the door of which was left ajar, he heard suppressed sobs. The faithful servant's unconcealed grief had well-nigh unchained the bitter sorrow in his own heart. He brushed the tears from his eyes, stepped to the couch, and drew the covering back.

He stood there long, lost in marvelling contemplation.

The beautiful lofty brow, overshadowed by the soft and abundant hair, the dark colour of which was not broken by one silvery thread; the daintily curved lips, that seemed about to open for some witty saying, lips the pallor of which was put to shame by the whiteness of the teeth, which were just visible; the broad-arched chest--what wonder that the man of fifty had felt in life like a youth--like the youth for whom Death had taken him.

From those pure and pallid features Death had wiped away even the faintest remembrance of the woe which had broken the noble heart.

Now it was still--still for evermore!

He laid his hand upon that silent heart.

"*Qui si sana!*" he said, very gently.

FOOTNOTE

Footnote 1: "Und immer ist der Mann ein junger Mann,
Der einem jungen Weibe wohlgefällt."